W9-AUZ-171

Always the Baker, Never the Bride

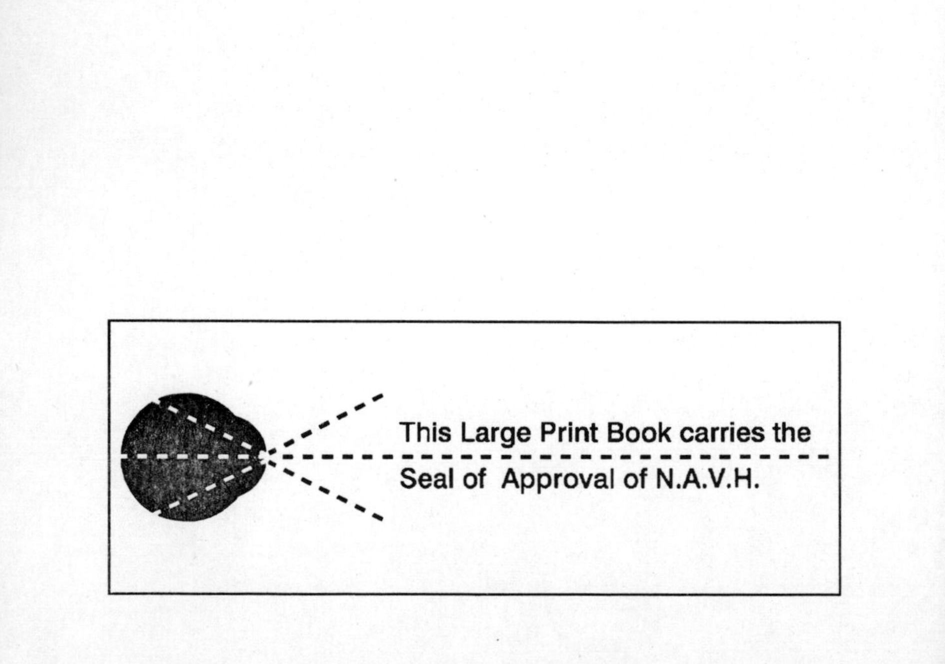
This Large Print Book carries the
Seal of Approval of N.A.V.H.

Always the Baker, Never the Bride

Sandra D. Bricker

THORNDIKE PRESS
A part of Gale, Cengage Learning

Detroit • New York • San Francisco • New Haven, Conn • Waterville, Maine • London

The persons and events portrayed in this work of fiction are the creations of the author, and any resemblance to persons living or dead is purely coincidental.

Thorndike Press® Large Print Christian Fiction.
The text of this Large Print edition is unabridged.
Other aspects of the book may vary from the original edition.
Set in 16 pt. Plantin.

LIBRARY OF CONGRESS CATALOGING-IN-PUBLICATION DATA

Bricker, Sandra D., 1958–
Always the baker, never the bride / by Sandra D. Bricker.
p. cm. — (Thorndike Press large print Christian fiction)
ISBN-13: 978-1-4104-3672-6 (hardcover)
ISBN-10: 1-4104-3672-1 (hardcover)
1. Confectioners—Fiction. 2. Women cooks—Fiction. 3. Diabetics—Fiction. 4. Hotelkeepers—Fiction. 5. Weddings—Fiction. 6. Atlanta (Ga.)—Fiction. 7. Large type books. I. Title.
PS3602.R53A49 2011
813'.54—dc22 2011001560

Published in 2011 by arrangement with Abingdon Press.

Printed in Mexico
1 2 3 4 5 6 7 15 14 13 12 11

Special thanks to the voice in my head.
Barbara Scott,
you're my editor/champion, friend, and sister-in-Christ.

To the Girl Power in my life.
By now, you chicks know who you are.
And Rachelle, you're the
icing on the cake
(pun intended).
Thank you so much for *getting me*
the way you do.

And to that little dash of
Boy SuperPower.
Thanks, D.

And to Candy, my personal assistant.
Bouncing around my house with the ear
buds in, she suggested I might like to
listen to her latest CD.
Michael Bublé, your *Crazy Love* album
inspired so much of the spirit
of this book.
And when Hollywood comes calling
to put it on film,
there's a part here for you, sugar.

All recipes contained herein
have come from the massive card file
of the late Jess Bricker.
As sweet as the cakes, pies, cookies, and
rolls she baked, my mother truly made
me what I am today:
a diabetic with a weight problem.

PROLOGUE

"She just went over like a lopsided sack o' corn. I tell ya, I never saw nothin' like it."

"Emma Rae? Can you hear me, honey? Emma Rae?"

Emma's eyes fluttered as she struggled to open them. Her mother's face came into focus just inches from hers, and she jumped.

"Here she comes, Gavin. She's coming around."

When Emma tried to speak, her tongue stuck to the roof of her mouth, and it made a sound like paper peeling away from plastic as she wiggled it.

"What . . . happened?"

"You fainted, Princess." Her father's pale face moved closer into view, and he took her hand. Emma realized she'd never seen him so obviously worried.

"I fainted?"

"How do you feel now?" After she had spoken, he looked somewhat relieved. "Still a little woozy?"

"A little."

She blinked a couple of times before she recognized the denim-clad form who peered over her father's shoulder. The way it stood on end, Danny Mahoney's wavy blond hair looked like a halo gone slightly berserk. His perfect square jaw clenched as he peered at her with those crystal blue eyes. Danny was the boyfriend Emma had dreamed about since the sixth grade. He was handsome and cool and just dangerous enough to make her parents worry and her girlfriends green with envy.

"Hi, baby. Whatcha need, huh?"

Gavin glared at Danny and separated him from Emma by repositioning himself. "Avery, why don't you and *The Boy,*" which Emma's father had insisted on calling Danny since their first date in sophomore year, "go and check on that doctor, huh? I'll stay with Emmy."

Just then an older man with a face like a bunched-up fist appeared from behind the yellowish curtain. His white coat and clipboard made him look a little like a butcher taking an order, but the stethoscope hanging around his neck provided the clarity Emma needed.

"How are you feeling now, young lady?

Better?"

Emma tilted her shoulders into a shrug. "I guess."

"Do you remember what happened?"

"Not really. Daddy says I fainted."

"She went down like a sack o' corn," Danny repeated, and then he snickered and looked around for acknowledgment. The only hint of it came from her father's menacing stare.

"What did you have to eat this morning?" the doctor asked.

Emma thought it over. "Nothing. I don't know. Except some cake. And a candy bar after second period."

"No breakfast? Any protein?"

"No."

"Well, that appears to be the problem. Do you know what it means to be *di-a-bet-ic?*" He said the word in a slow monotone, like Mrs. Prentiss presenting a new vocabulary word to her class.

Emma shook her head. "No."

"Oh, no, Gavin. She's diabetic."

"Calm down, Avery. Let's hear the man out."

"See, when you ate that cake and the candy bar, your blood sugar levels spiked very high, like they tend to do when we consume sugar. But after a spike, they tend to fall just as fast, and that's what's known as —"

Emma zoned out long enough to smile at Danny, and she didn't really hear the longest and most important part of Dr. Benjamin's explanation about the production of insulin within the body, the difference between *hypo*glycemia and *hyper*glycemia, or the body's natural this and that. She tuned back in about the time Dr. Benjamin told her parents how important it would be for Emma to monitor her blood sugar and stick to a diet created just for diabetics. But despite all the words bouncing around, all she really heard — *heard and managed to process* — were the two horrifying ones that came near the end of the monologue — the ones that made her mother cry and her father look like he'd been shot in the chest.

Daily injections.

"You can't be serious."

"Oh, I'm very serious, Emma Rae," the doctor told her. "It's good that we've caught this now because you need to get into a routine of nutrition and medication that will affect you for the rest of your life. Emma Rae, you have what is called Type 1 *diabetes.*"

No, Jesus. No, Jesus. No, Jesus. Please, Lord Jesus, noooooo.

"Does that mean we'll miss out on the prom?" Danny piped up from behind the others. "Because I'm already out for our share of the limo."

Aunt Sophie's Red Velvet Cupcakes

Preheat oven to 350 degrees.

1 1/2 cups granulated sugar
1 stick butter, softened
2 eggs
2 1/2 cups general purpose flour
2 tablespoons cocoa powder
1 teaspoon baking powder
1/2 teaspoon salt
1 cup buttermilk
1 bottle red food coloring
1 teaspoon vanilla extract
1 teaspoon distilled white vinegar

Beat butter and sugar on medium speed until fluffy.
Slowly add eggs while continuing to beat mixture.
Sift together flour, cocoa, baking soda, baking powder, and salt.
In separate bowl, beat buttermilk, vinegar, vanilla, and food coloring.
Add 1/3 of the dry ingredients to the wet, and mix on medium speed.
Continue adding dry ingredients in portions, mixing thoroughly.
Spoon into cupcake papers, just over half full.

Bake for 15 minutes and then rotate pan on oven rack.
Bake approximately 5 more minutes.
Allow cupcakes to cool in the pan for 10 minutes and then move to wire rack.
Do not frost until thoroughly cooled.

1

Emma cradled a single cupcake in her hands and lifted it within inches of her face to examine it with care. How she'd love to take a massive bite out of it and feel that moist, crumbly red velvet cake against the roof of her mouth, a flavorful burst of sweetness, and then the kiss of cocoa.

"You're not thinking of eating that, are you?"

Emma didn't even blink. Her focus remained fixed on the red velvet cupcake.

"Emma Rae? Have you had some protein? Because if you haven't, I'll tackle you right now and take that cupcake away from you."

The corners of her mouth quivered into a half smile before she set the confection on the wire rack beside the others.

"Calm down, Fiona. I'm not going to eat it. But you could let me dream about it for thirty seconds, couldn't you?"

Fee peered over square black glasses, a

short fringe of matching ebony bangs dangling inches above them. She stared Emma down, one colorful tattooed arm bent at the elbow, as her fingers drummed an impatient rhythm on her hip. Then she wobbled her head in that familiar way, the one that warned: *Next stop, a shaking finger, right in your face.*

"How about I go get you a protein shake," her friend suggested. "They have a new sugar-free flavor. Mango."

"Mmmm." Emma forced a sliver of a smile and shrugged.

"Dude, you'll love it. I'll be back in ten."

Emma glanced with longing at the wire rack before she returned to the sink to rinse the cupcake pans.

Diabetes. What a funny and cruel joke for God to play on a baker with a penchant for confections. For her recipes, the sweeter, the better. But Emma didn't partake. She'd won the Passionate Palette Award just last month for her crème brûlée wedding cake — a six-tiered, twenty-four-layer masterpiece filled with sweet custard that inspired one of the judges to remark, "This rocks my world." And yet Emma had never tasted more than a single, ecstasy-inducing bite.

She dreamed of sitting at one of the bistro tables beyond the swinging doors of her kitchen, a cup of coffee before her, a china plate adorned with an oversized hunk of cake, where the sweetness of each bite enveloped her and every forkful inspired a new creation.

The jingle of the front door beckoned, and Emma dried her hands before she abandoned her sugar-glazed dream and pushed through the kitchen door.

"Welcome to the Backstreet Bakery," she greeted the GQ cover model in the $600 suit. "How can I help you?"

"Coffee. Black. And one of those chocolate brownies."

He flicked the shoulders of his jacket with swift brushes that produced sprinkles of moisture. Emma darted a glance out the window; the sky had turned dark and rain drenched the streets.

"I didn't even know it was raining," she commented as she placed a paper doily beneath a large fudge brownie on a Staffordshire-inspired blue-and-white dessert plate.

"Came out of nowhere." He stood before the bakery case and peered at the confections on the other side of the glass.

"You know, these brownies are awesome with hazelnut coffee. Can I interest you in —"

"No, thanks," he said, cutting her off. "Just black."

Emma tried to resist the urge to tempt him further, and she was successful for about twenty seconds. Then, with a charming smile, she extended a glass coffeepot toward him.

"Dark roast. Extra bold. Hazelnut's perfect with chocolate."

He lifted his eyes and glared at her across the bakery case. "Just black. Thank you."

Emma shook her head and slipped the pot back into its place before grabbing the Colombian from one of the adjacent burners.

"Black it is."

He raked his dark hair with both hands, and his milk-chocolate brown eyes met hers without warning. A world of conversation passed between them in one frozen moment. She peeled her gaze away and tried not to stare at the slightly off-center cleft in his square chin.

"That'll be four dollars and eighteen cents."

He slipped a five toward her and muttered, "Keep the change."

She hesitated, wondering if she should bother to point out that she was the baker and not a waitress. And then she realized the tip was only about eighty cents.

Stand-up guy.

While GQ took his cup and plate and settled at a table near the window, Emma wiped down the counter and started a new pot of decaf.

A happy grunt called her attention back to her customer, and she tripped over the crooked grin he aimed in her direction.

"What's in this?" he asked, wiping a smear of chocolate from the corner of his mouth. "It's fantastic."

"Just your average fudge brownie," she replied, unsuccessful in completely masking her pride. "Well, actually, I use cashews instead of walnuts, and the frosting is a mixture of cocoa and —"

"I'd like half a dozen of them."

"Oh."

"Can you pack them up for me?"

"Sure. But wouldn't you like to try a variety? We also have a really nice blonde brownie with hazelnut cream —"

"What is it with you and hazelnut?" he interrupted. "Are you invested in plantations? I like the fudge brownie. I'd like to purchase six of them. Can you do that for me?"

Emma swallowed the answer that pressed against her lips and instead replied, "Yes, sir. I can do that."

"Good. Thank you."

Fee erupted through the door at just that moment, drenched from the downpour on the other side, oblivious to the obnoxious customer in their midst.

"I didn't get mango," she announced, rounding the bakery case and shaking her wet head until it splashed Emma. "They had the berry one that you like so much, so I got that one. Is that okay?"

"Yep," she replied, accepting the protein shake. "Thanks, Fee. Our customer would like six fudge brownies. Would you package them and collect his payment?"

Before Fee could reply, Emma turned her back and headed for the kitchen to enjoy her shake.

"You know," she heard Fee suggest just as the doors clanked shut behind her, "we have a really nice blonde brownie if you'd like to try a variety."

The snicker that popped out of her was certainly not ladylike.

Jackson climbed out from behind the wheel of his Altima and tucked the white bakery box of brownies beneath the shelter of his overcoat to protect it from the rain.

The moment he crossed the threshold of

The Tanglewood Inn, the familiar cackling of hens greeted him.

"Jackson, you're *dray-enched,*" Georgiann declared in her thick Southern drawl.

"It's rainin' cats and puppies out *they-ah,*" Madeline added.

Norma Jean tossed him a thick, white towel that smelled like flowers. "Dry yourself off, baby *bruthah.*"

All my sisters in one place, at one time. No good can come of this.

"What are you all doing here?" he asked them and then rubbed his rain-soaked face with the towel. "Did I forget something?"

"Norma Jean called us just this morning," Madeline explained. "I can't for the life of me figure out why you didn't rally the troops, Jackson. You know we offered to help you interview for staff."

"I appreciate that, I really do —"

"All evidence to the contrary," she crooned. "Norma said you have hotel staff interviews all day today."

"Yes, but —"

"But, nothing, do you hear me? We'll set up shop in three corners of the restaurant, and we'll just plow through those interviews until we find you just the right people."

Jackson knew better than to argue. He'd

learned to choose his battles in cases like this.

Norma Jean Drake Blanchette was the sister closest to Jackson's age, but being raised as the only boy with three older sisters and a single mom left him feeling a little bit like a lone sitting duck on top of a twirling birthday cake.

"What's in the box, Jack?" Georgiann asked. Her smile caused the deep dimples on either side of her mouth to cave in like bread dough pressed with two large thumbs.

Box? He'd almost forgotten.

"The most unbelievable fudge brownies you will ever taste," he announced. "Let's get some coffee set up in the dining room, and I'll grab the résumés from Susannah and meet you in there."

If his sisters were going to force their assistance upon him, the least he could do was wash it down with a few more delectable calories. And he supposed he could share the wealth as well.

The glass elevator up to his office groaned before lifting and then shimmied the rest of the way to the fourth floor. He was relieved when the doors opened at last.

"Coffee?" Susannah asked him as he crossed her office toward his own.

"No, thanks. I'm going to have some

downstairs with the Hens."
"I heard they were here."
"You heard?" And then he thought better of it. "Don't tell me. Do you have that file with the résumés?"
"On your desk with your messages."
Jackson dropped into the leather chair behind the large maple desk. Susannah had separated the message slips into two piles, based on priority. Inside the file folder were at least two dozen résumés, paper-clipped and categorized with small blue sticky notes, annotated in his assistant's perfect round handwriting.

Desk staff.

Bell staff.

Catering staff.

Susannah Littlefield was the best thing that had ever happened to Jackson's professional life. She'd been with him for all twelve years at his former job and had agreed to take a gamble and leave the security of corporate America to come along with him on this turkey shoot. Susannah was nearly sixty now, and Jackson was in a state of denial about the fact that she'd be thinking about retirement one day in the not-so-distant future. What in the world would he do then?
Susannah stood in the doorway and ad-

justed the wire-rimmed glasses on her knob of a nose, and then she smoothed the salt and pepper bun at the top of her head.

"I brought you a brownie," he told her. "But it's in a box downstairs."

"I hope to one day meet it in person," she replied with a grin.

"We live in hope."

Susannah handed him a typed schedule of interview appointments. "They're all confirmed except the two highlighted in blue."

"Thank you, Suzi. You take very good care of me."

"Somebody has to do it," she commented on her way out of his office.

Jackson closed the thick file and tucked it under his arm, waving at Susannah as he strode past her desk. Remembering his elevator ride up from the lobby, he made a quick right and headed for the stairs instead.

When he reached the dining room, Jackson stood in the doorway and observed his three sisters. Georgiann and Madeline had their mother's dark hair, light eyes, and porcelain skin, while Norma Jean's sandy hair and hazel eyes were reminiscent of the father who had passed away much too early with four small children still waiting to be raised.

Jackson watched them doctor up their coffee as they chattered with one another, oblivious to his presence. Each woman had a style that was all her own: George, in her ankle-length floral dress and single strand of perfect pearls; Maddie, wearing a smart sweater and pleated brown trousers; both women flanking Norm in her acid-washed jeans, tucked-in Henley and flat-soled suede boots. Each of them so different from the others, and all of them still polar opposites from the little brother they adored. Jackson knew he was fortunate to have them, a fact that was easy to forget some days.

"Jackson," Georgiann called out to him, waving her arms. "What are you doing standing over *they-ah?* Come on in and let's get down to business, huh?"

"Did you open the bakery box?" he asked as he joined them at the table.

"We were waiting on you," Norma replied. "But let's have at those brownies."

Madeline poured a cup of steaming coffee and slid it toward him.

"Mm!" Georgiann exclaimed in one short grunt, and then she repeated it. "Mm! These are fantastic. Wherever did you get them?"

"I forget the name of the place. A bakery down near the square."

"The Backstreet Bakery?" Norma asked, savoring her first bite with what appeared to be nothing shy of ecstasy. "Has to be. Oh, I love that little spot."

"Maybe."

"Jackson, you've got to steal away their pastry chef for The Tanglewood," Madeline stated. "These are amazing."

"Oh!" he snorted, setting down the cup and shaking his head. "N-nnnno."

"Why not?"

"I met their baker, and she was annoying."

"Oh, come on," Georgiann drawled. "How much time could you have spent with her when you stopped in a bakery for a coffee and a sweet? Really, Jackson. How annoying could she be?"

"Ha!" he blurted. "Pretty annoying."

Well. Besides those exceptional green eyes, and the chestnut silk she wore pulled back into a casual ponytail.

"Jackson."

"No kidding. She was pushy and tried to sell me something I didn't even want." The flour-dusted woman's green eyes flickered across his recollection, and Jackson shook his head. "And she has a strange preoccupation with hazelnut."

"Oh, I love hazelnut."

"Me too."

"Fine. But she's not an option for The

Tanglewood," he declared. "Let's move on. Here are the résumés for the interviews, and the candidates should start arriving in about thirty minutes. George, why don't you make recommendations for the bellmen, and —"

"Can I have another?" Norma asked, dipping her hand toward the bakery box.

"No." He laughed, snapping the lid shut before she could reach inside. "I'm saving one for Susannah."

"There are two in there," she objected.

"The delivery guy gets the last one."

"They were delivered?"

"Yes. By me."

"Oh. Well."

"Here. Console yourself with résumés for the restaurant positions. Maddie and I will talk to the desk applicants."

"Sweet tooth abuser!" Norma playfully accused.

"Just saving you from yourself," he said, tying up the box with the length of white string.

"Gee. Thanks."

"Saving you from yourself," Georgiann repeated, and then she clicked her tongue. "More like saving the brownie for *your*self."

"Yeah. There's that," he replied. And with one defiant flicker of a smile, he popped the last of the brownie into his mouth.

Important Tips for Cake Decoration

- Choosing the right bag for applying icing is crucial.
- A parchment bag is ideal; it can be used quickly and is disposable.
- A round tip is best for applying dots, making straight lines, or writing script.
- A star-shaped tip creates beautiful flowers and zigzag shapes.
- Use a leaf-shaped tip for a lovely garland design around edges.
- Decorate with *the V Principle,* making a "V" with thumb and forefinger.

Remember: Practice makes perfect!
Use a sheet of wax paper or an overturned cookie sheet to practice making designs before icing.

2

"My eyes look weird. Do I have bags under my eyes?"

"Not in real life."

"Well, what does that mean?" Emma asked as she scurried across the kitchen and yanked her favorite pot down from the rack above the prep island. Holding it upside-down and using the bottom as a makeshift mirror, she inspected her face. "Maybe I need more sleep?"

"Em," Fee groaned. "The picture is two inches square. And whether you look like you might possibly have bags under your eyes is really not the news here, is it?"

Emma thought better of it and sheepishly replaced the pot on the overhead rack. "Of course not." She sniffed. "No."

Fee spread out the food section of the *Atlanta Journal* in front of them. The headline sent a wave of excited shivers over Emma as she read it for the gazillionth time.

"Local Baker Makes Atlanta Proud."

Three columns and a baggy-eyed color photograph telling the world (or at least her little slice of it) that Emma Rae Travis had won the prestigious Passionate Palate Award for her crème brûlée "masterpiece." First, a finalist in the wedding cakes category, which had been all the award she'd dared imagine. But then she'd taken the whole enchilada, Best in Show, a national award that said she was the best there was.

"Why didn't they use a photograph of the cake?" she wondered out loud. "That's the real story, anyway."

"They really should have. Dude! That cake was magnificent."

Emma felt a rush of heat rise over her, and she shook her head. In her mid-thirties, she could still blush like a sixteen-year-old, and she hated that.

"Four layers of sinful confection," Fee read, pausing to shoot Emma a wide, toothy smile, "layered with some sort of vanilla miracle that stands on its own without daring to seep into this luscious cake. It even manages a whisper of the traditional brûlée crunch without intruding on the velvety softness of the overall experience. Judges scrambled to figure it out as they hovered over Travis's creation, planning weddings in their minds that would serve merely as an excuse to share this magic with friends, family, and an unsuspecting world. Emma Rae Travis is a confectionary genius."

It was the third time Fee had read the article out loud, but the excitement hadn't waned for Emma.

A confectionary genius.

Over the top, but really, really gratifying.

"They only mentioned the Backstreet in tiny letters after the close of the article," Fee pointed out. "Harry's going to go ballistic, you know."

"Yep." Emma glanced at her watch and nodded. "Any minute now, in fact."

When the front door exploded open and the bell flew off like a heat-seeking missile, Emma tapped the face of her watch and raised an eyebrow at Fee. "Right on schedule."

"Why are you standing around back here?" Harry blustered, propping open the kitchen door and filling the doorway as he stared Fee down. "Didn't you hear the bell in the front? I could have been a customer, and that's what you *do,* Fee. You wait on the customers. Now march your tail out there and *wait on customers!*"

"But you're the only —"

"Do you not speak English?" he sniped.

"Get out there."

Fee didn't say another word or even cast a glance in Emma's direction. Once she slipped past Harry, he stomped into the kitchen, letting the door swing shut behind him.

"So you've seen it," he growled, nodding toward the newspaper.

"Yes," Emma replied, folding the paper and tucking it into the drawer beneath the counter.

"Then you know that the bakery was barely given a mention."

"Yes, Harry, and I'm really sorry about that. I talked to the reporter and —"

"The Backstreet Bakery is practically a landmark in Atlanta!" he exclaimed, and then he rubbed his sandpaper face with both hands. "You'd be *nothing* without this place. You wouldn't even *have* that ridiculous award if not for the Backstreet."

Nothing!

"Well, I wouldn't exactly —"

"You think about that the next time you go looking for a little notoriety on your own, Emma Rae."

Emma heard the bakery phone ring, and she wished it had been her cell phone.

My kingdom for an interruption!

"This place gave you your start. I took

you in —"

— *when you were a nobody right out of cooking school.* Emma could say it with him, word for irritating word. She'd certainly heard it enough times to commit the diatribe to memory.

I took you in and gave you a kitchen to bake in, and this —

". . . is the thanks I get?"

Fee didn't set foot into the kitchen. She just called to her through a slight crack in the door. "Em? The phone's for you."

THAT's what I'm talkin' about! An interruption!

Harry was still grumbling as she moved past him and picked up the phone.

"Emma Travis."

"Ms. Travis, my name is Susannah Littlefield. I'm the administrator over at The Tanglewood Inn."

"How can I help you, Miss Littlefield?"

"Susannah, please."

"Susannah."

"I don't know whether you've heard about the redesign at The Tanglewood?"

"I think I read something," Emma said, trying to recall the article. "Some business tycoon bought it to turn it into an exclusive wedding destination hotel or something like that."

"Yes. My employer, Jackson Drake, has been completely refurbishing The Tanglewood, designing a five-star, one-stop shop for weddings and elegant affairs."

Emma's heart began to race, and she glanced at Harry as he leaned over the stainless-steel sink, scrubbing maniacally to eradicate some nonexistent blemish.

"I saw the article about your award," the woman continued. "Congratulations! It's quite impressive."

"Oh. Thank you," Emma replied. "So what can I do for you, Susannah? Were you looking for a wedding cake?"

"At least one," Susannah said on a chuckle. "Mr. Drake is interviewing for the catering staff tomorrow afternoon and I saw the article. I was hoping you might come in and meet with him."

Emma narrowed her eyes and grimaced. As Harry met her glance, he puffed his cheeks and shrugged. "What!"

"I'm sorry, I don't think I understand."

"I'm offering you the opportunity to run your own kitchen at The Tanglewood, Ms. Travis. Select your own staff, and work with Anton Morelli, one of Atlanta's finest chefs."

"I'm aware of his reputation. He's . . . gifted."

"I'd like you to consider coming to The

Tanglewood to create wedding cakes and pastries for us on a full-time basis."

Emma's eyes met Harry's again, and he glared at her. "Tick tock, Emma Rae. Is that a personal call?"

"Would you like to come and meet with Mr. Drake?"

"I'd love to, Susannah. What time tomorrow?"

Emma stood before the glass case, tap-tap-tapping her fingers on the top of it as she considered the array of baked goods before her.

"Let's do a selection of petit fours," she said. "Both kinds of brownies. A couple of the red velvet cupcakes."

Fee obediently removed each selection as Emma pointed it out, arranging the pastries atop a lace doily on a large aluminum tray.

"I'm going to take two of the mini wedding cakes out of the fridge. The crème brûlée, of course."

"Of course!"

"And the praline espresso."

"I thought you made that for the Reynolds tasting."

"I did, but that's not until Thursday. I can make another before then."

"Oh, Em," Fee said on an excited sigh.

"This could be huge for you."

"For *us,*" Emma replied. "If I go, you go. They said I could hire my own staff, and you can start out as a pastry apprentice."

Fee crumpled as she tried to stifle her enthusiasm, and then she popped up into a bouncing ball of excitement.

"Buh-bye, Harry," she sang. "Buh-*byeeeeeee.*"

"All right now. I don't have the job yet."

"But you will," she vowed. "Once the dude gets a load of what you can do, that job is yours, Em."

"From your lips to —" She couldn't even finish it. "Well, you know."

God hadn't been paying much attention to Emma for a while. Or maybe it was the other way around. Either way, she had no reason to believe He'd be interested in starting again now.

"Will you help me load my car?"

"Is that what you're wearing?"

It was a simple question, but fully loaded.

"Yes. Why? Is it all wrong?"

"It's not wrong. It just needs . . . *something.* It doesn't scream, *Emma Rae, Cool Baker Dudette.*"

Fee's silent scrutiny caused Emma to look down at her clothes. Navy blue linen trousers and a pale pink silk blouse.

"I know it's a little more dressy than normal," she explained, fidgeting with the lone wrinkle she spotted on the sleeve of her blouse. "But this is an important job, in an elegant hotel, and —"

"No, no," Fee interrupted. "I mean, it's too much *color.*"

"Pink and navy blue is too much color?" Emma asked on a chuckle. "This, from the girl wearing so much black that she disappears if the lights go dim?"

"Hey. It's a look."

"Yes, it is. But it's not *my* look, Fee."

"Do you want to borrow my choker? Just to jazz it up a little?"

Emma stared for a moment at the jagged silver rendition of thorny barbed wire circling Fee's throat, and then she shook her head. "Thanks anyway. I'm thinking I'll go simple. Help me load the car?"

"Sure."

They carefully transferred the sample tray to the passenger seat, and Emma double-checked the plastic-domed lid to make sure it was secure before setting the lipped platter bearing two miniature wedding cakes on top of it.

"Too bad we can't belt them in," Fee observed. "Do you want me to ride over with you and sit in the backseat to anchor them?"

Emma looked at her Mini Cooper, then at Fee, and back again. "Where will you sit?"

"Good point."

"Besides, you have to mind the store," Emma reminded her. "I'll just drive very slowly."

"Slower than your usual? You should have left yesterday then if you wanted to make your appointment."

"Hey. I'm careful."

"You're in slow-mo, Em."

"I am a cautious driver."

"Yes, you are. Cautious and *s-l-oooooow.*"

Emma chuckled and then closed the bright red door with care. She stood before Fee for a silent moment, trying not to look as nervous as she felt, and then she realized that she was biting her lip.

"You'll do great," Fee promised. "Just remember: you're a confectionary *genius!*"

"Yes, I am."

"Knock 'em dead."

"I will," Emma stated with gusto. "I'll knock 'em —" and she jabbed the air with her fist for emphasis "— dead!"

Fee raised two fists before her, and nodded her encouragement. Emma grinned as she tapped them with her own. It was a ritual for them, a secret handshake of sorts that they'd been sharing since very soon after they'd first met. *Tap-tap.* Then both palms upright, two slaps, two more slaps returned, a couple of quick hip bumps, and "Hoo-yeah!" in unison.

"Go get us that job!"

When she wasn't shifting gears, Emma kept her hands at ten and two o'clock all the way over to The Tanglewood. It was a short drive, but it seemed like a long winter's trek with the volatile cargo on the seat behind her. And it didn't help that the young guy in the SUV on her bumper kept honking his horn. What did he want? She was going the speed limit. Almost.

She'd only just pulled into the circular drive in front of the hotel when a smiling woman stepped up to her car and tapped on the window. Emma rolled it down tentatively.

"Yes?"

"What a cute little car," the woman said in a deep Southern drawl. "You can park it right *heah, sugah.* The hotel isn't open yet, so we don't have to worry about parking. Just pull it up in line after the others."

"Oh. Well, thank you."

Emma did as she was told and then slipped out of the car.

"I'm Madeline Winston. My little *bruthah* owns The Tanglewood."

"Pleased to meet you. I'm Emma Rae Travis. I'm here to interview for the pastry chef position. Susannah Littlefield called me?"

"Good gracious, yes," Madeline cooed. "You're the young lady who won the award for the best baker! Susannah was so excited that you agreed to come and speak with us, Miss Travis."

"Emma."

"And I'm Madeline."

Emma tugged open the back door, then slid the trays toward her.

"What have you got there, Emma?"

"Oh, I brought samples."

"*Sam–ples!* How lovely! Can I help you carry them?"

"I think I've got it. Just point me in the right direction. That would be a great help."

Madeline took her assignment very seriously, gently touching Emma's arm and guiding her every step.

"Right *ovah hee-ah.* A tiny step up. That's right. Now just let me get in front of you and I'll open up that side *do–ah.*"

Over the top of the tray and right between the two small cakes, Emma spotted an arched entry to what appeared to be the restaurant.

"Shall I set up in the dining room?" she asked.

"Please," Madeline replied. "It's off to the left. Just be careful as you go through, because there are —"

A sudden crunch against both of her knees sent Emma teetering off balance. As she struggled to keep the trays from toppling, her upper body continued forward while her foot suddenly wedged itself beneath an enormous soft mound.

"Whoooooooaa!"

"Oh, no!" Madeline cried from behind her, but it was too late to stop the crash.

First, the cakes hit the carpeted floor, and then Emma's body as she demolished one of the cakes with her elbow and landed face-first in the other.

Madeline shrieked, and after several moments, Emma realized the woman was using her own sweater to swipe the streaks of fondant from Emma's cheek.

"I'm so sorry," she told her as she wiped off her face. "I'm so very, very sorry. I was just about to tell you the linen company had left a bundle of table linens right in the middle of the lobby."

Emma glanced back at the toppled mound of tablecloths and embroidered napkins and then clamped her eyes shut so tightly that they ached.

"I'm so sorry, Miss Travis. Are you all right?"

"What on earth is going on out here?"

Emma looked up to find a man standing over her, arms folded and glaring down at her like the giant looking at Jack from the top of the beanstalk.

Except Jack's giant probably didn't look like this! This giant bore a striking resemblance to . . . *last month's cover of GQ!*

"This is Emma Rae Travis," Madeline told him, still wiping Emma's face with the sleeve of her sweater. "She's the baker Susannah told you about this mornin'. She was kind enough to bring us some samples of her work, Jackson. But the linens were delivered and left right here in the middle of the lobby. And I think you can guess what happened next."

"You're the hazelnut girl."

Emma looked up at him and cocked her head. "Pardon?"

"The fudge brownies and the hazelnut coffee pusher. From the bakery down on the square."

Hazelnut —

"Oh! It's you," she said as she struggled to find her footing.

"It's me."

"You're the one who made those scrumptious brownies Jackson brought us last week?" Madeline exclaimed. "Isn't that something, Jack?"

"It's something, all right," he muttered and then appeared to compose himself. "Are you hurt?"

"Yes," she replied. "My ego is crushed. Surgery may be needed."

He laughed in spite of himself.

"Madeline. Why don't you call for someone to come and clean up this mess?"

"Wait!" Emma cried. "Let me see if there's anything that can be salvaged."

Clearly, the point was moot.

"No. I guess there's not."

"Come on, sweet pea," Madeline crooned. "Come upstairs with me, and we'll get you cleaned up. Then you'll come to Jackson's office for a proper meeting."

"Maddie, I don't think —"

"Hush now," she chastised. "We'll meet you in your office in two shakes of a little lamb's *tay-il.*"

Madeline placed a firm arm around Emma's shoulders and led her past the front desk and down the hall toward the elevator. Emma couldn't help herself, she looked back, wondering for a moment if the storm brewing in Jackson Drake's chocolate brown eyes would turn her straight to a pillar of salt just for looking.

Espresso Fondant

2 pounds powdered sugar (sifted)
1/4 cup chilled water
1 tablespoon gelatin (unflavored)
1/2 cup white corn syrup
1 1/2 tablespoons glycerin
2 tablespoons shortening
1/2 cup cocoa powder
1 teaspoon vanilla extract
3 tablespoons espresso

Sift powdered sugar into a large bowl and make a well in the center. Set aside.
Pour water into a saucepan and sprinkle the gelatin lightly across the top.
Let soften for approximately 5-8 minutes.
Heat and stir until dissolved and clear. DO NOT BOIL.
Remove from heat and add corn syrup, glycerin, and shortening. Blend well.
Pour the gelatin mixture into the sugar well and mix until blended, working from the well out so that the fondant will be pliable.
Knead with your hands until stiff, and then knead in cocoa and espresso.
Use powdered sugar in small amounts to keep mixture from being sticky.
Shape into a ball and wrap tightly with plastic wrap.

Place in airtight container and let it rest at room temperature overnight before rolling out and fitting over cake.

3

Madeline's sister Georgiann had a pink sweater with pearl buttons in her car that fit Emma as if it belonged on her. Their other sister, Norma, was able to scrub the fondant from Emma's dark blue trousers and blow them dry with a hair dryer, while Susannah Littlefield helped her brush the clumps of icing out of her hair. Less than twenty minutes later, Emma had reapplied a pink frost to her lips and pulled her hair back into a neat ponytail, and when Susannah escorted her into Jackson Drake's office, Emma looked for all the world as if she'd just arrived.

"Have a seat, Ms. Travis."

"Thank you," she replied, and then slipped down into the leather chair across from him. "I'd just like to say how sorry I am, Mr. Drake."

"No need to apologize," he said without looking up from her résumé. "We'll be lucky if you decide not to sue us." His eyes darted upward and he regarded her seriously. "You're not going to sue us, are you, Ms. Travis?"

"Oh! No. I'm not."

Emma's heart was pounding so hard against her chest that she could see Georgiann's cashmere sweater pulsing along with it.

"Good."

And just like that, his focus was back on the parchment paper in his hands.

"Knock, knock," Madeline announced in a sing-song voice as she pushed the office door wide open.

She held a small china plate with both hands; on it were several petit fours, two small brownie squares and a hunk of praline espresso wedding cake.

"What's this?" Jackson asked her.

"Well, everything wasn't completely ruined," she explained, setting the plate on the desktop, and then running a reassuring hand over the slope of Emma's shoulder. "We cleaned up the mess, and then saved a bit of what didn't hit the carpet."

While her brother regarded the plate before him, Madeline winked at Emma.

"Thank you," Emma mouthed with caution.

"Now I'll just leave you two to your meetin'," the woman said, rolling around the edge of the door and disappearing without another peep.

Jackson looked up at Emma, shook his head, and peered back at the sweets on the plate.

"Oh, um. Let me just tell you what these are," Emma stammered, standing up and leaning across the desk. "This is a blonde brownie with walnuts, butterscotch and chocolate, iced with hazelnut cream."

"Of course it is."

"And the petit fours are red velvet, carrot cake, and pumpkin spice. It looks like they managed to save the espresso wedding cake with praline filling. The fudge brownie you've tasted already, but I didn't know that when I brought it."

His eyes felt like a steam iron being pressed against her, and Emma sat down in the chair again and folded her shaking hands in her lap until he looked away at last. She regarded him closely as he reached down and picked up one of the petit fours and popped it into his mouth.

"That one is pumpkin spice," she commented, but he didn't reply.

After what felt like a week or so of agonizing silence, the door to his office creaked open again. This time, it was Susannah who peered at them through the crack.

"We've got a problem, Jack. Could you step out for just a minute?"

Without so much as a by-your-leave, Jackson Drake got up from his chair, crossed the office, and left Emma sitting there. She turned and looked at Susannah, still standing in the doorway.

"Sorry, sugar. Someone's caught in the elevator."

"Oh!"

Emma hopped to her feet and followed Susannah around the corner where Jackson stood at the closed elevator door with Madeline and Georgiann, both of the women cringing at the sounding buzzer.

"Did you push the emergency call button?" he called, and someone from the other side confirmed that he had. "Then someone should be here in just a few minutes. Hang tight."

The buzzer ceased at last, and Jackson stared at the floor, shaking his head.

"The thing was doing a shimmy earlier in the week," he told Susannah. "I should have had you call the service company then."

"Oh, well, that wouldn't have anything to do with the door being jammed," Emma stated, and then she realized both Jackson and Georgiann were staring at her as if her hair was on fire.

"How do you know that, pumpkin?" Madeline asked her.

"When the car shimmies," she began, and then she interrupted herself. "I mean, I'm assuming this is a hydraulic system, right?"

Jackson Drake looked at her as if she'd just spoken to him in a foreign tongue.

"Well, it probably is. Anyway, I'm thinking it's likely that the rails are just dry. A little oil can take care of that for you. But the door jamming like this is probably your drive belt. The service guy will take care of that when he gets the passengers out."

"The drive belt," Madeline repeated. "Aren't you just the handiest little pastry chef that there ever was?"

Emma shrugged. "My dad was in construction. One of the companies he owned a long time back built elevators for small commercial buildings."

"My daddy was in banking," Madeline commented. "But I can't balance my checkbook without help."

"Ms. Travis," Jackson piped up. "I hope you won't mind if we cut our meeting short."

"Oh. Certainly. You have things to deal with here, don't you?"

"Thank you for understanding."

"Nonsense," Madeline said, taking Emma's hand into hers. "Why don't you come along with my *sistah* and me, and we'll go down the street and grab some lunch. Maybe some sweet tea and a sandwich and, by the time we get back, you and my *bruthah* can pick up right where you all left off."

"Oh, well, I can't really —"

"Don't be silly. Of course you can. Let's go, ladies. Susannah, will you join us? And Jackson, we'll bring you something back."

"Yeah, it's a simple fix," the serviceman told Jackson as he scribbled on the yellow paper on the clipboard in his hand. "Just the drive belt."

"The drive belt," Jackson repeated. "That's what kept the door from opening properly?"

"Yep."

"And the car shaking?"

"Yeah, that's another issue."

"Dry rails?" Jackson suggested.

"Right."

"You'll see that they're oiled?"

"That's my job."

Jackson wanted to laugh, but instead he just shook his head.

A pastry chef who knows about elevator

cables and drive belts. Now if I can just hire a front desk manager who can rotate the tires on my car.

Jackson strode down the hallway and into his office. He'd forgotten about the plate of cakes on his desk until he sat down in his chair, and then his sweet tooth got the better of him, inspiration to fetch himself a cup of coffee.

He popped a square of blonde brownie into his mouth, and then he leaned back against the chair and closed his eyes while he savored it.

What do you know? Hazelnut really could be the answer to all the world's confectionary needs!

Jackson gulped down some coffee and then picked up the résumé of Emma Rae Travis.

Graduate of Le Cordon Bleu College of Culinary Arts; certified in Patisserie and Baking; six years as Head Baker for The Backstreet Bakery in Roswell; three-time finalist in the wedding cakes category of Atlanta's Passionate Palate Award competition; grand prize winner of the award just this year.

"She is fabulous, Jackson," Madeline whispered as she stepped into his office. "Is that her résumé? Aren't you impressed? We all just love her to death, I tell you. If you don't hire that woman right this very minute, you're a bigger fool than Catfish Walter."

Catfish Walter. Jackson hadn't thought of the old toothless guy who'd worked for their grandfather in more than a decade.

"Why did they call him Catfish, anyway?" he asked.

"You stop that," she chastised him. "She's downstairs with Georgiann, looking around the kitchen. You take yourself right on down there, Jackson Drake, and you offer her a job."

"I'm sorry, Maddie. The last I knew, this was my hotel, and I get to choose the staff."

"Stop it right now," she said, and then she gave his hand a quick, tender rub. "You and I both know this was Desiree's dream, and not yours. And if that angel had had all of the bakers east of the Mississippi to choose from, I'm telling you she would have chosen Emma Rae Travis. Now you go down there right now and offer her the job, Jackson, and make Desi proud."

Jackson arched an eyebrow at his sister, but the rest of the glare he'd been planning fell short in the light of the charming grin she flashed at him.

"You are a very bossy woman."

"I know I am, pumpkin. Now get along

downstairs."

Jackson planted a peck on Madeline's cheek as he passed.

When he finally made it down near the kitchen, the scrape of furniture drew his immediate attention. Inside, Emma Travis was giving directions while two workmen hoisted a heavy metal island across the floor.

"What's going on here?" he asked Georgiann, who was standing back and watching from the sidelines.

"Oh. I'm sorry," Emma said. "I just thought I'd help you get this part of the kitchen set up for easier use."

"Did you?"

"Chef Morelli's kitchen is perfect for what he does," she explained. "But in here, for the purposes of baking, it's all wrong. The prep station is on the opposite side of the room, too far away from the refrigeration unit. Wedding cakes, in particular, can sometimes weigh up to a hundred pounds or more, and you're not going to want to have to transport them across the length of the room to get them chilled. And the cupboard for the —"

"I have an idea," Jackson interrupted. "Why don't we let the person who is offered the job, and actually accepts it, set up the kitchen the way *they* want it?"

"Oh. I . . . uh . . ."

"Jackson, this is not Ms. Travis's fault," his sister objected. "I asked for her opinion, and then called Frank and his carpenter in from the dining room for their help moving things around so I could see what she meant."

"She's got a good point about the flow in here, Mr. Drake."

Jackson turned and looked the workman squarely in the eye. "Thank you, Frank. And this would be your professional opinion based on all your experience as a baker?"

"Well, no. But I'm a contractor. I've built more than a hundred commercial kitchens."

Jackson felt something thud inside him. He wondered if he might have to hire Emma Travis, just so he could be around on the off chance that she was ever wrong about anything.

"Why don't we go sit down and have a chat, Ms. Travis?"

"Emma."

Her hazel-green eyes hinted at a twinkle before she dragged them away from him. He noticed a slight tremble to her hands as she ran them through her dark brown hair and then folded them in her lap when they settled across from one another in the dining room. He couldn't seem to catch her eye as she fidgeted and darted her attention from the draperies to the doorway to the carpet.

"Something else that doesn't look quite right, Emma?"

"Oh. No. I was just thinking."

"About?"

"About your linen delivery service. They shouldn't have been allowed to just drop the delivery in the lobby and leave like that. I was thinking that if I were you, I'd fire them and sign a contract with Indelibles down in Dunwoody. They have great prices and color selection. With them, you could have your tables dressed in one color for brunch, for instance, and then another for more elegant dinners."

"I didn't see anything on your résumé that would indicate any job experience running a restaurant," Jackson noted. "Yet you seem to be an expert on this topic, as well as many others."

"The Avery Chronicles," she replied, and the sliver of a smile that she delivered charmed Jackson to the very core.

"Pardon me?"

"Avery Travis. That's my mother."

"Avery Travis from Savannah?"

"Well, she grew up in Savannah, so . . . yes. The very same. She's the queen of fundraisers, worthy causes, and cotillions. You can't be her daughter without picking up a vast array of useless information about hosting parties, setting up buffets, and assembling celebrity auctions."

Avery Travis. Emma Rae Travis's mother? It seemed almost impossible.

"You are a wealth of surprising knowledge and information, Ms. Travis."

"Emma."

"I assume my sisters have filled you in on the destiny of this endeavor?"

"They have."

"And your thoughts?"

"I think it fills a niche that no one really knew was there. It's quite brilliant, actually. Who else in Atlanta has a hotel where you can have your bridal shower, the rehearsal dinner, your wedding, reception, and your honeymoon if you want to, all in one location?"

"And this is something you would like to be connected with? Help build this business and make it thrive?"

"I would. Very much."

"When can you start?"

"I think I already did," she said with a grin. "Now, can I go back in there and have my kitchen set up the way I like it?"

"Stop by my office afterward," Jackson

suggested. “We’ll talk about salary, staff, and calibrate our expectations.”

“I’ll do that,” she said, hopping to her feet and extending her hand toward him. “I’m really excited about coming to work at The Tanglewood. You won’t regret hiring me.”

Jackson shook her hand and smiled. “Is that a promise?”

“Yes, sir. It is.”

“We’ll get along just fine then.”

The Top Ten Most Popular Wedding Themes

1. Whimsical or fairy tale
2. Holiday focus (such as Christmas or Valentine's Day)
3. Victorian or medieval setting
4. Hollywood glamour
5. Beach or seaside
6. English garden
7. Winter wonderland
8. Black & white ball
9. Hawaiian or luau
10. Sports-related

4

"Baseball." Emma repeated it again just to be certain. "They want a baseball-themed wedding?"

"I'm sorry to tell you, yes. They are Atlanta Braves fanatics, and they met at one of the games," Jackson explained, and then he leaned back in the leather chair behind his desk until it creaked. "My sister Madeline is going to be working as an overall coordinator for the weddings. She'll sync everything up for these events as they unfold. Any further details can be had by talking to her."

Emma had the distinct impression that she'd been dismissed. She didn't know whether to hop up and run out of the room, or switch to one of the dozen other topics she'd brought with her to the first meeting with her brand-new boss.

"Was there something else?" he asked, running a hand through his thick hair.

"Oh, yes," she said. "A whole lot of something elses, actually."

"Can you give me the abbreviated version, then? Or maybe it's something Maddie can handle? My plate is a little full today."

The skin on her face and chest heated up like someone had switched on the burner.

"I thought this was a status meeting," she said in controlled-courtesy mode.

Jackson sighed. "That would indicate that I know what our status is. And I don't quite have a handle on that at the moment."

Emma took a deep breath and held it. When she finally released it, she did so with slow and deliberate consistency.

"You called this meeting," she reminded him. "Perhaps you have questions for me?"

"No."

A long moment of silence ticked between them.

"No?" she clarified.

"Not right now. No."

"Can I ask why I'm here?"

Jackson propped both elbows on the desk, and then dropped his face into his hands and rubbed it briskly. When he finally lifted his gaze again, his mouth tilted into half a smile.

"You are here, Ms. Travis, because I'm told you're the best. Beyond that, I'm afraid . . . I've got nothin'."

Emma couldn't help herself, and she popped out a chuckle in rhythmic spurts. She stood up and leaned across the desk, touching him firmly on the shoulder. "Honesty is good."

This time, it was Jackson's turn to laugh. "I apologize, Emma. I'm in a little over my head at the moment. And I'm not accustomed to being in over my head."

"I sense that," she replied. She stood, folded her arms, and faced him. "What can I do to help?"

He screwed up his mouth and narrowed his eyes. "I have *no* idea."

"Well, when you do," she offered with a nod toward the door, "I'm just downstairs."

Emma emerged from Jackson's office to find Susannah wide-eyed and hurrying toward her. Placing one finger over her lips, she nodded Emma toward the hallway in a conspiratorial fervor and, outside the door, Susannah looped her arm through Emma's and led her toward the elevator.

"Our boss is in a pickle," she told her. "There's a meeting in the courtyard in ten minutes to talk about it."

"Thank goodness," Emma returned.

The Tanglewood was a box of sorts, all four sections of the historic building wrapping around a large, open brick courtyard. Tall, leafy trees were draped with strands of a thousand small lights and nearly as many tweeting birds with high-pitched little voices. Thick bars of sunlight forced their way through the branches from the bright blue Georgia sky, landing on the brick as if illuminating a portion of a stage that was ripe for the first act.

"Oh good!" Georgiann exclaimed as they arrived. "Now we're all here."

Norma wiped off the top of one of the bright-white bistro tables as Madeline appeared with a tray of china cups and a large flowered pot.

"Sit down, you two," Madeline urged them as Norma poured. "We've got tea now. It's time to get down to business."

"Well, somebody has to," Susannah chimed in.

Emma peered into one face after another, all of them contorted with a mix of worry and amusement.

Georgiann stepped into her Big Sister role and pointed her finger at Madeline. "Maddie, you start."

"Okay," she complied, opening a leather portfolio and turning over page after page of notes. "We've got to make plans for the opening night party. And then we have seven confirmed weddings scheduled for the next three months after we open."

"What?" Emma interrupted. "I've only heard about one of them."

"I'll go over them with you in detail," Madeline promised. "But the first thing we have to do is decide on how we can make the most of our opening to let Atlanta know we're here."

"Isn't this something your brother should be tending to?" she asked with a gentle cringe punctuating the end of the question.

The sisters all chuckled, and Susannah squeezed Emma's hand.

"Maybe we should give Emma a bit of background," she suggested, and Georgiann nodded as if giving her permission.

"Well," Norma began, combing her already-perfect hair back with the tips of her fingers, just the way Jackson often did. "Desiree, my brother's wife —"

"He's married?" Emma interrupted.

"His late wife, *sugah,*" Georgiann offered.

"Oh."

"She used to work here at The Tanglewood," Norma went on.

"It was a little boutique hotel back then," Madeline added. "And Desiree was the assistant manager."

"She used to dream about buying this

place and turning it into a wedding destination hotel," Georgiann took over again. "She'd tell him all about her plans. Oh, they were just fantasies, of course, but Desi loved to dream about what she was going to do *he-ah.*"

Susannah leaned closer to Emma, and her floral scent tickled Emma's nostrils. "She died of cancer, just a couple of years ago."

Emma's eyes widened, and then regret took the form of a salty glaze. "That's awful."

"In her final days, Desi told Jack that it was her one and only regret in life," Madeline drawled, "that she never followed through on those plans."

"So once she was gone and the grief was stranglin' him like a weddin' corset," Georgiann piped up, "sure enough, this place went on the auction block for sale. Jackson hasn't done three impulsive things in his whole entire life, but he snapped up The Tanglewood faster'n a gator snags meat."

"I think he thought it was a tribute to Desi's memory," Madeline told her, scrunching up her nose and pressing her turned-down lips together. "But the truth is Jack doesn't know two licks about romance, so him operatin' a weddin' hotel?"

"Well, that's just about as crazy as tryin'

to milk a three-legged dog," Georgiann finished.

Well, that IS crazy, Emma thought. But she didn't quite see the whole connection between milk and a handicapped canine.

"I think he's just realized he's up a creek without a paddle," Madeline explained. "And we're makin' it our jobs to help him row."

Emma nodded. Now *that* she could understand.

"He's hired that crazy chef. What's his name, Susannah?"

"Anton Morelli."

"Morelli. That's it. Well, you just meet that man for twenty-seven seconds, and you know he's gonna spot Jackson as a fish outta water in nothin' flat. He'll slice and filet that boy before the first appetizer is ever served in this place." Madeline placed her hand around Emma's wrist and looked her hard in the eye. "We've got to get things organized before he comes on board next week."

"What can I do to help?" she asked them.

Georgiann smacked her hands on the tabletop and grinned. "That's the spirit."

"We've got to make a plan for the opening gala," Norma told them. "We need a theme and a plan."

"And it had better be a doozy," Georgiann

added. "Atlanta needs to get the new and improved Tanglewood Inn on their radar, and fast."

Two hours later, each of the women gathered around the courtyard bistro table had a list of responsibilities assigned to them. Even in the management of the meeting itself, Jackson Drake's sisters were a well-oiled machine. Norma cleared the tea service while Madeline gathered their notes and Georgiann straightened the chairs. Emma was reminded of a synchronized swimming exhibition she'd once seen as they met up once again, said their hasty good-byes, and floated from the courtyard to the lobby before separating and going in three directions. The only thing missing were the swimsuits and bathing caps with matching rubber sunflowers on them.

Susannah's focus dragged to the lobby as an awkwardly tall gentleman emerged and looked around.

"That'll be Edward," she said, gathering her notes and poking her pen behind her ear.

"Edward?"

"Jackson's ten-thirty," she replied as she scurried toward the door. Then she tossed her hand into the air and wiggled her fingers as she sang, "Hotel insurance."

Emma folded her notes and, on her way back to the kitchen, tucked them into the file folder of impending weddings that Madeline had provided. She'd want to go over them with Fee when she arrived for her first official day in the employ of The Tanglewood Inn. Emma glanced at her watch and wondered what Fee's take on the place would be.

Less than an hour. Not nearly enough time to file down the jagged edges around her.

Emma took a slow stroll down the wide hallway from the lobby that led toward the restaurant and kitchens. Two swinging doors stood before her, both of them freshly painted white, identical with their round acrylic windows and stainless-steel kick plates, not a smudge in sight. She smiled as she softly nudged the one on the right, taking such pleasure in the gentle whoosh as the door separated from the rubber insulation around the jamb. On the other side: Emma's personal nirvana.

Two rows of stainless-steel work tables reached all the way down the length of the kitchen, like a shiny highway stretched across the desert at dawn. A perfect row of glass-paned cabinets framed with glossy hunter green trim sported brushed silver pulls. Bakeware was stacked inside a floor-to-ceiling cupboard, peeking out at her from behind a rectangle of streak-free glass. Emma tugged open one of the dozen drawers and brushed her hand along the variety of stainless-steel spoons positioned neatly like a museum display. She admired the bright apple-red tiles behind the deep porcelain sinks; a perfect match to the small diamonds of detail spotting the reflective black and white checkerboard floor.

At the other end of the kitchen sat an office (a cubbyhole really) open to the kitchen with one glass wall and three others freshly painted cream. The room was just big enough for a small desk, two upholstered chairs from the restaurant, and a mint green four-drawer file cabinet. It was small, but it was hers. She'd never had a kitchen *and an office* before. Just the sight of it made her feel all trembly and official inside.

"Ahhh-gguh!"

Emma turned just as Fee dropped two enormous canvas bags to the kitchen floor with a clunk and leaned against the doorway looking stunned. She shook her head slightly, and then clutched her own throat, propping her mouth open into a perfect round O.

"This is our kitchen??"

"It is," Emma grinned. "Isn't it just —"

"Yes. It is," Fee replied on a sigh. "It really is."

Fee hopped from foot to foot and then skittered across the length of the room toward Emma. The two of them smashed into something that resembled an embrace, and then they began to jump up and down in perfect unison.

"We are going to be *baking* here, Em," Fee told her, as if Emma didn't already know. "Here. *In this kitchen.*"

"Yes, we are!"

Both palms upright, two slaps, two more slaps returned, a couple of quick hip bumps, and "Hoo-yeah!" in unison. Their private language for celebrating the score.

"And not a comb-over in sight," Fee added, referring to their former boss's questionable hairstyle.

"Nope. Our new employer has a full head of gorgeous hair," Emma beamed. "Wait until you —"

The kerplunk of the swinging door drew them to immediate silence as they both spun around and faced the man standing in the doorway. His comb-over inspired a wayward snicker from Fee, and Emma punched her in the ribs with her elbow.

"Can I help you?" Emma offered.

"Don't bother telling me who you are," the man demanded. "Just leave my kitchen *at once!*"

The smile Edward Beemis had pasted on his face melted away the instant he swaggered out the front doors of the hotel. Jackson felt pretty certain Beemis thought he hadn't spotted it, but he caught it all right. Insurance guys and realtors — they all had the same air about them as far as Jackson was concerned. Unfortunately, they both were quite necessary in his new world.

Just as he turned back with the intent of heading toward the staircase and back up to his office on the fourth floor, an explosion of voices erupted and the kitchen doors flew open.

"Come osarla!"

"Chef Morelli, please come back!"

Jackson looked on as Anton Morelli skidded to a stop a few yards ahead of him, followed by Emma and a strange-looking character out of a gothic nightmare he'd once had.

"Sono uno dei massimi chef nel mondo!" Morelli shouted at them, waving his arms, his face turning a scarlet shade of frustrated.

The Goth with the silver hoop through her nose whispered something to Emma, and then Emma responded, telling Anton, "I know! You are!"

Her helpless, hopeful eyes landed on Jackson, and he asked, "What did he say?"

"Oh," said the Goth in monotone, "he's appalled. And he's the greatest chef in the universe."

"Oh," he replied. "*WHO* are you?"

"Fee Bianchi," Emma said. "Meet Jackson Drake."

Fee nodded at him with limited interest.

"Bianchi," Morelli repeated. *"Il suo nome è Bianchi?"*

"Yep," Fee answered. "That's my name."

"Italiano?"

"Si."

"E lei parla la lingua?"

"Yep. I'm fluent."

Morelli moved in on the woman as if she were his long-lost daughter, grabbing her with both hands and dragging her into an awkward embrace. The two of them began chattering unintelligibly while Jackson and Emma looked on.

"Fee is my assistant," Emma told him.

He blinked hard and swallowed his initial impression. "She any good?" he asked in hope.

"The best. I met her straight out of cooking school. She applied at the bakery, and I snapped her up. She's been my right hand ever since."

Jackson lifted one shoulder into a shrug. "Good."

"I know!" Fee exclaimed. "But your kitchen is even better than ours. We're just pastry chefs. You're The Big Cheese. *Il Formaggio Grande!*"

Morelli clanged like a fire engine, and then he tugged Fee toward him again and kissed her cheek. As an afterthought, he held her away from him and looked her over.

"You look very interesting," he told her in English, with only a slight Italian accent. "Do you do this on purpose, this look?"

"Oh yeah," Fee told him. "It's my personal style."

Morelli considered it, shrugged and then laughed again. "*Si.* You do have the style. Now you show me my kitchen, Fee Bianchi."

Fee looked back at them over her shoulder. Softly, toward Emma, she asked, "His kitchen *is* better than ours, right?"

Emma looked at Jackson, and he nodded.

"Yes!" Emma reassured her, and Fee disappeared around the corner, swept along by Hurricane Anton Morelli.

Jackson sighed. "Have you got this?"

"Well," she said, glancing down the hall

toward the kitchen. "Fee seems to."

"Good."

He started to turn away when Emma reached out and touched his arm. "If you have a minute?"

He didn't, but he didn't tell her that. "What's up?"

"I was thinking about the opening. Your sisters mentioned that you want to have some sort of party to introduce the new Tanglewood to Atlanta."

He sighed again. "It seems to be the consensus that this is a necessity."

"I have an idea about that."

"You do?"

He looked at Emma, and collided with the excitement sparkling in her stormy green eyes.

"I was thinking, since this is going to be a wedding destination hotel and everything, maybe we could have a sort of wedding reception. You know, following the marriage of the new Tanglewood with Atlanta. We could have a live band and dancing, and we could send out wedding-type invitations to everyone on the social register. It could be a sit-down dinner to show what Anton can do for a really elegant reception, and I can make an elaborate, one-of-a-kind wedding cake to —"

"You know, that's a pretty great idea," Jackson admitted, a little surprised to feel his own enthusiasm kicking in. "Could you run that by my sisters?"

"Sure," she said, and a smile peeled across her face, from one apple cheek to another.

Jackson started away from her, and then stopped in his tracks. Turning back, he said, "Thank you, Emma. And welcome to The Tanglewood."

The grin deepened across her fresh face. Something about it pinched him, and in that moment he was reminded of Desiree.

"Thank you, Mr. Drake."

"Jackson."

"Thank you, Jackson."

He nodded before heading for the stairs. Emma Rae Travis was quite a surprise. She hadn't turned out to be at all like his first hazelnut impression of her, and he was relieved about that. He could only hope her *assistant* turned out to be a surprise too. Black eyeliner, a nose ring, and fluent in Anton Morelli. The big picture didn't compute, but it didn't have to, as long as she lived up to Emma's confidence in her.

As he turned the corner, Norma met up with him and matched him stride for stride.

"Emma had a pretty great idea about the opening night shindig," he said.

"Well, for starters, let's not call it a shindig."

"Point taken," he replied. "How about the very elaborate opening night hootenanny?"

"Oh, Jackson," his sister sighed.

"I want you to talk to her more about it."

"Got it. And what about the restaurant? Have you made any decisions about opening it up to the public?"

"I don't know. Let's schedule a meeting with Anton once he's calmed down."

"Calmed down?" Norma glanced over at him as they walked along. "He's not calm?"

"Some mix-up about the kitchen."

"He's here?"

"He is."

"Two weeks early."

"Yes."

"We were also discussing the possibility of opening the courtyard a couple of afternoons during the week for high tea."

Jackson stopped, and then just stood there, kind of frozen. "High tea?"

"Emma had some really good ideas about it, and I thought —"

"She is just a font of inspiration, isn't she?"

"She's fantastic, Jack."

"Have you met her assistant?" he asked her.

"Fee?" Norma chuckled. "She's unique."

"She is that."

They reached the elevator and Jackson pressed the call button. "Let's schedule a meeting with Emma too. We'll discuss what she has in mind."

"Great!"

"But don't get your heart set on high tea, Norm."

"As long as you don't set your mind against it."

"I will listen with an open mind."

"Sure you will."

"Don't I always?"

Norma sniggered. "You don't want me to answer that, right? It's rhetorical?"

"Right."

"Thought so."

Afternoon High Tea
at
The Tanglewood Inn

An Assortment of Tea Sandwiches
Asparagus & Prosciutto ~ Cucumber Mint ~ Chicken Almond Salad

Scotch Eggs and
Dijon Deviled Eggs
Blueberry Scones with
Devonshire Cream

An Assortment of Delectables
Miniature Fruit Tarts ~ Petits Fours ~
Cashew Fudge Brownies
Chocolate-drizzled Strawberries ~
English Shortbread Cookies

5

"I was thinking something midweek, like Tuesday and Wednesday afternoons in the courtyard, weather permitting; in the restaurant, if not. Something very special, by reservation only. We could set the tables with fresh flowers in crystal bowls, and mismatched place settings of china with Battenberg lace table linens. The biggest expense is for a couple of misters."

"Misters?"

Georgiann patted Jackson's hand. "Outdoor fans with a faint mist to keep things cool, *sugah.*"

"Oh, right."

"We could easily wait until the spring to get them, though," Emma added, "before the weather gets too warm. I left those in the column on the right as a future expense." She waited a moment for some reaction, but nothing came. Jackson Drake's handsome face was a blank canvas. "So.

What do you think?"

"Oh, honey, Jackson didn't understand a word you said other than *afternoons* and *weather permitting,*" Georgiann teased. "We'll leave the style to the women in his life and just let him make the business decisions. What do you say, Jackson? Is there a little money in the budget to light a fire under this good idea?"

"I think it would be a great sideline for bridal showers, or bridal party and mother-daughter events," Emma added. "It could be a great resource to build clientele if we offered this as a little something extra."

Jackson leaned back in his chair and sighed. He propped his chin atop his clasped hands and looked at Emma until she felt a spark ignite from the heat of it.

"And this will be separate from the restaurant," he clarified. "Anton will not be involved at all."

"Right. I'll hire just one server. Fee and I will do all of the prep work and the baking."

"Fee?" Georgiann asked, looking around at them. "Who's Fee?"

"My assistant."

"You met her," Norma reminded her sister. "Yesterday in the kitchen."

Georgiann thought it over, and then the

light appeared to dawn with the odd expression that rose over her. "Oh. Really? That's your assistant, Emma Rae? She's . . . she looks interesting."

"Fee is a dream," Emma assured them. "She's gifted, and she's my right arm."

"Well, all right. I suppose if —"

"And you think you can manage this, along with the wedding cakes and the daily desserts for Morelli's restaurant."

"I do," she replied. "It's not really that much more work, just a couple of days a week."

"Exactly how much would you need to set this up?" Jackson asked Emma. "Table doo-dads and the like."

Emma pulled the budget sheet from the file folder in her lap and slid it across the desk toward him. "The setup is on the top, then a small amount for advertising and staples."

Jackson picked up the paper and turned it over. "This is it? This is all you'll need?"

"Yes, sir."

He glanced at Georgiann, and his sister grinned at him. "It's a dazzler of an idea, Jack."

"It's got our vote too," Madeline announced from the sidelines, where she and Susannah were quietly seated.

Emma hadn't realized she was holding her breath until Jackson smiled and the air sputtered out of her lungs.

"Let's do it."

"Oh, that's great!" she exclaimed, hopping out of the chair to her feet, and Georgiann clapped her hands.

"I'll rely on you to set it up and keep to this budget," he said, holding up the sheet of paper she'd handed over. "Not a nickel over these figures without coming back to me first."

Emma nodded. She could hardly wait to tell Fee. Their own kitchen, a line of specialty wedding cakes, and now their own tea room? It was almost more than she could contain, and she wanted to burst out of there and take the stairs in leaps, two at a time. Instead, she dropped back down into the chair and sighed happily.

"That's just great," she told him. "Thank you."

"Now let's move on," Jackson said, all business once again. "Let's review the plans for the opening. You're up, Maddie."

Madeline dragged her chair over to the side of the desk and opened a thick file folder. "All righty," she said as she began handing over paperwork. "Emma and I have been kicking around some really wonderful ideas to expand on her wedding theme idea. Norma has worked with Anton to develop the menu. And here is a sample of the invitation, based on a classic wedding announcement. And . . . oh, where is it? Here is the suggested guest list that Susannah has put together."

"We thought we'd go very exclusive," Susannah chimed in. "A sit-down meal, dancing, champagne; an elegant reception with one of Emma's crème brûlée wedding cakes as the grand finale."

"I thought I could design a cake version of The Tanglewood," Emma added.

"Can you do that?" he asked.

She nodded, then plucked the sketch from her file and pushed it toward him.

"You can make a cake that looks like this?" he exclaimed.

"My assistant is an artist when it comes to sculpting three-dimensional cakes."

"Is this three-dimensional?"

She nodded again and grinned.

"That's . . . *amazing.*"

"That's why we hired her, Jack," Georgiann told him on a chuckle. "Emma Rae is *amazing.*"

"Tell him your other idea, Emma," Madeline said with a nod of encouragement.

"Oh!" she exclaimed, pulling another page

from her file and holding it up toward him. "I was thinking something like this. It's put together on an acrylic stand, and it holds up to two hundred individual wedding cakes. That way, we could do several different varieties so that people could really sample what we have to offer."

"How many different kinds of cakes are there?" he asked, and the women in the room chuckled in unison.

"Jack, it's limitless," Madeline answered. "Cake flavors and fillings and icings."

"Let Emma tell him, *sistah.*"

"I could work up maybe five or six of my specialties and —"

Jackson leaned forward and groaned, causing Emma to stop, mid-word. The look on his face was ominous, and she found herself holding her breath again.

"I think I owe you ladies an apology," he said at last. "I jumped into this thing and . . . well . . . most of the burden has been resting on all of you, and I'm really sorry for that."

"Jack."

"No, George. Let me say this," he insisted, running his fingertips through his hair with a worried frown. "You've rallied around me. My sisters, Susannah, and even you, Emma, a virtual stranger. All of you are the ones making Desi's . . . well, making this happen. Not me." Emma felt the weight of his emotion, and it closed in on her like the locked door of a very small room.

"I just want to thank you. All of you."

"We're happy to do it," Madeline said as she rounded the desk and wrapped her arms around her brother's neck.

"We've got your back," Susannah added.

"Don't you worry about a thing, little *bruthah,*" said Georgiann.

Emma felt a little pinch to her heart as she looked on, wondering for the countless time in her life whether this scene represented what *real families* were like. She'd really have no way of knowing, after all, being the only child of Gavin and Avery Travis.

Living at opposite sides of the country and never having been in the same vicinity since the ink was dry on the divorce decree eight years back, their names still fit together like one word. *GavinAndAveryTravis.* Even as the thought comforted her in that odd and somewhat disturbing way, Emma was fully aware of how ridiculous the dynamic actually was.

With a sigh, she attributed yet another awkward moment in her life to the dysfunction that was The Family Travis.

It's all a rich tapestry, she decided.

Trying to figure it out had led to far too many headaches over the years. She brushed thoughts of *GavinAndAvery* aside with a wisp of hair from her face, and she smiled.

"I've got a meeting downstairs," she announced as she rose from the chair.

"The baseball wedding?" Madeline asked.

"The very same."

"I can't wait to see what you do for them."

"Fee and I have come up with several options for the cake," Emma said as she headed for the door. "Now, if we can just convince Anton to get behind a menu of hot dogs, Cracker Jack, and beer —"

They all hooted with laughter, and Emma shrugged.

"Maybe we can leave him out of this one and just contract a street *vendah,*" Madeline teased.

"It's okay. I have a plan to let Pearl break the news."

"Pearl?" Jackson inquired.

"That's Anton's sous chef," Susannah told him.

"She doesn't wear a dog collar, does she?" Georgiann asked, wide-eyed, and everyone broke into laughter.

"It's not really a dog collar," Emma said, leaning in toward Georgiann. "It's just . . .

well, Fee has a unique personal style."

"Oh. All right."

Emma gave Georgiann's shoulder a pat as she grinned at Jackson. "Thank you so much."

"A baseball-themed weddin'," Georgiann drawled as Emma headed down the hall toward the stairs. "Can you *imagine?*"

As Emma hurried across the courtyard, Fee tossed her a fragmented smile.

"This is Callie Beckinsale. Ms. Beckinsale, this is Emma Travis, our resident cake genius."

The perky blonde's grin swallowed most of her face, and over-whitened teeth flashed at Emma unexpectedly, like a surprise out of a children's pop-up book.

"It's such a pleasure to meet you," she sang at a high pitch. "I was maid of honor in Susan Reese's wedding last year, and you did the English garden cake? You were at The Backstreet then, of course. It was the one with the ivy around the bottom and the sugar flowers and the luscious fresh raspberries between the layers?"

"Yes," Emma said, scraping back a wrought-iron chair and joining the others at the bistro table. "I remember."

"Well, Dan and I — Dan, that's my fiancé — well, neither one of us had ever seen a cake like that one." The woman spoke in fast spurts. She looked at Fee, tucking a strand of hair behind her ear, and told her, "It was like a piece of art or something."

Fee handed Emma her sketch pad. "Ms. Beckinsale, we're going to be serving some samples. Can I get you some coffee to go with it? Or some tea?"

"A soda would be fine. Or just some water." She shrugged at Emma and added, "I don't drink coffee. Dan says I'm just a big kid that way. Twenty-six years old, and still drinking soda with everything. But that's just the way I am, you know?"

Emma smiled, certain that Callie Beckinsale had the ability to make caffeine feel jumpy.

"Some cold water would probably be best," she said. "It keeps the palate clean."

"Oh, right. Okay. Whatever."

As Fee went off to the kitchen, Emma peeled back the first few pages of her sketchbook.

"I took a look at the notes from your meeting with Madeline," Emma said. "She tells me you and your fiancé met at a baseball game, and you'd like the reception to reflect your love of the game."

"Yeah, Dan and me have season tickets to the Braves games. Our whole relationship revolves around baseball, really. So we'd like to tie that in to our after-party, you know? My cousin Lisa is making these darling little home plate centerpieces with these little tomahawks."

"Tomahawks?"

"The Atlanta Braves? Tomahawks?"

"Oh, of course."

"And we're thinking about barbecue for the food."

The corner of Emma's mouth twitched as she realized her joke about hot dogs and Cracker Jack wasn't so far off after all.

"We want it very low key, you know? Just a real kick-butt party with our friends."

"Can you tell me something about the wedding itself?" Emma asked her. "Is it in a church, or outdoors?"

"Oh, it's an outdoor wedding," she replied with a sniff. "Dan went to high school here in Atlanta, and he was a big star on their baseball team, so we're getting married right on the home plate where he used to play. It's going to be very romantic."

Emma stared at her for a long moment, wondering whether Callie was joking.

Pressing her lips together, Emma forced herself to blink. "Okay. Well, here's a couple of ideas that I have for you." She slid the pad across the tabletop toward Callie.

"They each serve up to one hundred people, as you requested, and you said you wanted something nontraditional."

"Dan and I are not traditional people."

The mother of all understatements.

"This first one is more of a sleek, high-end wedding cake, but with baseball diamond-shaped layers, kind of topsy turvy, with bases and a home plate."

"Oooh," she exclaimed as she peered at the sketch pad. "That's so cute."

"Then the next one," Emma continued, flipping over the page, "is a little more unusual."

Emma couldn't get another word in before Callie squealed and snatched the sketch pad from the table to get a closer look at the large sculpted baseball glove holding a pitcher bride and a catcher groom.

"This is the one."

"Well, there's a third —"

"No!" Callie exclaimed, and she slammed the pad down on the table and smacked it with her fist. "This one. This is the one!"

Emma chuckled. "All right. Let's talk about the fi—"

Her words were chopped in half as Callie hopped over to Emma and thumped both arms around her, still hopping and yelping something unintelligible. When she finally let her go, Emma was still bobbing.

"You're a *geeeeeenius!* She's a genius!"

Emma followed the path of Callie's excitement and her eyes met Jackson's where he stood at the entrance to the courtyard, his charcoal gray shirt sleeves rolled to the elbow and his textured tie loose around his open collar.

"So I've heard," he told Callie with a smirk. Nodding at Emma, he added, "Can I see you when you're through?"

"In a few minutes?"

He nodded. "In the restaurant."

"Sure."

Jackson closed the doors, and Emma watched him through the glass as he sauntered across the lobby toward the kitchen.

"Who is *THAT?*" Callie asked her.

"My boss."

"Lucky you. He's fine."

Fee turned the corner holding a tray of samples and a crystal glass of iced water.

"I'm going to leave you to Fee to decide on your cake flavor and fillings," Emma said, clutching her sketch pad. "It was a pleasure to meet you, Ms. Beckinsale."

Callie nodded her head enthusiastically and angled that full grill of bright-white teeth toward her.

Just as Emma started to leave, Callie

stated, "Soon to be Mrs. Daniel Mahoney," and then she giggled.

Emma turned back and stared at her. "I'm sorry. What did you say?"

"Callie Mahoney. That's what my married name will be."

"Danny Mahoney?"

"Yes."

"You said your fiancé went to school here in Atlanta."

"Yes, at George Washington High."

Emma drew a shaky breath and smiled. "I went to Washington."

"Did you? Did you know my Dan?" What were the odds? The same Danny who had watched her do a face plant on the floor the night she found out she was diabetic.

Emma nodded. "Yes. I did."

"What a small world!"

It took her a moment, but Emma found her game face again. "It sure is. Please give Danny my best."

Jackson knew if he spoke out loud the thoughts he was having just then, he would come off as selfish or ungrateful. It wasn't like he didn't know good and well that he was the luckiest so-and-so on the planet, having the sisters he had. Georgiann, Madeline and Norma Jean had been rallying around him all his life, and he'd often wondered what in the world he would do if he didn't have their support.

"You can do it, baby *bruthah!*"

"Go get 'em, Jackson."

But right then, in those few quiet moments alone in the restaurant, it was just him and the cup of coffee he'd scored from Fee in the kitchen. There was no backdrop of chatter or decisions being forced upon him that had been made in the name of Jackson's own good. There was a calendar in front of him, scribbled with four different shapes of penmanship, cluttered with appointments and reminders and updates. Just coffee and a few chunks of cake samples he'd nabbed from the tray Fee had been preparing. As he popped the last bite of something lemon-filled into his mouth and drew a slow sip of coffee to wash it down, Jackson smiled. If only for that one tranquil moment in his empty restaurant, he'd found sheer bliss.

His twelve years at Drummond & Associates, with Susannah by his side, had been organized and chaos-free, but tossing three opinionated Southern belles into the mix had made even his routine with Susannah seem strained and unfamiliar. For the umpteenth time since he'd taken the leap,

Jackson found himself wondering why he'd been so impulsive in this massive career change; but deep inside, he knew the answer. After spending his entire fourteen years of marriage devoted to making things right for Desiree in every way possible, that one niggling residual thread left undone in her life had choked him.

"I don't have any regrets, Jackson," she'd said to him, so beautiful even perched on the edge of her death. "My life with you has been more than I ever could have hoped for."

"You don't mind that we didn't have children?" he'd prodded, and she shook her head with assurance. Trying to smile at her but failing miserably, he had asked, "Or that we didn't buy that house in Buckhead before property values skyrocketed there?"

"Well, maybe that," she conceded with a grin. "And, of course, *The Tanglewood.*"

Desiree had started out as a desk clerk at the small boutique hotel, and made concerted efforts to construct a career there. She'd celebrated the second anniversary of the assistant manager promotion just a few days before the cancer was diagnosed.

"I've been dreaming for so many years about buying the hotel and converting it," she reminded him, and then paused to take a few deep breaths from the tube of oxygen gripping her nose. "It would have been so romantic, Jackson. I wish we'd done it together when the place was for sale a few years ago. Now Rupert Duncan is the owner, and the man has no imagination whatsoever. He just sees The Tanglewood as rooms, a restaurant and a front desk."

"You really love the place," he'd responded, and Desiree had looked up at him with a teary glaze in her dim eyes. This time, she was the one failing at her attempt to emit a reassuring smile.

"It's been the second love of my life."

And so, with those words the net was cast. Jackson's love for his wife dragged that moment and those words right out of the air between them, and he'd clutched them to his heart for safekeeping until the afternoon just a few short months ago when he carelessly opened the newspaper and caught sight of a headline:

ROSWELL'S TANGLEWOOD ON THE AUCTION BLOCK AGAIN

Jackson's thoughts were interrupted when Emma plunked down into the chair across the table from him with no warning at all. He swallowed around the lump in his throat in hopes of washing away the cloud of emotion before his employee picked up on it.

But on second glance, he realized Emma seemed a little too preoccupied to pick up on anything going on with him.

"You all right?" he asked her, and she scrunched up her face like Norma's five-year-old grandson Brant. "I'll take that as a no."

"You know that baseball wedding?"

"The Braves fans."

She leaned back into the plush scarlet chair. "Turns out I know the groom."

"Really."

"Yep. Danny Mahoney. My high school boyfriend."

Jackson thought it over for a moment, and then nodded. "Ahh. So you're just realizing, if things had gone differently, it could be you having a baseball-themed wedding. That's rough, huh? I guess you really missed out."

A chuckle popped out of her, and she melted into a full grin as she covered her face with both hands and peeked at him through her fingers.

"A little perspective," he reminded her, and then he gulped down the last of his coffee.

"Okay," she replied with a giggle. "Point taken."

"Listen, I wanted to discuss something

with you. I was contacted earlier by an attorney here in town, a guy named Vincent Lewis."

"Vincent Lewis," she repeated. "Why does that name sound familiar?"

"He's representing the owner of The Backstreet Bakery where you used to work."

"Harry?"

"Yes."

"Why would Harry's lawyer be contacting you?" she asked him, her hazel eyes flashing bright green emotion.

"Well, it would appear that your former boss is planning to sue your current one."

"I'm sorry," she said, leaning across the table with a look of surprise. "He's what?"

"He's suing me for stealing you away. It seems I've ruined his business."

"Oh, for crying out loud," she groaned. "Is he kidding with this? What a piece of work!" Emma slammed back against the chair again and dropped her head. "I am so sorry."

"An interesting guy, your Harry?" Jackson asked her. "He's the gift that just keeps on giving."

The Most Important Things to Remember about Crumb Coating a Cake

- Crumb coating is a thin, even layer, usually made out of frosting, that acts as a primer for the application of frosting.
- The crumb coat is applied with a flat spatula in swift, firm movements.
- If your cake will be filled between layers, be sure to *fill it first,* and then add a crumb coat to a completely cooled cake.
- Crumb coating is particularly important as the first step before adding fondant to a cake.
- Since fondant is sweet, but often lacks real flavor, jam or a fruit glaze makes a wonderful crumb coat for a fondant-covered cake.
- If you choose a jelly or jam such as apricot or raspberry, heat it up first and strain out any small seeds or pieces of fruit.
- The crumb coat should be very thin, just thick enough to spread.
- After the crumb coat is applied, refrigerate the cake for 20–30 minutes, until the coating has completely set.

6

Emma checked the results of her glucose test on the monitor: 94. Right where it should be first thing in the morning.

After her morning injection of insulin, she tossed the used test strip into the trash, zipped the monitor back into its small case, picked up her bowl of oatmeal, and headed for the living room. She curled into the comfy easy chair by the window and set the bowl on her knee while she pulled the phone toward her.

The Ercol Bergere chair around which her small living room now revolved used to grace her father's massive library, and she held fond memories of climbing into his lap and leaning against him as he read to her from one of his favorite books. Hemingway, Dickens, Twain; Emma knew now that these books weren't exactly bedtime fare for the nine-year-old that she was in the final months while they still lived as a family, but at that age, she was none the wiser. The soothing sound of her father's gravelly voice was the only lullaby she ever needed back then, and she'd fallen asleep within the arms of that chair, and those of her doting father, on many happy evenings.

By the time she was ten, however, her father had moved out of their Washington, D.C., colonial. When she was eleven, he moved back in, just two days after Emma and her mother had made the trek back to Avery's Southern stomping grounds to begin anew. After a short stop in Savannah, they'd settled in Roswell, just in time for Emma to start high school. Her father had followed for a trial reconciliation a few years later, but it didn't take, and he'd headed back to D.C. just after her high school graduation.

The telephone rang right on schedule: 8:30 a.m. every Sunday morning like clockwork.

"Hi, Daddy."

"Morning, Princess. Oatmeal or eggs?"

"Oatmeal."

"Raisins or walnuts?"

"Both," she replied, digging a mouthful out of the bowl with her spoon. "And a splash of milk."

"Good girl. Blood sugar?"

"94."

"Atta girl."

"And you? Are you having coffee or coffee?"

"I decided on coffee this morning."

"Black?"

"What else?"

As volatile as his relationship with her mother had always been, there was steel security for Emma in theirs.

"How's work, Daddy?"

"I've sold my last business," he announced. "Travis Development is no more."

Emma plopped the bowl of oatmeal to the table next to her and shook her head. "What?! I thought that was the one you were keeping."

"I've spent too many years in real estate and construction, Emma Rae. It's time for a change."

"A change? To what?"

"A few good steaks, a cigar every now and then. Maybe some travel. I've decided to take it easy and see how that feels."

"Red meat and cigars!" she exclaimed. "Remember your blood pressure."

"My blood is pressing on just fine now that I've decided to retire."

"Well," she said on a chuckle, "no one deserves it like you, Daddy. But I sure can't envision this new lifestyle on you."

"Stay tuned, Princess," he declared. "Now tell me about your new venture. What's this corporate tycoon-turned-hotel-renovator like?"

"He's . . . confusing," she admitted. "He doesn't seem to know a thing about the hotel business, yet he jumped in with both feet just the same."

"A visionary."

"Or an idiot," she giggled.

"Mmm," he considered. "Or that. Is he treating you right?"

"He is. I have the most amazing kitchen. Top of the line. And he let me bring Fee over with me."

"Ah, Fee. How is she? Still dressed in black, I'm guessing."

Emma laughed. "She's still Fee."

"It works for her."

"Yes, it does."

"I'm happy to see you making a clean break from that other one."

"Harry."

"Yes, Harry."

"Well, I made a break, but I'm not sure how clean. It turns out he's suing my new boss for something like alienation of employment."

Gavin spouted a low-pitched, one-syllable

guffaw. "He's nothing without you. I guess he's finally realizing it. Too little, too stinkin' late."

"I just feel bad for Jackson."

"Jackson, is it?"

"That's his name, Dad. He told me to call him Jackson."

"I bet he did."

A click interrupted the conversation, and Emma didn't need to even look. It would be Fee calling, as she did every Sunday morning, to invite Emma to join her at church.

"You have a call," her father stated.

"It's okay. I don't need to pick it up."

"You're sure?"

"Yes. Tell me about you, Daddy. What led you to this monumental decision to sell Travis Development?"

A second click broke through, then Emma leaned back into the chair and closed her eyes, ignoring it as she listened to her father's dramatic tale of industrial espionage, corporate competition, and general incompetence, none of which had a thing to do with why he'd decided to retire.

After they hung up twenty minutes later, she took a shower and threw on some jeans and her Falcons jersey, tidied up the kitchen, made her bed, and took two laps around the apartment. After her weekly call from her father was through, Sunday was Emma's least favorite day of the week. She never quite knew what to do with herself. Fee had surmised that it was her work/life imbalance at the root of the trouble, and Emma didn't entirely disagree. But she put the thought out of her mind as she grabbed her purse and keys and took off for The Tanglewood at eleven o'clock that morning.

Christening her new key to the back door of the hotel kitchen, Emma beamed as she let herself in and punched in the security code on the wall pad, then locked the door behind her again. She grabbed a Coke Zero out of the refrigerator, and then hopped up on the prep table in the middle of her kitchen before popping the top and gulping down half the contents of the can. She looked around at the place, her brain humming with plans for the tea room and the upcoming weddings, so consumed that she jumped when she realized she wasn't alone.

"You scared me!" she exclaimed. "How long have you been here?"

"Hours," Jackson replied and nodded toward the can of Coke Zero resting on her knee. "Can I have one of those?"

"Help yourself."

She watched him as he yanked open the

refrigerator door and pulled one of Fee's orange sodas from the door. He looked good in his street clothes, she decided. Smiling, she realized she never would have imagined the weekday Jackson Drake in a pale chambray shirt, tails out, and black jeans that were worn through at the knees. His Nikes had seen better days, and Emma liked his dark hair a little tousled the way it was just then.

He leaned against the counter and threw back several gulps from his drink before asking, "So, what are you doing here today? It's your day off."

"I was a little restless," she told him. "My head was all full of cakes. What about you?"

"I got to wondering about converting that back room into a consultation room for people who come in to book their weddings. Don't you think we should have somewhere that they can go without having to seat them in the restaurant or out in the courtyard?"

"I didn't know there was a back room," she told him. "Where is it?"

"Right off the entrance to the restaurant."

"I thought that was a supply closet."

"No, it's a whole room with built-ins and plenty of room for . . . well, come on. I'll show you."

Emma's tennis shoes squeaked as she

hopped down from the table, and she followed Jackson through the swinging door and off to the right. He pulled the oak door open and the two of them stepped inside.

"I figure it's about twelve feet by twelve feet," Jackson told her. "We could put a table and chairs over there, and then maybe a couple of comfortable chairs or a sofa over there."

Emma looked around, catching his vision. "Oh, you know, we could get some really nice still photographs of a few of my wedding cakes, maybe a couple of Anton's specialty dishes, and we could frame them and hang them on that wall. I have a friend who is a wonderful photographer."

"Maybe we could have your friend create some albums for them to look through, add in some sample menus for the receptions, that kind of thing," he added. "You know, this could really be a functional room."

"That was a pretty great idea you had," she told him with a grin.

"You know, you're right," he said, returning her smile. "I normally save my strokes of brilliance for weekdays, so this is a Sunday bonus."

"Those are always a nice surprise."

"I'll get Norm working on converting this room first thing tomorrow," he remarked as they headed out of the room. Then suddenly, he stopped so unexpectedly that Emma smacked right into him from behind.

"Ohh. Sor—"

"Back!" he exclaimed, then he barreled backward, taking Emma right along with him, back into the office before he yanked shut the door.

"What is it?" she asked. "What's going on?"

Jackson spun toward her, and there was barely a break of air between them as he shushed her with an urgency that confounded Emma. She took two steps away from him.

His masculine scent was resolute with hints of wood and spice and underlying notes of citrus. Emma breathed it in casually, and then held it there for a moment.

"Emma's nose always knows," her mother used to say, and it was true. If she hadn't become a baker, Emma might have been a professional *nose* for a perfume company.

"Why are we hiding?" she whispered, and Jackson turned two shades of embarrassed.

"Ah." He didn't seem to want to tell her, but then he admitted, "My sister's just arrived."

"Which one?"

"George."

"Oh." She nodded. Georgiann really was the sister most likely to induce hiding.

"You're a little afraid of her too?" she asked.

"Afraid? No." He looked at her with an odd arch of his eyebrow. "No. She's got her son-in-law with her."

She considered that for a moment and then asked, "You're afraid of him?"

Jackson sighed. "Not afraid. I'd just rather avoid him if I can. It's a long story."

"Ohh." Emma sounded as if she understood, but she really didn't, so she started to inquire further. "I don't think I —"

The door flung open just then, cutting her words clean in two.

"Jackson, I thought that was you," Georgiann crooned. "What in the world are you two doing locked up in here?"

"Hello, Jackson," the young man beside her said, and then he smiled at Emma with an aura of sweetness, not very scary at all. "Hello."

"Emma Rae Travis," Georgiann announced. "Meet my son-in-law. Reverend Miguel Ramos."

Jackson figured Emma must have thought he was some kind of heathen, running for cover at the mere sight of a pastor! He wished he could explain, tell her that it wasn't like that.

Well. Not exactly.

Miguel was a good man. He'd officiated over Desiree's funeral, said the most beautiful things about her, and then he'd phoned Jackson every week for months afterward just to see how he was doing. But all of those encouraging words about how God had a plan and how God turned all things to good if you believed, no matter how impossible that might seem — those words acted as an irritant against Jackson's wounded heart.

He didn't want to hear that God had a plan; not if that plan included taking away the only woman Jackson had ever loved completely, who had somehow been able to see past all the garbage, straight into Jackson's shell of a soul, and love him in return. He never was one of those hearts-and-flowers believers in soul mates or destiny, but the fact was that Desiree had been the one and only love of Jackson's life. When she was taken from him, he was left with nothing — or so it had felt for a very long time. So platitudes from a young pastor with a beautiful wife and two small children, words that said God had a plan and that Jackson would somehow recover after losing her felt as hollow as he did. After a while, he associated that vacant feeling toward God with the messenger. With Miguel.

When he bought The Tanglewood and set it up as the wedding destination hotel that Desiree had dreamed it could be, Georgiann had come up with the idea of bringing Miguel on board as the official wedding pastor. She'd been campaigning for the idea ever since, and Jackson had been able to consistently avoid the meeting she wanted to arrange. Three Sunday mornings in a row, the two of them had shown up at his house after services. He'd felt like a Class A jerk, hiding out in his home office until they finally stopped ringing the bell, but he just couldn't face Miguel and his *God is good* mentality. Maybe one day, but not yet.

So with that in mind, he'd left home early that morning, hiding out at The Tanglewood, certain that he'd outsmarted them. But as usual, Georgiann had shown who was really boss in the outsmarting department.

"I just had a feeling we'd find you here," she said as the four of them gathered around a bistro table in the courtyard.

"I was just taking care of some planning with Emma," he explained. Never mind that it had been an impromptu meeting rather than a scheduled one.

"I really wanted to put you and Miguel together to talk about him performing the weddings here."

"What's to talk about?" he asked casually. "We'd love to have you on board, Miguel."

"I'm happy to hear that," Miguel replied. "I've been trying to reach you to find out how you've been doing, but —"

"You know," he interrupted, "this place has taken up every bit of time I ever thought I had. In fact," and he glanced at his watch for good measure, "I have to get going right now, but it was really great to see you again, and I'm glad to know you're on board. George will take care of all the details with you."

"Wait a second, Jackson," Georgiann exclaimed. "Where on earth are you off to?"

He stared at her, not an answer in sight.

"We're going shopping!" Emma piped up.

"Shopping?"

"Yes, I know a couple of great thrift stores where we can get some vintage china and linens for the tea room."

Georgiann arched an eyebrow and deadpanned, "Jackson is shopping for linens."

"You know how he is about budget," Emma teased. "He's afraid I'll go overboard, so he's strictly there as my financial watchdog."

Relief flooded Jackson's senses, and gratitude pinched inside his gut as she asked him, "Can we get going now? I really am in a time crunch today."

"Jackson —"

"Sure, sorry," he said. "Miguel, good to see you again. And George, I'll talk to you tomorrow. We have a ten o'clock with Anton about the menu, right?"

"Uh, yes."

"I'm parked right out front," Emma said as they made their getaway, just loudly enough for Georgiann and Miguel to hear. "I know right where we're headed, so I can drive."

"Be sure to set the alarm when you leave," Jackson called to them over his shoulder, but he didn't dare turn all the way back and risk meeting Georgiann's stare. He already felt the full heat of it on his neck.

Outside, Emma headed straight for a bright red Mini Cooper, and Jackson wondered if his six-foot frame was going to fold down enough to fit inside. It was a challenge, but he managed it. Once inside, Emma turned over the engine, and the two of them sat there in silence, staring straight ahead. Emma's hands clutched the steering wheel; Jackson's were curled into fists.

"Why did you do that?" he asked softly.

In the close quarters, he felt the shrug of her shoulders. "You said you were avoiding Miguel. I thought I'd help."

Jackson's mouth twitched. "I guess you'll want to know why."

"Not particularly."

Curious, he turned in his seat and looked at her. "Really?"

She let go of the wheel long enough to turn her hands over. "I'm sure you have your reasons. But your sister doesn't strike me as one who takes that into consideration when she wants your ear."

Jackson let out a little laugh. "No. She's not."

"Listen," she told him, tucking a wisp of straight, silky hair behind her ear, "I know all about family pressure. If you'd ever met my mother, you'd understand."

Jackson grinned, watching her closely as she grabbed the rectangular tortoiseshell eyeglasses from the drink holder in front of the gearshift. Without looking back at him, she unfolded them, placed them primly on her nose, then pulled the parking brake, pressed down the clutch and shifted into first.

"We'll start at a shop I know nearby," she

told him, her hands placed firmly on the wheel. "If we don't find anything there, we can make a run out to Alpharetta. There's a great little place over there that's —"

"You mean we're really going shopping?" he blurted.

"We told them that's where we were going," she said with a sniff. "They'll expect us to come back with something."

Jackson couldn't think of a thing to say back to that. Facing forward again, he pushed the seatbelt buckle into place and leaned back against the red leather seat with a sigh.

I guess I'm going . . . shopping.

And from the looks of things, he'd be getting there at a snail's pace. Emma Rae Travis drove like Jackson's 83-year-old grandmother.

Emma's Cashew Fudge Brownies

Preheat oven to 350 degrees

2 sticks butter
2 cups granulated sugar
4 eggs
1 cup cocoa powder
1 1/4 cups flour
1 teaspoon salt
1 teaspoon baking powder
1 teaspoon vanilla extract
1/2 cup halved cashews

Melt butter and pour into large bowl.
Add sugar and cocoa, mixing with wooden spoon or rubber spatula.
Add eggs and vanilla, continuing to stir.
In separate bowl, sift flour, salt, and baking powder, then add dry ingredients to bowl and stir in cashews.
Mix well, and pour mixture into 9″ × 13″ baking pan.
Bake for approximately 30 minutes.
After cooling, cut into small squares.
Layer two squares and fill with cocoa icing, then frost top and garnish with cashew halves.

7

Emma couldn't stifle her pride as Blythe set down the tiered crystal service of sweets atop the large center table in the courtyard. She'd asked the English-born server she'd hired to make this dry run as close to perfection as possible, and Blythe had not disappointed her. Wearing a ruffled white apron and white gloves, she created a scene straight out of *Remains of the Day.*

"Cashew fudge brownies, a specialty here at The Tanglewood Inn," Blythe said in her very proper English accent. "And we have fruit tarts in apricot and blueberry; petit fours in red velvet, lemon and hazelnut cream; traditional English shortbread cookies; and fresh strawberries drizzled in dark chocolate."

Madeline swooned, while Susannah and Georgiann beamed beacons of sheer pleasure. Emma and Fee casually lowered their hands beneath the Battenberg tablecloth and tapped out a silent low-five of victory.

"Well, honey, this has just been magnificent," Madeline said as Blythe filled her cup with hot tea. "You've outdone yourself."

"One cube?" the server asked, offering a square of sugar held by sterling tongs.

"Thank you," Madeline replied with a nod. "I just wish Jackson was able to break away to enjoy this."

"He's up to his chin with permits and licenses until after four o'clock," Susannah told them.

"Maybe we could put together a doggie bag," Fee suggested, "and deliver it to his office door."

"Oh, I don't think —" Madeline began.

"What a wonderful idea!" Georgiann chimed, cutting short Madeline's objection. "Would you do that, Emma?"

"I hate to interrupt him, but if you think —"

"Anyone who can get my *bruthah* to go shopping for *table linens,* well. There's a magic to you, child."

"I'm sorry," Susannah interrupted. "You did what?"

"This girl managed to get Jackson Drake out on a Sunday afternoon, shopping for these very platters and linens that you see here."

"No, you didn't," Madeline exclaimed.

"I saw it with my own eyes, Sissy."

"Is this true?" Susannah asked, leaning over toward Emma. "How on earth did you do it?"

My reward for saving his rear end.

"It was two hours out of his life. No big deal," she said instead.

The three women chuckled as if Emma had delivered a savvy one-liner. She turned and looked at Fee, who gave her a shrug.

"Put together a little of everything on a tray?" she asked.

"Sure." Fee took off immediately for the kitchen.

"Oh! Fee?" Fee came to a full stop and looked back at her. "He doesn't like tea. So can you put on some coffee?"

"You got it."

When she turned her attention back to the table, all three of the women were staring in disbelief.

"What?"

"He doesn't like tea?" Georgiann repeated.

"We talked about it when we were shopping. He's not a tea drinker. Just coffee, strong and black."

"She's right." Susannah glanced at Georgiann.

"Indeed." Georgiann turned to Madeline.

"Mm-hm," Madeline said with a nod.

It was no wonder that Jackson tended to hide from the women in his life every now and again, Emma thought. If there was a closet or a back room close enough, she might consider ducking into it now herself.

"You know," Georgiann said, tapping her index finger against her chin, and Emma held her breath for whatever might come next. "I think you're right about that Fee. I like her."

"I love Fee!" Norma chimed in.

"She's not nearly as frightening as she looks."

Emma grinned, deciding not to tell her that it depended on the day whether Fee was frightening or not.

By the time Emma reached the kitchen, Blythe had prepared a beautiful presentation with one of the tiered trays Emma had purchased at the thrift store. The top layer offered chocolate-drizzled strawberries, the second was covered with finger sandwiches, while the bottom tier displayed an array of desserts set in tiny scalloped papers. Fee put the final touches on a small platter bearing a steaming cup of coffee, utensils, and a creased linen napkin.

"Shall I deliver this?" Blythe asked her.

"No, I can do it." Emma said.

Fee helped her balance the coffee tray atop her palm, and then she picked up the food service by the sterling triangle at the top. "Back in a minute."

The elevator, glass on one side, looked out over the courtyard, and Emma watched the threesome of women with their heads together right where she left them as the car glided up to the fourth floor. She wondered about their conversation as Georgiann chattered fifty miles per hour, and then the three of them tossed their heads back and laughed.

"Knock, knock," she sang softly from the doorway of Jackson's office.

He looked up from the stacks of paperwork in front of him, narrowed his eyes, and then waved her inside.

"Mohammed can't come to the tea room, so the tea room will just come to Mohammed," she quipped. "I thought you might be hungry."

He leaned back in his chair and let the shadow of a smile cross his face.

"The menu was a big success," she told him as she laid it out in front of him. "I'm sure you'll hear all about it soon enough."

"No doubt," he replied. "Is that coffee?"

"Yes. No special flavor, no added anything,

just strong, black and Colombian."

He sighed, then grabbed the cup and waved it beneath his nose. Closing his eyes, he took a strong whiff and sighed again.

"Enjoy," she whispered as she backed out of the office.

"Wait. You don't have to go right away. Have a seat."

"Susannah said you were buried. I don't want to sidetrack you."

"I can use a little sidetracking right now, Emma. I've reviewed and signed so much paperwork today that my eyes are a blur and my hand is cramped."

"Poor little hotel owner," she teased.

He shook his head and pasted a mock-serious grimace on his handsome face. "And here I thought I might get a little sympathy."

"What made you think that? Silly man," she returned, and he shot her a good-natured grin.

"So did my sister hit you up about your mother?"

Emma's eyes darted from the desktop to Jackson's face. "Pardon me?"

"I guess not. George has this crazy idea that having your mother come to the opening night gala might help put us on the map, socially speaking."

"Oh." Her thoughts were suddenly like a

crazy, offbeat railroad hub where trains just barreled in, smacking into one another on every side. "I really don't think . . . I mean . . . How does Georgiann know who my mother is?"

"I guess I told her," he admitted. With his face tilted downward, Jackson lifted his eyes and squinted slightly as he gazed at her. "Sorry."

"How did you know?"

"The day you came in to interview. You mentioned it."

"I did?" She strained to remember what would cause her to do such a thing. She normally liked to keep her family tree planted behind a brick wall and an imposing fence.

"There's no obligation," he assured her. "I mean about inviting your parents."

"My parents?" she exclaimed, and she reached out and held the edge of the desk with both hands. "Both of them? Well, that could just never . . . it couldn't . . . they wouldn't."

Jackson's laughter was lyrical, yet really irritating at the same time. What on earth could he find to laugh at? What could be funny about the horrifying picture he'd painted on her black-black mind's eye! Gavin and Avery Travis in the same place, *the same room,* at the same time?

"Don't panic, Emma. Calm down. No family reunions, I get it."

"It's just that . . . you don't understand how . . . how . . ."

"Relax," he said with a chuckle. "It's okay, I do understand. Family, over there." And he waved his arm at the doorway and down the hall. Then he mimed a circle in front of him and added, "Work life, here. Worlds colliding, bad."

"Yes," she nodded emphatically, and then transitioned to shaking her head. "Very, very bad."

"You're singing to the choir, my friend. Singing to the choir."

The familiar jingle from the bell on the front door of The Backstreet Bakery brought a sort of hollow nausea to the pit of Emma's stomach. She thought she would never cross this particular threshold again but, as her Aunt Sophie used to say: *"Never" can be a very short surprise.*

"Well, look what the cat dragged in."

It had only been a couple of weeks, but Harry looked different to her. His comb-over was particularly sparse, and the sour expression on his scrunched-up face appeared just a little more tart.

"Hi, Harry. How are you?"
"How am I?" he exclaimed. "You take off and leave me in the lurch like that, and now you darken my door to ask me how I am?"
"I referred three wonderful bakers to you, Harry. It's not my fault that you ran every one of them out of the place with your sparkling personality."
"Incompetents! All of them."
Emma found herself wondering, just for a moment, whether Harry and Anton Morelli were related.
"Harry, what's this nonsense about suing Jackson Drake?" she asked, stepping toward him, just the display case standing between them. "Please don't do that."
"He stole my whole staff right out of my kitchen."
"He didn't. He made me an offer, and I took it. I stole Fee, Harry."
"So you admit it. I'll just name you in the suit then."
Emma sighed. "I don't know why I thought coming here to talk to you would help the situation. I guess I just hoped you'd surprise me and sprout a conscience."
"I made you, Emma Rae. You'd be nothing without The Backstreet."
She swallowed hard. "You're probably right. Maybe that's why I'm here."

Harry glanced down at the floor.

"Please tell me what I can do to make this right, Harry. The Tanglewood is such a great opportunity for me. And I'm sorry for the effect it's had on you, but I had to take the chance and move on. You can understand that, can't you?"

No reply.

"I went to culinary school with a girl named Delilah," she said, rooting around in her bag until she found the slip of paper with her friend's name and phone number scribbled on it. "She is a wonderful baker, Harry; probably better than me. I've told her all about you, and she's waiting for your call."

Harry glared at her, but he took the paper from her hand.

"Don't mess this up," she warned him gently. "She'll keep this place on the map."

Harry sniffed and gave her half a nod. "I'll think about it."

"Hire her, Harry. And then call off your attack dog and leave Jackson Drake alone to get his hotel up and running." They stared into each other's eyes for a long moment, and then Emma smiled. "Please do this for me?"

He nodded, and made a sort of a grunt that Emma decided to take as a verbal agreement.

"Thank you."

Emma headed for the door, and just as the bell jingled overhead, Harry called out to her. "Emma Rae?"

She turned back toward him and waited.

"You're, uh," he muttered. "You're the best there is."

"Thank you, Harry."

On the drive back over to The Tanglewood, while stopped at a light on Holcomb Bridge Road, Emma did something she hadn't done in a very long while. She closed her eyes and asked God for His help in placating Harry and convincing him to drop the ridiculous lawsuit against Jackson.

"Jackson has his hands full right now," she reminded Him. "I can't stand being the root of one more crisis for him."

A honk from the car behind her jerked her eyes open, and she pressed the gas and eased back on the clutch. "All right already. I'm going."

Fee had several tables dressed and ready to go for the photo shoot by the time Emma returned to the hotel and made her way into the restaurant. She'd called on her old high school friend, Peter Riggs, for photographic help, and he was now placing lights on tall stands around the crème brûlée wedding cake she'd finished just that morning. Fee had placed it on a high table draped in a yard of scarlet velvet cloth that perfectly matched the color of the sugar roses climbing the tiers of the cake.

"Hi, Petey. Thank you so much for coming."

"Glad to do it, Emma Rae. How are you?" Peter pulled her into an embrace, and one of the two cameras hanging around his neck dug into her arm. "Congratulations on your new job, by the way."

"Thanks. Listen, I've got a meeting upstairs that starts in about three minutes. Fee will get you anything you need, and I'll try and get back down here before you finish up."

"No problem. Do what you need to do."

"Fee, be sure and get the cakes out of the lights and back into the fridge as soon as Peter shoots them?"

"Chu got it, boss lady."

"Thanks, both of you," she called to them as she jogged out of the restaurant and across the length of the lobby.

She caught her breath on the elevator ride to the fourth floor, and then took several deep breaths and released them slowly before turning the corner into Susannah's doorway.

"They're waiting for you."

Emma nodded, then walked into Jackson's office with a smile. Norma and Anton Morelli flanked Jackson's desk, and he nodded Emma toward the empty chair to one side.

"I'm sorry if I'm late."

"Where is the other one?" Anton demanded. "Fiona Bianchi."

"Oh, she's downstairs overseeing a photo shoot for me," Emma replied, and then she turned toward Jackson. "For the framed photographs in the consultation room."

"Good. Glad you're on that."

"We were just going over Mr. Morelli's exquisite wedding menus," Norma said, and she handed a stack of them to Emma. "Have a look."

As she pored over them, Emma wondered who would have the task of suggesting barbecue and cole slaw for Danny's baseball wedding.

Pumpkin tortellini with chestnuts.

Herbed pork loin with praline mustard sauce.

Pan roasted Georgia rainbow trout with Granny Smith apple and walnut chutney.

Roasted prime rib of beef with wild mushrooms and caramelized onions.

Glazed duck breast with roasted eggplant.

"This is staggering," Emma told Anton. "You're a master. An absolute artiste."

His very straight face slowly tilted upward into a sort of smile, and she heard Jackson sigh as it did.

"Now you tell me," Emma suggested. "Out of my list of specialty cakes, which ones would create the best marriage with your entrees?"

Out of the corner of her eye, she saw Norma shoot Jackson a look, and she imagined that it meant they were pleased. At least she hoped that's what it meant.

"Let's start with the crème brûlée cake," she said. "What would you think of suggesting a pairing with the duck?"

"No!" The three of them jumped when the word popped out of him like a sharp, pointed sword. "They must pair crème brûlée with the prime rib of beef!"

Emma cast Norma a quick glance. Then she shook her head, chuckled and nodded. "Of course. You're one hundred percent correct."

"A gentler taste with the duck," Anton insisted, pulling one of the description cards from the pile on the desk. "This one, with pistachio filling."

"Perfect." Emma nodded, handing the card to Norma. "The champagne and pistachio cake with the glazed duck breast entrée. Of course, we can never guarantee that they'll take our suggestions, but —" His expression changed as fast as a dark storm cloud appearing on the horizon. "— we'll always nudge them toward good taste wherever we can."

Anton surprised her with a laugh. "One man's praline sauce is another man's beef barbecue, ehh?"

Emma looked up into Anton's eyes, and he winked at her. "Fee Bianchi told me of the baseball disaster. But we will please every customer, not just the ones who are right in the head."

A string of chuckles tumbled out of Emma, a sort of blended mixture of relief, amusement, and averted panic. Pulling it together again, she told him, "I think that attitude just reinforces why you're such a master, Mr. Morelli."

Anton tweaked her cheek just a little too hard, and Emma glanced over at Jackson just in time to catch the silver flecks of glee flashing in his dark brown eyes, which caught and held hers.

"Now for the daytime weddings," Norma interjected. "Mr. Morelli has created some simpler menus for brunches or luncheons."

Emma tried to concentrate on Norma's words —

Smoked salmon bruschetta, cocktail meat-

balls in black pepper cider sauce, chicken roulade with rice pilaf . . . something about stuffed chicken breasts . . .

— but all she could really hear was the annoying pound-pound-pound of her own heartbeat in response to Jackson's tender hold on her eyes. Emma couldn't look away, and it was frustrating. She was reminded of the time she and Danny had been arguing, and he used duct tape to bind her wrist to his so she couldn't escape. No matter how hard she twisted and pulled, Jackson Drake's eyes had her in an infuriating lock.

"Emma?"

"Hmmm?"

"Anton asked if you had a pastry with a Southern slant. Something traditional to go with his rainbow trout."

"Oh!" she exclaimed, peeling her gaze away from him like gray duct tape from her wrist. "Yes. Umm, I have something here . . ." She fumbled through the cards until she found it. "It's a pecan praline filling with a caramel glaze."

"Exceptional," Anton rumbled, and he gave Emma's hand a harsh little pat.

STACKING MULTI-TIERED WEDDING CAKES

- A cake with multiple tiers often looks as if the layers have simply been placed one on top of the other; however, this is not the case. To do so would ensure a cake avalanche effect as the weight of the upper layers crumbled into the lower ones.
- The bottom tier of the cake is affixed to a cake board with a thin layer of icing to hold it in place.
- The upper tiers are supported with three or four wooden dowels per layer, carefully placed and measured, so that the weight of the upper layer is supported.
- Remember that tiered cakes tend to be quite heavy, so if the cake has to be transported, you'll want to consider that carefully. You may choose to disassemble the layers before transporting, and then reassemble them when you reach your destination.
- Always advise the bride and groom to cut the cake at the *bottom layer first.*

8

Norma had transformed the room that had once been an office into an inviting consultation room for planning receptions, banquets, and special events. Steel-blue walls set a backdrop for an arrangement of six 11″ × 14″ photos in identical brushed nickel frames displaying an array of banquet possibilities, from buffet tables brimming with choices to elegant place settings bearing gourmet meals.

A cherry table and three chairs angled into the corner, and on the opposite wall hung another arrangement of six framed photos, those showcasing Emma's abilities as a baker and wedding cake designer. Beneath the display sat an overstuffed floral sofa between two indigo easy chairs and a cherry coffee table set with glossy flyers and brochures detailing what The Tanglewood Inn had to offer.

"It's really beautiful," Emma told her as

they stood inside the doorway and inspected the finished room.

"I tried to make it into a place where clients will want to relax and spend time pulling together the details."

"You certainly accomplished that."

Fee poked her head through the doorway. "Wow!"

"Isn't it great?" Emma asked her.

"Amazing." She tossed a smile toward Norma before catching Emma's eye. "You have a call."

Emma rubbed Norma's arm on her way to the doorway. "You done good."

"Thanks, Emma."

She rounded the corner and crossed her kitchen, then sat down behind her very own desk with a sigh.

"Emma Travis," she said as she picked up the phone.

"My daughter, the professional."

Emma grinned and leaned back into the chair. "Mother."

"It always sounds like you're calling me a bad name when you say it like that, Emma Rae."

"How would you prefer me to say it?" she laughed.

"Mother, darling!" Avery exclaimed. "I've missed you so."

"Well, I have. How are you, Mother darling? Are you in town?"

"No, I'm in Savannah with your Aunt Sophie, sweetheart. I'm thinking about bringing her with me to Atlanta."

"It would be nice to have her visit."

"Not for a visit, Emma Rae. I'm thinking of bringing her there permanently."

Emma chuckled. "Have you discussed that with her yet? I can't imagine Aunt Sophie packing up and leaving Savannah behind after all these years. Has she ever even left the city limits?"

"Yes, she has. But she's not doing very well, and I'm worried about her. I thought I might be able to get her one of those apartments in the Sandy Springs complex where Delores and Beauregard Denton moved last year. Peachtree something."

"Everything in Atlanta is Peachtree something, Mother."

"It's one of those communities; a retirement village with a penthouse."

"Assisted living?" Emma asked.

"Yes, that's it. Sophie can't live on her own anymore, Emma Rae."

"It's that bad?"

"She wandered off in her nightclothes last week, and they found her waiting outside Nieman Marcus for the doors to open."

"Oh," Emma groaned. "That's not good."

"No, it's not. I'm very concerned. I'm going to call the Dentons and see what they can tell me about the place. I visited them last year, and we had a very nice luncheon in the restaurant downstairs."

"The cafeteria?"

"Yes, I suppose so."

"Give Aunt Sophie my love?"

"I will, sweetheart. Now tell me how your new job is coming along. When do you open?"

"Next week we have an official opening," she replied, and then she opened the desk drawer and propped both feet on it. "The first hotel guests are booked the week after, and our first wedding is on the eighteenth. You'll never guess whose wedding it is."

"Tell me."

"Danny Mahoney."

"Mahoney," Avery repeated. "Mahoney. Where do I know —"

"My high school boyfriend."

"Oh! Sweet Ivy James, you can't be serious. Remember how your father abhorred that boy?"

"Well, he needn't have worried. Apparently, Danny has found the woman of his dreams in a tiny blonde named Callie, and their wedding theme . . . wait for it! . . . is the Atlanta Braves."

"Why am I not surprised?" Avery said with a chuckle. "Didn't he play baseball in school?"

"He sure did. I'm designing a sculpted wedding cake for them in the shape of a baseball glove."

"Please. No more."

"Oh, there's more, Mother. The reception food?"

"Chicken wings?"

"Barbecue."

Avery began to chortle, and Emma could just picture her there, her hand to her slender throat, her dark brown hair pulled back into a perfect, elegant bun, her sparkling smile lighting up three or four rooms around her.

"What a shame, sweetheart. No wedding barbecue for you. Are you heartbroken?"

"Deep despair. When will I see you?"

"Another week or so, I imagine. I'll let you know. Perhaps you can give me a tour of your beautiful new hotel."

"It's not my hotel, Mother," Emma said with a laugh. "But I'd be happy to show you around." Thinking better of that, she added, "Maybe on the weekend, when no one else is here."

"Why? Are you ashamed of me?"

"No," she replied, and it bounced on a nervous chuckle. "Of course not. Give me a call."

"I will. I love you, sweetheart."

"Love you too."

The weight of the situation began to press in, and Emma replayed her conversation with Jackson in spurts. Georgiann had wanted Avery to attend the opening; now Avery was coming to town right around the time of the opening.

"Worlds colliding, baaaaaad," Jackson had said.

Emma popped her feet from the desk drawer to the floor and groaned. "Very, very bad," she said out loud.

"What's bad?"

Emma jerked her attention to the doorway, where Fee leaned on the jamb. "Huh?"

"You said something was very, very bad. What is?"

"Oh." She dismissed her with the wave of her hand. "Nothing."

"Can we talk?"

"Sure. Come on in. Is this bad news?"

"I don't think so," Fee answered with a slight cringe.

"Oh, no."

"Dude. Don't get all bunged up. I just want to ask you something."

"So ask."

"You know how, when you meet someone and you're really attracted to them, but maybe they might already be tagged by someone else?"

Emma cocked her head slightly and grimaced. "No."

"Come on. Sure you do. Like if I've met someone, but you might already be, you know, *attracted* to them. I can't just move in before I ask you about it. It's part of the Girl Code."

"The Girl Code." Emma wasn't following.

"Emma Rae. Is there anyone that you're *attracted to* at the moment? Someone you wouldn't want me, you know, going out with?"

"No."

"There's no one?"

"No one."

Fee raised her eyebrows and stared at her until Emma's skin started to feel tight.

"Anyone . . . *around this place?*"

Thud!

"Fiona, I am not attracted to Jackson Drake!" she exclaimed. "I can't believe you would even ask me that, or that you would —"

Something began to dawn.

"Wait a minute. Are you going to *date*

Jackson, Fee?"

"Good grief, no. Why? Are you?"

"No."

"Are you sure?"

"Yes! Is that who you're talking about?"

"No," Fee replied.

"Then who?"

"Peter."

Emma fell silent, scratched her head, then squinted her eyes at Fee. "You want to date Peter Riggs? My photographer friend?"

"So much."

She wasn't sure why the idea surprised her, but it really did.

"Go for it."

"Honest?"

"Yes. Go for it."

Fee stretched across the desk and squeezed Emma's wrist. "Thank you!"

"Uh, sure."

At the doorway, Fee turned back toward her and shot her a crooked little smile.

"What?"

"You and Jackson Drake," she said as if she were trying it on for size. "Dude."

"Get out of here."

"Emma, he's hot."

"He's also our boss. Get out. Call Peter."

"I already did. He's picking me up in an hour."

■ ■ ■ ■

A glimpse of red drew Jackson's attention as he stepped outside. Emma's miniature car was parked out front and, to his surprise, he saw that she was seated behind the wheel, her head tilted back and her eyes closed. She jumped when he knocked on the window, then she rolled it down halfway.

"Power nap?" he asked with a smile.

"Dead battery," she replied, and her warm breath steamed from her lips as it hit the cold night air. "I called the auto club an hour ago, but they haven't shown up. I guess I drifted off."

"Come on," he said with a nod. "I'll give you a ride home."

"But —"

"But nothing," he interrupted. "We'll leave your key under the back seat and lock all the doors except that one. I'll have someone take care of this in the morning. It's late and you're exhausted. Let me drive you home."

She didn't even try to talk him out of it; she just pushed open the door and climbed out of her car. "Thank you," she said, twisting off the key and handing it to him. "I'm so tired."

"I hear you," he groaned.

She followed him around the curve of the driveway to where his car was parked, and she let out a long, appealing sigh once they were inside.

"We should have heat in just a minute," he promised after turning the ignition. "Have you had dinner?"

"Dinner?" she replied. "What's that?"

Jackson unbuttoned his overcoat, then slipped his cell phone from the breast pocket of his jacket. "I just ordered takeout," he told her. "I'll add to it, and we can have dinner together at your place."

She appeared slightly taken aback, but she didn't object.

"Hi, Serena. It's Jackson Drake again. Will you double that order I just placed? I'll be there in fifteen minutes to pick it up." Pressing the phone against his shoulder, he asked Emma, "You're not a vegetarian or anything, are you?"

"Nope. Full carnivore."

"Shrimp?"

"Yum."

"Excellent." He brought the cell back to his cheek and thanked the hostess before disconnecting the call.

"So what's on the menu?" she asked him. "Shrimp?"

"Chu Chee."

"Oh. Do I like that?"

"Yes, you do," he replied, punctuating it with a wide grin. "It's one of your favorites, in fact."

"Good to know," she replied, her head bobbing in a slow nod.

Emma was quiet on the drive over to the restaurant, and when Jackson returned to the running car with their dinner in hand, she was curled against the passenger window, sound asleep. He almost hated to open the door and wake her, but the sting of recent cooler temperatures made him do it anyway.

He set the bag on the back seat and slid behind the wheel. As he shifted the car into gear, Emma's green eyes fluttered open and she half-smiled at him.

"Chotchke," she muttered. "Smells good."

"Not Chotchke," he chuckled. "That's what my buddy's Jewish mother keeps on her mantle. *Chu Chee.*"

"Right." She closed her eyes again as she asked him, "What is that, anyway?"

"Shrimp," he answered, and she nodded. "With snow peas, string beans and green pepper in coconut milk and red curry."

"Mm. You're right," she said without opening her eyes. "I do like it."

Jackson sent a grin in her general direction. "Emma?"

"Mm?"

"Where do you live?"

After a moment's processing, she sat straight up and giggled. "Oh, sorry. Make a left at the light."

Emma's building reminded Jackson of the tiny brownstone he and Desiree kept in Manhattan during their short time there. A string of six entrances, each of them with five brick steps leading to their leaded-glass doors; Emma's was the one on the end.

The interior was warm and inviting, more like a cozy library than a woman's home, a startling contrast to the large, gold filigree heart hanging on the door by a paisley wired bow. He'd expected something different somehow. Ribbons and lace perhaps? Pastel colors and floral prints?

No, he decided. *Not that.*

But certainly not the rich color palette grounding sturdy-yet-comfortable furniture, floor-to-ceiling bookshelves and a heavy stone fireplace.

"Make yourself comfortable," she told him. "I've got to do the insulin thing. Then I'll get some plates and silverware."

Jackson watched her until she disappeared around the corner. He recalled a family friend who'd lost her eyesight to diabetes when he was just a kid. And he thought he remembered that his paternal grandfather had actually lost a leg because of diabetes that wasn't kept under control. He didn't know much more about the disease than that, but Emma appeared to have it well in hand. At least, there were no apparent signs of those beautiful eyes of hers going dark any time soon.

The mantle was lined with framed photographs depicting an adolescence much less humiliating than one might expect to hear Emma tell of it. And there were graduation photos of embracing friends, Fee Bianchi in a costume of some kind, an erect, hair-laden sheepdog whose eyes were obscured by a mop of unruly white fur.

An elegant woman gave a proper smile from a carved wooden frame at one corner, while an older gentleman with the disheveled appearance of a news bureau chief grimaced from the opposite end of the mantle.

Probably her parents, Jackson decided, and the metaphoric placement of their photographs was in no way lost on him. *Keeping them in separate corners.*

"Your father?" he asked her when Emma leaned across the small dining table off the kitchen, setting placemats with ivory china and frosted glasses.

"Yes," she said with a nod, then she stepped up beside him and peered at the photo with a tentative smile. "He's one of a kind."

"Just like your mother?"

Emma chuckled. "Avery Travis was the first like her, and the last of her species. Southern royalty meets old world elegance."

"They don't sound so terrible," he observed.

"Not as long as they're kept at a distance," she revealed. "And as far apart as humanly possible."

Jackson laughed at that. "Maybe you could give me lessons on how to do that."

"For your sisters?"

"Yes."

"Not possible," she said on a giggle. "They've already united. They're a force of nature now."

"You learn fast, Emma."

"I do, indeed. Come on over to the table and let's have some of that Chotchke."

"Chu Chee."

"Right."

Jackson served two plates while Emma poured water for the both of them.

"You keep glasses chilled and frosted?" he

commented. "Just in case foreign dignitaries come to call?"

"Or employers bearing Thai food."

His grin turned into a smirk as he tried to hold it back, but Emma returned it with a full, toothy smile that lit up the whole room.

"You mentioned doing the insulin thing," he remarked. "What does that involve?"

"Oh. Taking my glucose level before every meal."

"That's the pin-prick to the finger?"

"Right. And then an injection of insulin if it's necessary, which it wasn't tonight."

"How long have you had it, Emma?"

"Since high school," she replied. "Sort of cruel irony for a baker, isn't it? But let's talk about something else, shall we?" Emma lifted her glass toward him. "To cars that start, and food that's hot."

"And to keeping our family members in cages where they belong."

"Salut!" she exclaimed, and they both took swigs as they nodded.

Dinner conversation ebbed and flowed, from shop talk to musings about the cold weather, from Jackson's teenaged artist dreams to Emma's days in culinary school. Even the silences were comfortable ones, and it occurred to Jackson that it had been a very long time since he'd shared one of his many, many takeout dinners with a companion.

Emma Rae Travis, Jackson admitted to himself, was a really beautiful girl. If her résumé hadn't betrayed her age, he'd never have thought she was older than her twenties; there was something so girlish about her with that sleek brown-and-golden streaked hair that she kept tied back in a ponytail or knotted in a messy loop at the top of her head most of the time. Except now, of course. Now it was hanging free across her shoulders, parted on one side and tucked neatly behind her ear. Emma's clear porcelain skin was luminescent, and those glistening emerald eyes of hers always seemed to draw a dusting by the long fringe of bangs.

Beautiful, he thought.

"What?" she asked just then. "What are you thinking?"

He popped a shrimp into his mouth and smiled as he chewed it, biding his time to find an answer.

"Because you look like you've just had a serious revelation of some kind."

"Do I?" he asked, wiping his mouth with the paper napkin she'd folded beneath his fork.

"Mm-hmm," she nodded. "And I

wouldn't want you straining anything, so spill it."

"Really?"

"Yes, really."

"I was thinking of a way to ask you whether you had some coffee."

He waited, hoping she bought it.

"Nope," she replied, leaning back into her chair. "Besides, the way you like it, thick and practically free-standing, well, it's too late for that sort of caffeine, don't you think?"

He raised a brow and tilted into a partial smile. "Yes?"

"How about you surrender a little and let me make you a cup of tea."

"Tea!" he exclaimed, and then laughed right out loud. "I'll pass."

"Come on." And then with an inviting smile, she added, "I have cinnamon sugar cookies."

"That, I'll take." With a second thought, he added, "But you're diabetic. What are you doing with cinnamon sugar cookies in your house?"

"There are only two," she defended. "They're Peter's favorites. I made them as a thank-you for the fast turnaround on the photographs he took for us. I kept a couple because I like to keep something sweet in the house, just in case."

"Just in case, what?"

"In case my battery goes dead on my car, and someone is nice enough to give me a ride home and buy me dinner and I need to provide dessert."

"That's what I call thinking ahead," he teased. "Can I have them? The cookies?"

"Not without the tea," she replied with a mock-serious shaking of her head. "It's tea and cookies, or nothing at all."

"Emma Rae Travis. Are you really giving your employer an ultimatum?"

"I know," she said with a shrug. "I know. Fire me if you will, but there are no cookies without tea in this house."

Jackson mulled that over, then finally asked, "What kind of tea?"

"I'll surprise you."

While Jackson cleared the dinner plates, Emma filled a stainless-steel kettle with water and placed it over a low gas flame on the stove. When the cookies finally arrived at the table, they were accompanied by two heavy stoneware mugs of something that smelled of spicy fruit and cream.

Jackson scrunched his nose and looked up at Emma. "Fruit tea? Are you kidding me with this?"

"Cinnamon plum," she replied. "Just try it."

He reluctantly took a sip from the cup. It wasn't terrible, but it sure wasn't as appealing as a cup of black coffee might be with one of those cookies on the plate across from him.

"Milk in it?" he asked her.

"Cream. It's the English way."

"I'm American. Can I have coffee now?"

"You may not. Drink your tea, or there is no cookie for you."

"I had a schoolteacher like you once."

"Then you probably know better than to argue with me."

Jackson laughed as she offered him the plate.

"Just one," she said, smacking his hand lightly when he reached for the second cookie. "Don't be a piglet."

Emma's Famous Cinnamon Sugar Cookies

1 1/4 cups flour
1/4 teaspoon salt
1/4 cup granulated sugar
1 egg
1/4 teaspoon baking soda
1/2 cup butter
3/4 cup light brown sugar
2 teaspoons vanilla extract

Outer mixture: 1/2 cup granulated sugar and 3 tablespoons cinnamon

Sift the flour, salt, and baking soda into a bowl.
In a separate bowl, mix the butter, sugar, and brown sugar until creamy.
Add the egg and vanilla.
Add the dry flour mixture slowly and continue to mix thoroughly.
Break the dough into three or four sections, rolling each into a log about two inches thick.
Wrap them in wax paper and refrigerate overnight (or for at least 3–4 hours).
The next day, mix the cinnamon and sugar together, and roll each log in it.
Cut the logs into quarter-inch slices and

place on an ungreased cookie sheet. Bake at 350 degrees for 15 minutes.

9

"Admit it! You're obsessed with hazelnut!"

"I am not."

"You are!"

Emma rubbed both cheeks with her hands. She hadn't laughed so hard, or for so long, in years. Leaning back against the cushions they'd pulled down from the sofa, she stretched her legs out on the carpeted floor and clutched her stomach.

"Stop it. I can't laugh anymore," she pleaded, then she proved herself wrong with a bumpy string of laughter.

Jackson's long legs were extended alongside hers, crossed at the ankle, his feet resting on the shoes he'd removed hours before. Sitting beside him there on the floor in front of the fireplace, Emma wondered for the first time all evening what time it had gotten to be.

"12:30 a.m.," she said out loud. "I can't believe it's after midnight."

"It can't be," he replied, looking at his watch, and then groaned. "Emma, I'm so sorry. I had no intention of staying this late."

"It's okay."

"It's not," he said, pushing upward, then placing his stocking feet into his shoes. "You were half asleep when you left work at seven-thirty, and now I'm sitting here talking your ear off at twelve-thirty."

"Honestly, it's fine," she reassured him. "I enjoyed it."

"Really?" he asked with a sort of curious, vulnerable curve of a smile.

"Really. I haven't laughed this much in I don't know when."

"I'm not sure I ever have," he commented, then he sighed. "Definitely not since I lost Desi."

Emma stood up and began gathering Jackson's belongings: his tie from the back of the sofa, his suit jacket from the dining room chair, his overcoat from the pewter hook near the front door.

"I think it's sweet the way you call her that," she said.

"Pardon?"

"Desiree. How you call her Desi."

"Oh." His smile was laced with equal measures of happy nostalgia and sour regret. "She hated it at first. But it always seemed to fit."

"I didn't know her," Emma remarked, "but it does seem to fit. It's very sweet."

"Sweet," he said with a sigh. "There's something I don't think I've ever been called."

Emma's heart began to pound as she watched him slip into his jacket. "I find that hard to believe."

"Oh, believe it," he replied, sliding into his overcoat. "There's nothing sweet about me, Emma Rae."

"You just look at yourself and the world around you through eyes of . . . disappointment," she told him, straightening the folded collar of his coat. "So you can't see what the rest of us see."

When she released the collar and pulled back her hand, Jackson's eyes caught hold of hers in one of those invisible grips that were starting to become somewhat familiar to Emma. Once again, she tried, but she couldn't look away from him, and so she just stood there, tied to him, the green of her eyes swimming around in the gold-flecked brown of his.

"Thank you for the chotchke."

Jackson's sudden smile beamed. "Chu chee. You're welcome."

For a fragmented moment, she was convinced that a kiss was about to follow. Her pulse raced, her heart pounded, her palms began to perspire. And against her better judgment, when Jackson moved closer to her, she pursed her lips in preparation.

"See you in the morning," he said suddenly, breaking the spell by planting a platonic sort of peck on her forehead, stifled by a thick fringe of bangs. It made a sort of thud as he did it. "I'll pick you up at eight."

"Okay."

"Thanks for everything," he told her.

"Even the tea?"

"Well, not so much for the tea. But the cookies and conversation were first-rate. G'night."

She watched him head down the stairs and out into the bitter cold.

"Good night, Jackson."

Emma closed and bolted the door, then slipped the chain into place. Instead of turning out the lights and heading straight to bed, she grabbed the chenille throw from the back of the sofa and wrapped it around her shoulders as she plunked down into her father's easy chair and sighed. Outside the bay window, Jackson's taillights flashed and then disappeared around the corner of her street.

Emma folded her legs beneath her and

stared at the last glowing embers in the fireplace. With opposition pressing in against her efforts not to sit there and replay every word, every inflection, every sparkle in Jackson Drake's gorgeous eyes, Emma lost the battle and surrendered to warm, smile-inducing thoughts of him. Oh, she knew how ridiculous it was; how utterly pointless and possibly even dangerous. But did she stop herself and send herself to bed?

Curling into the chair like a cat near a hearth, Emma closed her eyes and purred softly. When she'd turned over the key and her car just clicked, Emma had expected the worst: a long wait for the auto club, numb fingers and a runny nose from the cold. Instead, a handsome rescuer had appeared, and she'd been given the unplanned opportunity to know Jackson on a more personal level.

Emma had never been one for warm, gushy feelings, but there in the dim midnight rays streaming through the window of her apartment, she had to admit there was a bit of a marshmallow forming around her heart. In fact, in retrospect, the whole evening with Jackson had taken on the feeling of an unexpected gift dropped right in her path, and if a girl couldn't get a little mushy about that, well . . .

Really now, Emma Rae. Get over yourself.

Ah, there she was. The real Emma had at last stood up inside her.

What took you so long?

The sarcastic, cynical Emma had finally arrived; the one who knew that fluffy visions and starry-eyed notions about broad-shouldered rescuers and happily ever afters were best confined to romance novels and Jennifer Aniston movies.

"Better late than never," she muttered, and she tossed the chenille blanket aside, unfolded from the chair and trudged off to bed.

"It's not even eight in the morning," Emma growled as she looked out the window and jumped at another blast of Jackson's car horn. "Oh, man! My neighbors are going to love me."

She snapped the lock on the front door and slipped into her coat, hurrying down the stairs.

"You're early," she managed to say, one of her gloves flopping out from between clenched teeth.

Jackson glanced at the clock on the dash. "I said eight."

"Yes," she replied, pulling the door shut

and fussing with the seatbelt. "It's not eight yet."

"It's seven forty-six."

"That's not eight."

She noticed a slight roll of the eyes.

"Tea with cream and sweetener," he mumbled, and he shifted gears and eased out into traffic.

"Beg your pardon?"

"I stopped for coffee," he said with a nod toward the two paper cups tilted against the dash. "I got you tea with cream and sweetener."

"Oh!" she popped, grabbing the cup with the string hanging from it. "Thank you. You're forgiven."

"Forgiven," he repeated. "For what?"

"For being early."

"I'm not early."

"Is it eight o'clock yet?" she asked. She sniffed the steam from the cup and sighed. "No. It is not. That means you're early."

She thought she sensed a response making its way out of him, but instead he focused on the road ahead in silence.

This is sure a different guy from the one who left my house last night.

"A lot going on today," he grumbled a few minutes later.

"Oh?"

"Orientation for the wait staff and housekeeping."

"That's today?"

"Do you know anything about the fire marshal?"

Emma chuckled. "Not a thing. Why?"

"Well, you knew what was wrong with the elevator, and you directed me to a linen service. I just thought you might know about the fire marshal too."

"No," she assured him. "Are the inspectors coming today?"

"Ten thirty."

Emma sipped her tea and glanced at the rolling gray clouds on the horizon. "Looks like rain."

"Norma e-mailed about a tentative wedding group," he said. "Did she cc you on that?"

"I haven't checked yet today."

"The couple is local, but they have family coming in from three states."

"Mmm," she perked up, taking another sip from her cup. "They'll need rooms then."

"The bride and her mother are coming in this week for a tour. Oh, and your friend Harry dropped the lawsuit. Did I tell you that?"

"No, you didn't. That's great."

He sort of grunted in agreement, and Emma shook her head. What in the world had happened to him in the last twelve hours?

Jackson pulled into the circle in front of the hotel and parked behind her Mini Cooper. Emma had cranked open her door, unlatched her seatbelt, and flung her legs out before she realized he wasn't moving.

"Jackson?"

"Yeah."

"Are you all right?"

"Yeah."

"You might want to get out of the car then."

He seemed to think that over before responding. "Yeah."

Emma slipped back into the seat and closed her door, then turned sideways toward him. "Can I help?"

"No."

"Really? Because you look like you might need some help." When he didn't reply, she touched his arm. "You're kind of freaking me out."

He tilted his head downward and released a puff of a chuckle. "Welcome to my world."

"What, you're freaking out?"

"Little bit, yeah."

"Why?"

Jackson shook his head slowly before finally raising his eyes and looking at her. "I'm trying to figure out what on earth I was thinking when I bought a hotel."

"Well, that's easy," she said on a sigh. "You were taking a chance." He turned his glance toward her. "You were stepping out into an arena where you'd never been before to honor your late wife, and to break out of the corporate rut you were stuck in. You were thinking you would build something brand new, from the bottom up."

"Sounds pretty ignorant when you put it like that, doesn't it?"

"No," she reassured him. "It sounds brave."

Jackson looked away for a long moment, and then he sighed. "Are you a praying person, Emma?"

"Not so much in recent years, no."

"That's a shame."

"Why's that?"

Madeline and Georgiann appeared at the driver's window and began to knock, Madeline shooting one of those big toothy smiles of hers right at them, while Norma jogged around the car and pulled open Emma's door.

"I don't know," Jackson said without looking back at her. "I just found myself wishing for a miracle all of a sudden."

Emma chuckled, and then looked into the side mirror just in time to see Reverend Miguel climb out of the car behind them.

"You might want to talk to him about that," she suggested with an over-the-shoulder nod.

Jackson groaned slightly as he climbed out of the car.

"Here are your keys, Emma," Norma said, placing the car key into the palm of her hand. "Jackson had me meet the auto club this morning, and they've replaced your battery. It was dead as a doornail."

"Oh, thank you . . ."

Everyone seemed to be talking at once, and Jackson reached the front door and raised both hands. "Hang on! One at a time."

Emma lowered her head as she moved around them toward the hotel. "Have a nice day," she muttered, and Jackson gave her arm a soft poke with his elbow as she passed.

Every table in the restaurant was occupied, and a large rectangular one at the front held piles of uniforms and stacks of paperwork. Norma flew past her into the restaurant, and then skidded as she turned back toward her.

"Oh, Emma, good morning. Is there any chance you might have time to help me?"

"Sure."

Norma turned around and raised her voice to the group gathered inside. "Everyone. Attention please, everyone!"

The rumble of voices faded down to nothing, and Norma thanked them. "I'd like you to meet Emma Rae Travis. She is our award-winning pastry chef and baker. When you've finished filling out your paperwork, please go and hand it to Emma behind the table —" Making circles with her arm, Norma motioned Emma over toward the table at the front of the room. "— and she'll help you find your uniform."

Emma looked up just in time to catch sight of Fee heading for the kitchen, and she found herself making the same flailing circular motion with her arm that Norma had made. Obedient to the call, Fee tossed her backpack through the kitchen door and joined Emma at the front of the restaurant.

"What's all this?"

"Orientation."

"To what?"

"I'm not sure. But you're helping."

"Oh good. I was hoping for a confusing task to start my day."

"Fee," Norma breathed when she saw her.

"Lovely." Appearing somewhat frantic, she pointed in opposite directions and instructed, "Fee, you can take the serving staff, and Emma, you take the housekeeping table. Each uniform package contains two uniforms and a folder with regulations, their hours and scheduling and general information about The Tanglewood. They are each labeled with the person's name. Collect their paperwork, hand over their uniform package, and then —" She leaned in and whispered, "— get them out of here."

A couple of dozen housekeepers and three supervisors later, every one of the uniform packages had been dispersed from Emma's table, and she moved over to Fee's to help her do the same.

"Fourteen waitresses, seven waiters, twelve busboys and six dishwashers," Norma read from a list at the top of her clipboard. Flipping the page, she added, "Four hostesses and six bartenders."

Emma was tempted to shout, "Hike!" But she resisted.

Norma looked at her watch and frowned. "It's not even eleven o'clock, and I'm exhausted."

"How about I go and put together a little sustenance," Fee suggested. "Some coffee and a snack for the three of us?"

"That sounds lovely."

"Tea for me?"

"You head 'em up, and move 'em out," Fee said to Emma as she passed.

"Okay!" Emma exclaimed, prodding the thick of the crowd like cattle. "Everyone has their initial schedule, their uniforms and their hotel packet. If you have questions, there's a number to call inside the folder. Use the side door to the parking lot, and have a great day."

When Emma had seen the last of them out the door, she returned to the restaurant to find Norma moving from table to table, collecting pens and scraps of paper and pushing chairs into place.

"Thank you so much for your help, Emma."

"Happy to."

Norma sank into one of the chairs and propped her feet on another. "Really, you were hired as a baker, not an assistant recruiter or a security officer."

Emma chuckled. "It's a new business, Norma. We all pitch in; that's how it works."

"Well, thank you." Fee entered with a large tray, and Norma brightened. "Oh, halleluiah. Thank *you,* too!"

"Em, your mom called," Fee announced as she set the tray on the table. "She left a message with the service. Something about your Aunt Sophie's new digs over in Sandy Springs. I guess she's in town, huh?"

"Oh, that's wonderful," Norma commented as she creamed her coffee. "My sister will be so pleased."

"Yeah, she said she'll call you this afternoon."

Oh, good.

They'd no sooner gathered around the coffee and scones than Emma glanced up and noticed Norma brighten again, and she turned around to see what had caused such a beaming smile.

"Hello, Princess."

Emma hopped from her chair so quickly that she nearly fell over it. "Dad!"

"Mister Travis!" Fee exclaimed, and then her face melted into a mixture of horror and disbelief. "Uh-oh, Em. This is *not good.*"

Emma jerked her head over her shoulder and met Fee's eyes with her own flaming ones. "I know!"

"This is your father?" Norma asked.

"What are . . . what are you doing here?" Emma asked, using the table to balance herself upright.

"What do you think? I'm visiting my daughter. Come here and give your old man a hug."

Emma's heart pounded with foreboding as she moved toward him, sort of like the soundtrack of a movie when the tuba and trombone let the audience know that the plot is about to take a menacing turn.

Gavin and Avery Travis in the same town, at the same time?

There wasn't anything Emma could think of that was more menacing than that!

FOR IMMEDIATE RELEASE

One-Stop Wedding Hotel Gears for Opening in Historic Roswell

ROSWELL, Ga. — The Tanglewood Inn of Roswell, once known as a premiere Georgia boutique hotel, was bought earlier this year by corporate raider Jackson Drake (formerly with Atlanta's Drummond & Associates), whose late wife Desiree Drake worked at The Tanglewood until her death in 2008. Drake is in the process of converting the inn into a full-service bridal nirvana of sorts offering clients event planning for parties, pre-wedding events and showers, as well as the ceremony, reception, and honeymoon.

The new Tanglewood boasts 144 unique guest rooms, including 20 Grand Suites, and features four-poster beds, gas fireplaces, carved armoires, and the elegant Victorian flair for which the hotel has always been known. Some of the rooms have wrought-iron balconies which overlook a New Orleans-style courtyard, while others include bay windows large enough to stand in and beautiful city views.

The overhaul of the establishment will introduce an exclusive 100-seat restaurant operated by world-famous chef Anton Morelli (open to outside patrons from 5 p.m. until 11 p.m. Sunday through Thursday) and an English tea room (open on Tuesday and Wednesday afternoons from 1:00 p.m. until 4:30 p.m. by reservation only). Facilities include three ballrooms, a 200-seat theater, a guest library, and a brick courtyard for private social events hosted beneath the open Georgia sky.

Weddings and events booked at The Tanglewood will have menu choices from chef Anton Morelli's gourmet repertoire, as well as custom wedding cake design by Emma Rae Travis, this year's recipient of the coveted Passionate Palate Award for her six-tiered crème brûlée wedding cake masterpiece.

The new hotel opens the first weekend of next month with an invitation-only wedding-themed kick-off event which is meant to celebrate the marriage of the historic Roswell community and its newest and most exclusive setting for *Happily Ever Afters*.

Contact: Connie Edison
Edison Public Relations
(770) 888-3321

10

"Dad, the hotel isn't even officially open yet," Emma told him. "You can't stay here."

"All right then, I'll stay with my little girl."

"But my place is so small. Let's get you a room at The Grapevine. It's nearby, and you'll be more comfortable there than at my place."

"Don't be ridiculous!" Norma interjected, taking Gavin's hand between both of hers, she told him, "You'll stay with my husband and me. We have more than enough room, and we'd be so happy to have you."

"Oh. Norma. Really." Emma felt a little faint. "Y-you don't want to do that."

"Of course I do. I won't hear another word, Emma. Gavin will just come home with me and stay with us for as long as he'd like."

"How long will that be, exactly?" Emma asked her father, trying her best to sound casual, knowing that she'd missed that mark by leaps and bounds.

"Oh, I don't know," Gavin replied. "I thought I might hang tight for the opening of this place. See my little girl in her element."

"Dad! That's two weeks away!"

"That's wonderful," Norma chimed in. "Just wonderful. We'd love to have you attend the opening, Gavin."

"What's that about the opening?" Georgiann asked from the doorway to the restaurant.

"Oh, Georgiann, you'll never guess who this is!" Norma sang. "It's Gavin Travis, Emma's father."

Georgiann inflated like a helium balloon and then bobbed her way across the room to Gavin's side. "What a *pleashuh* to meet you, Mr. Travis."

"Mr. Travis died a decade ago," he told her. "You call me Gavin."

"All right then, Gavin. I'm Georgiann Markinson. My little *bruthah* Jackson owns this establishment."

"A pleasure to make your acquaintance," he said, lifting her hand and kissing it softly, an action that caused Georgiann to giggle, pushing Emma's eyebrows straight up into a curious arch.

"Gavin is going to be staying with Louis

and me," Norma announced to her sister.

"That is really just so . . . umm . . . nice of you, Norma," Emma sputtered. "Really, really nice. In fact, there's still time to change your mind about that. I'm sure The Grapevine would be —"

"Don't be silly," Norma replied. "Louis and I will love having your father as our houseguest."

"Oh. Well. If you're sure."

"In fact, we should all have dinner together tonight," Norma exclaimed.

"What a wonderful idea!" Georgiann concurred.

"Everyone must come to my house for dinner," Norma told them, and she grabbed Fee's wrist and shook it.

Fee scrunched up her face in a forced excitement, and she nodded so eagerly that it made Emma a little dizzy. When Norma looked away, Fee and Emma exchanged wide-eyed stares tainted with panic.

"Emma, I'll drive your father out to the house and get him settled, and you all come along whenever you're ready. Dinner will be at seven sharp."

"I'll tell Jackson and Maddie," Georgiann told her. "Shall I invite Susannah?"

"Of course!"

"Good then."

Emma just stood there, feeling a little like an empty plastic bag swept up by a gust of wind as they all moved around her. Gavin kissed her cheek and squeezed her arm, but Emma still didn't move a muscle except for the weak little smile she managed to give him.

"I'll see you at dinner, Princess."

"Okay, Dad."

"I'll just walk you two out," Georgiann said as she headed for the front door, arm-in-arm with Gavin, Norma on the other side of him.

Emma and Fee stood glued to their spots, side by side, watching them go.

"Uh," Fee said. "You remember that your mother is in town as well, right?"

"Yeah. I remember."

"What are you going to do?"

"I thought I'd go upstairs."

"To see Jackson?"

"No. To jump."

Jackson escorted Leo Finch to the lobby and shook his hand, thinking that this man looked more like the prototype for an Internal Revenue Service auditor than a fire marshal. He could almost picture Finch on the cover of the government recruitment brochure for the IRS, smiling just enough to tip the hand of that chipped yellow front tooth, but not enough to inspire any real confidence.

"Thank you for everything."

"Sure thing," Finch replied, and then he pulled a very serious face, eyebrows pointing downward at his nose. "And remember. Only *you* can prevent hotel fires."

The fire marshal quoting *Smokey the Bear?* It was too strange to be real.

"Ha," he managed. "Good one. Have a good day."

Not a great day. Just a good one. Preferably somewhere else.

Jackson watched the man fuss with his tweed jacket as he headed down the hotel driveway toward the street, and he wondered where he was parked. His musings were cut in two with the distant click of heels top-noted by Georgiann's sing-song voice.

He knew better, he really did. After all, he was an adult, the owner of the place, but Georgiann's approach sent anxiety coursing through him. The second heel click heading around the corner would be Miguel, and he'd been successfully dodging him all day.

What was it about mild-mannered Miguel Ramos that could make a successful grown man hightail it and duck for cover?

Jackson knew the answer, but he didn't stop to ponder it. He didn't tiptoe away; oh no, there wouldn't be any tiptoeing for him. But he did manage to keep contact between his shoes and the shiny marble lobby floor to a minimum as he made a beeline for the converted office that used to be his supply closet of choice in moments like these.

He eased open the door, slipped inside, and closed the door again. He didn't mean to hold his breath, but he realized that's just what he was doing.

"Oh, I'd forgotten Miguel Ramos was in the house."

His hand still poised over the doorknob, Jackson closed his eyes and dropped his head against the door. He hadn't noticed that the room was illuminated, or that Emma was sitting there. One deep breath of composure, and he turned around and gave her a clumsy smile.

"No judgment here," she said with a grin, seated on the floral sofa in the corner, looking quite prim with her legs crossed and her arm draped over the back of the couch.

"Who are *you* hiding from?" he asked her.

"My family tree. You?"

Jackson nodded. "You had it right. My nephew."

"Share my soda?"

"Sure."

Jackson crossed the room and took a seat in the deep blue wingback chair while Emma refreshed her glass of cola, then handed him the can. Once he'd taken it, she raised her glass toward him, and he clinked the can against it with a nod before taking a drink.

"So, Jackson," she began, then she leaned back into the couch and arched her brow at him. "How are we going to get you through this debilitating fear of the clergy?"

Jackson snickered and rested an ankle on the opposite knee. "I wish I knew."

"Any other uniformed figures you hide from? Postal workers, dog catchers, maybe a medical professional or two?"

"No. No, it would appear to be an aversion to well-meaning pastors alone."

He found himself carefully examining the fabric on the arm of his chair as she asked him, "Do you want to talk about it?"

After a long moment of consideration, he replied, "Not really."

"Okay."

"Do you want to talk about your reasons for hiding in this room?"

Emma chuckled, then she closed her eyes and tilted her head to the back of the couch with a sigh. "My family tree has root rot."

"I understand," he told her with a grin.

"Oh, no," she replied, lifting her head and braising him with the fire in her eyes. "Your family is just big and quirky, with a somewhat dim view of boundaries." Jackson laughed right out loud at her perceptive analysis. "My family doesn't know what boundaries *are.* And to make it worse, I don't have a group of sisters to ease the burden of being the only child of Gavin and Avery Travis. You don't understand. It's just me, Jackson. No one else. Just me, wedged between these two great big —" she waved her arms in opposing circles, as if depicting a tornado in pursuit, "— *big* personalities."

Jackson couldn't help himself — he guffawed, then slapped the arm of the chair to punctuate his amusement.

"Oh, laugh it up, buddy," she told him, her expression trapped somewhere between hilarity and utter panic. "But you're going to be dragged into this vortex of human dysfunction. At this very moment, *Norma* is playing hostess to my *father!*"

"What —"

"Oh yeah. My father came to town today, and your sister took him home with her. Like an orphaned child headed for Disneyland, talking about having dinner and taking him to see the sights."

"Well, that's not so . . ."

"No, wait. There's more."

"More?"

"My Aunt Sophie isn't doing so well in Savannah," she said. Then wandering off on another trail of thought, she continued, "I think she might have Alzheimer's, actually. They found her at the mall in her pajamas, I guess, waiting for the stores to open. That can't be good, right? I mean, she wasn't just walking in her sleep or something. She was confused, and she just —"

Their eyes met, and Emma stopped herself mid-thought.

"Sorry. Anyway. My mother got the brilliant idea, with the impeccable timing that she's always possessed, to choose this exact moment in time to bring Aunt Sophie to Atlanta and get her settled in some assisted-living facility she knows about."

"Well, that part is good, right? She's taking care of your aunt, seeing to it that —"

"No. You don't understand. My parents can *not* be here at the same time. It's just a whole . . . a whole . . . recipe for *disaster!*"

"And you don't think you're just the slightest bit over the top with this?" he asked with a grin.

"Oh, fine. You hold fast to that, Jackson. I want to hear more from you once you've been in a room with both of them at the same time. I give you five minutes."

"Until what?"

"Until you run screaming into the night."

Something in her expression drained the amusement out of the conversation, and Jackson reached over and touched her arm.

"They're that horrible?"

"The truth is, they're wonderful people. Both of them. My mother is refinement and grace, with this really keen sense about decorum and courtesy. She's lovely, she really is." She smoothed her hair back with both hands and sighed. "And my dad is one of the greatest men I've ever known. He's smart, and he's well traveled, well read. He's not refined like my mother, but he really knows what's what. Do you get what I mean?"

Jackson nodded tentatively. "I think so."

"They're fantastic people, they really are. But you put them in a room together, Jackson, and it's like . . . like . . ."

"Like you want to lock yourself in a supply closet?"

She pressed her lips together and nodded. "At the very least."

"When does your mother arrive?"

"Any minute."

Jackson got the feeling from her reply that

Houston command was at the ready, counting backwards toward liftoff.

"Do you want me to wait with you?"

"Oh," she said on a sigh. "No. There's no use in that. Go on. Save yourself."

Jackson grinned. He drained the last of the soda from the can and set it down on the coffee table before standing up and facing her. When she looked up at him, he stretched out his arms for a moment, then tapped his chest with both hands before opening his arms again.

"Come on. Let's hug it out."

While chuckling, Emma groaned and pushed herself up from the sofa and smacked into his embrace.

"Everything is going to be okay," Jackson told her, suppressing the smile that threatened to turn into full-on laughter.

She groaned again, then she nodded unconvincingly. "Yeah, yeah, whatever." As she pulled away from him, Emma looked up at Jackson and brightened. "Hey, can I go find Miguel for you?"

Jackson planted his hands on her shoulders and braced her before him with a grimace. "That was just mean."

"I know. I'm sorry," she surrendered. "You just make it too easy."

He patted her shoulders before releasing

her and heading for the door. "I'll see you later."

"Oh right," she said. "At dinner."

He turned back and tilted his head. "Dinner?"

"Oh yeah, buddy. We're *aaaaall* invited to your sister's house. Won't that be special?"

Jackson opened the door. "I'm concerned about you, Emma Rae," he said with his back to her. "The pleasure you find in taking down the people around you isn't healthy."

"I know."

"You should get therapy for that."

"Maybe your nephew does counseling," she exclaimed. "We could get a group rate. Want to go find him and talk to him about that right now?"

Jackson didn't look back at her, so she didn't get to see the grin spread across his face. It wasn't lost on him either, the way Emma was able to amuse him that way. The muscles in his face actually ached a little from the uncharacteristic action they were getting.

"I'll bet he's still here," she added. "I could go and have a look around."

Jackson shook his head and stepped through the doorway.

"See you at seven!" she called after him.

"Don't be late. You don't want to miss the floor show."

Adorable, he thought as he closed the door behind him. *Somewhat neurotic. And unbelievably adorable.*

Five Effective Ways for a Bride to Eliminate Wedding Day Stress

1. Plan an extra hour into her morning for soft music, a pot of tea, and quiet time to prepare for the day ahead.
2. Write in her journal, citing all of the things for which she is grateful.
3. Meditate on the things that matter. She should spend some time sitting quietly, putting all thoughts of cakes, flowers, and centerpieces aside in order to think about her goal of committing to the person she loves.
4. Take a warm bath. Fragrances such as lavender, sandalwood, and citrus are soothing aromas which bring about relaxation.
5. Have a nutritious breakfast. Include more protein than carbohydrates, and drink an extra glass of cool, clear water with the meal.

11

"Emma Rae Travis, let me look at you."

Avery rested one hand on her hip, and the other covered her heart as she smiled in that elegant way she had about her, a mixture of appreciation with unmistakable traces of pride in a job well done. Her ivory skin was flawless, from the curve of her oval chin to the slight widow's peak at the top of her forehead. She always looked a little like a silhouette on a cameo to Emma, with her raven hair combed smoothly back into a perfect bun, just a few stray wisps curling at the back of her neck and in front of her ears.

"You're just lovely, darling."

"You act like it's been years since you've laid eyes on me," Emma teased. Stepping toward her mother, she wrapped her arms around her and kissed her cheek. "It's only been a couple of months."

Avery reached out and freed the hair Emma had tucked behind her ear. "It feels like years. But look at you, with a prestigious new job in this lovely hotel; a kitchen all your own. I'm so proud of you."

"Thank you, Mother."

A gasp turned their attention to the doorway of the kitchen, where Georgiann stood planted, her hand over her mouth.

"This is your mother?"

Emma's heart dropped an inch or two. "Yes. Mother, I'd like you to meet Georgiann Markinson. Georgiann's brother is my boss, Jackson Drake."

Georgiann scurried across the kitchen, closing the gap between them, and gently took Avery's hand. "Avery Buffington Travis. It's such a pleasure to meet you at last."

"Why, thank you so much, Mrs. Markinson."

"Georgiann, please. It's just a thrill."

"And you will call me Avery."

Georgiann beamed as if she'd just been presented to the queen.

"Well," Emma began, drumming her fingers on her hip, striving to gain control before it completely eluded her.

"I've been to the Hoyte Museum in Savannah. Your tireless efforts toward the restoration work there was inspiring. Just inspiring."

Avery's smile ignited like a gas flame

turned to High. "Ah, a woman of culture," she surmised. "You have a taste for the arts, then."

"Indeed! In fact, I've used your work in Savannah as a blueprint in my effort to help restore The Grayden here in Atlanta."

"The Grayden!" Avery exclaimed. "I saw my first ballet at The Grayden Theater. Are you familiar with the Atlanta Women's Preservation Guild?"

"I've served on the board for the last six years."

Avery took Georgiann's arm and led her toward the door of the kitchen. "You must tell me all about it. I was elected president of the guild in 1997."

"Oh, yes, I know."

Emma just stood there and watched them disappear as the kitchen door flapped behind them. After a moment, she lifted her head and looked at the ceiling.

"Really, God?" she remarked. "Seriously?"

After two deep breaths and a stretch of her neck, Emma proceeded through the kitchen door.

"You must come!" Georgiann exclaimed just as Emma reached them.

"I'd be delighted," Avery replied, and then she turned to Emma with a meaningful grin. "Georgiann has just invited me to join all of you for dinner tonight at her sister's home."

"Oh." Emma's mouth went completely dry. "No." She cleared her throat, and then bit the corner of her lower lip. "That's not really . . . No."

"No?" One of Avery's eyebrows formed a perfect raised arch.

"No, Mother. The thing is . . . the fact of the matter is . . ."

"Emma Rae, if you don't want me included on your dinner with your friends, just say so. I can easily drive out to Brookhaven and fend for myself this evening."

"No, it's not that, Mother."

"Then what is it? Georgiann has extended a perfectly lovely invitation and, if you don't want me to accept, you'll have to give me a reason."

Emma shifted all of her weight to one hip, lowered her head and tucked her hair behind one ear. When she looked up again, both Avery and Georgiann were staring her down.

"It's Daddy."

"Gavin? What about him?"

"Well, he's in town."

"What is *that man* doing in Atlanta?" she asked, as if the divorce decree had only allowed him access to the portions of the country that were north and east of Georgia.

"He wanted to surprise me."

"Your father never could comprehend the discourtesy of surprising a woman on a whim."

Emma cleared her throat again. "Well, the truth is . . . Georgiann's sister, Norma, invited Dad to be her houseguest."

"I see."

"And the dinner is sort of . . . he's kind of . . ."

"The guest of honor," Avery finished for her.

"Yes."

"I see."

Emma didn't like it when Avery went quiet that way. She shifted to one leg, and then the other. "But you know —"

"Your father is so fond of surprises," Avery interrupted. "What do you say we give him one tonight?" Emma's heart palpitated. "What would surprise him more than you showing up for dinner with me on your arm?"

"Oh, Mother, I don't —"

"What a wonderful idea!" Georgiann exclaimed. "I was just about to head over there myself. Avery, why don't you ride with me, and Emma can follow in her little toy car."

And before the tornado siren in Emma's head could sound the alarm of approaching disaster, Avery had kissed her daughter on the cheek and crossed through the lobby with Georgiann.

"There's my Princess!" Gavin exclaimed as Norma escorted Emma into the parlor.

"Hi, Daddy." She kissed his rough cheek and squeezed his arm.

"Your father has been regaling us with tales of life in our nation's capitol!" Norma announced. "He's quite the business tycoon, your father."

Emma nodded, then glanced around the room to make sure she hadn't just missed Georgiann's car out in the drive.

"What do you have there, Emma?"

"Oh!" She'd almost forgotten that she had brought something along for dessert. "I've been experimenting with a new recipe, and I think this batch turned out very well. I'm calling them Mocha Latte Cookies; they're dipped in chocolate. I thought you might like to have them for dessert, or perhaps just keep them around for another time."

Norma peeked into the open box and swooned. "I don't know how you do it, Emma. They're just beautiful. I'll have Harriet put them on a tray to serve with coffee after dinner."

Emma handed over the white box and moved toward her father. "Dad, there's something I need to tell you," she whispered under the guise of an embrace.

"What is it, Emmy?" he asked her, and his brown eyes sparkled at her as he ran a hand over the dark gold and silver-streaked hairline that had receded more than an inch since the last time he'd come to town.

"I didn't plan this. I mean, I didn't even know she was —"

"Greetings, Gavin." Her mother's smooth, low voice sliced Emma's warning right into pieces.

Gavin's face glazed over, and he looked down at Emma and groaned. Under his breath, in his signature gravel-and-molasses tone, he muttered, "Hide the women and children."

"I'd like you all to meet Emma's mother, Avery Travis," Georgiann announced. "Avery, this is my sister Norma, her husband Louis, our other sister Madeline, and Jackson's longtime assistant Susannah."

Avery spread her greetings around the room, and then landed back on Norma. "I can't thank you enough for allowing me to join your festivities."

"We're happy to have you."

Gavin took a step back when her gaze found its way to him, and Emma bristled.

"No need to stand guard, darling," Avery told her. "Your father and I are civilized Southern people." With a sassy little grin, she added, "Oh wait. That's just me." Moving toward him, she took his hand. "How are you, Gavin?"

"That depends. Does your kind still devour their prey?"

Avery smiled. "Only if it's appetizing, so I think you're safe."

Amusement popped around the room, then Emma realized that hers was the only laughter fraught with tension. Everyone else seemed to be taking this meeting in stride. She hoped they wouldn't end up strangled by their own cluelessness in the next several minutes.

"So where is the man of the hour?" Avery asked as she turned toward Georgiann. "Wasn't your brother supposed to be here tonight? I'd like to shake the hand of the man who recognized the mastery in my daughter, the baker."

"He just called a few minutes ago," Susannah answered. "He should be here any minute."

"Pork tenderloin for dinner," Norma announced. "I hope everyone likes pork?"

"My favorite kind of hoof," Gavin replied, and Emma masked the cringe that involuntarily popped up to her face.

"Why don't you help me with beverages," Norma said as she touched Emma on the arm.

"Um, okay," she replied.

"You can stop hovering, Emma Rae," her mother assured her. "We can be trusted."

Emma puffed out a little chuckle and followed her hostess across the room to the carved wooden cart set up next to the fireplace. As Norma filled several crystal glasses with sparkling water, Emma's eyes meandered across the room to where her mother joined the other women. Her father stood across from Louis Blanchette, entertaining him with conversation that she couldn't quite make out.

The sleeves of Gavin's expensive suit jacket were pushed up toward his elbows, and his dark brown tie was knotted loosely beneath an open collar. He'd always been one to tell a story with his hands, and she noticed as he moved them that his breast pocket was stuffed with several cigars. She had still been holding out hope that he'd given them up.

"These are for Louis and your father, dear."

Emma accepted the glasses and delivered them to the men at the other side of the room.

"Thank you, Princess." Gavin took a sip and then pulled a sour face. "What is this?"

"Mineral water."

"Mih-neral water," he repeated with a grunt. "I thought people still drank bourbon in Southern parlors."

"Not this one, Dad," she replied in a whisper. "Behave yourself."

His chuckle and the glistening spark in his eyes told her he'd just been teasing her, and Emma shook her head and sighed as she walked away from him.

Once she'd delivered a tray of drinks to the women, Emma straightened and her eyes met Jackson's where he stood in the entryway. Just the sight of him caused her heart to leap a little. Suddenly, she wasn't alone in this. Relief pushed a grin up and over her face that Jackson returned with a reassuring nod.

"Jackson, come in here!" Georgiann exclaimed, and she hurried to his side and planted a kiss on his cheek. "You have to meet Emma's charming parents."

His eyes had darted back to Emma on the word "charming," and just as fast he headed straight for Avery and took her hand in both of his.

"Mrs. Travis, I'm so happy to meet you."

"Well, well, aren't you just as handsome a man as I've ever seen here in Atlanta," she returned. "It's such a pleasure, Jackson."

"And this —" Norma said, leading him by the arm to the back of the sofa. "This is Emma's father, Gavin Travis."

"Mr. Travis," Jackson said, and Emma watched as her father sized him up over their handshake.

"Good to know you."

"Your daughter has played a very big part in making The Tanglewood even more than I'd planned it to be," he told them. "I'm very fortunate to have her on board."

"Yes, you are," Gavin replied gruffly, and then he and Jackson exchanged smiles. "I'm probably a little biased, but I happen to think Emmy's the cream of the crop."

"Well, I agree," he said, and Emma's pulse fluttered. "I hope you'll both be able to stay for the opening?"

"I wouldn't miss it," Avery chimed, and Georgiann clapped her hands in response.

"I was hoping you'd grace us," she said, and then looked toward Gavin hopefully.

"I'll do my best," he added.

Jackson followed Emma to the beverage

cart, and she poured him a glass of sparkling water.

"No bloodshed yet," he softly observed. "How long before the lions are released?"

She handed him the glass. "Shouldn't be long now."

A gentle knock on the door hushed the hum of conversation.

"That will be Fee," Emma announced.

"I'm sorry. I should have told you," Georgiann said. "I invited her, but she already had plans tonight. She said to tell you she was very sorry she missed the fun, but she wanted to hear all about it in the morning."

"Oh." Emma was disappointed. Fee was so familiar with her family history that she would have been a nice buffer for her. "Then who's at the door? Are we missing someone?"

"Yes. I invited —" The entrance of the final dinner guest halted Georgiann's words. Then she lifted a wide grin and finished her thought. "— my nephew. Miguel, come in and meet Emma's parents, Gavin and Avery Travis."

Emma watched as Jackson's solid shoulders sank ever so slightly.

"You're just in time," Norma said as she greeted Miguel. "We were just going to sit down to dinner."

Emma took her father's arm, and they followed Louis into the rectangular dining room. A beautiful mahogany table occupied the center of the room, comfortably flanked by twelve chairs with generously padded rose tapestry seats. A starched-white tablecloth was set with deep indigo placemats embroidered at the edge with tiny white flowers, and the blue-on-white place settings glistened beside crystal goblets and shiny silver flatware. The centerpiece, an arrangement of burgundy and steel-blue flowers, was impeccable in an oblong crystal vase.

"Your china is exquisite," Avery said as she and Norma passed through the entryway. "Is it Churchill?"

"You have a wonderful eye!" Norma exclaimed. "English Blue Willow Ware."

"It's just stunning."

Louis pulled out a chair and motioned for Emma to take a seat beside her father. She sighed as Avery sat down at the opposite end of the table. If one of them couldn't be seated at a table in the next county, she'd take whatever distance she could get.

Jackson's eyes met Emma's and she smiled, but just as he headed toward the empty seat next to her, Avery caught him by the wrist and looked up at him.

"Jackson, will you sit beside me?" she asked. "I'd like the chance to get to know you."

He hesitated. The empty seat beside Avery was flanked on the other side by dark-haired, dark-eyed Miguel, and his thought process was unmistakable.

"Of course," he finally replied, and he exchanged a nod with Miguel when he took the chair.

Jackson glanced at Emma, and she could almost hear the soft click as their gazes locked for one frozen instant. The twitch of his eyebrow and the upward tilt of one side of his mouth told her everything he might have said aloud if they were alone.

Two uniformed servers filed into the dining room, one with a large platter of sliced pork tenderloin balanced on her arm, the other bearing lovely china bowls. They announced the menu items as they approached Georgiann first, at the head of the table.

"New potatoes with rosemary and minced garlic, and steamed asparagus with your choice of butter or hollandaise."

"Lovely. Thank you."

Gavin leaned in close to his daughter and whispered, "Tomorrow night, it's Morton's for a rib eye."

"Just what you need, Dad. A pound of red

meat to clog up your arteries."

"At what point when I wasn't watching did you transform into your mother?"

Emma's Mocha Latte Cookies (v.4 — Final)

Melt 2 squares (2 ounces) of unsweetened chocolate in a small pan, and let cool.
Combine 2 cups flour, 1 teaspoon cinnamon and 1/4 teaspoon salt.
In a large bowl, beat 1/2 cup shortening and 1/2 cup butter until soft.
Add 1/2 cup granulated sugar and 1/2 cup brown sugar, and mix well.
Add 1 tablespoon double-strength espresso to the butter mixture with 1 egg and the melted chocolate.
Fold in the flour mixture and mix well.
Cover the bowl and refrigerate for two hours.
Shape the dough into two equal rolls and seal in plastic wrap.
Chill overnight.
Cut the rolls into 1/2-inch slices.
Bake at 350 degrees on ungreased cookie sheets for 10–12 minutes.
Remove and cool.
Heat 1 1/2 cup semisweet chocolate chips and 3 tablespoons shortening over low heat until melted.
Dip 1/2 of each cookie into the chocolate mixture and place on wax paper to cool and set.

12

The French doors from the dining room to the veranda were propped open, and Jackson had a clear line of sight of Emma where she sat outside and sipped from a cup of tea, gazing out over the grassy slope of Norma and Louis's backyard.

He popped the last bite of her cookie concoction into his mouth and picked up his coffee cup. Stepping out onto the veranda, the soft clink of spoons against china cups harmonized with the hum of conversations behind him. He grinned at Emma as she looked up at him.

"It's a beautiful night, isn't it?" she asked as he sat down on the iron bench beside her.

"It is."

"It's been so cold lately. But tonight is really mild."

"And no bloodshed," he pointed out. "I'm thinking you may have overstated the rot in your family tree branches, Emma Rae."

She chuckled, then sipped again from her tea. "Are you disappointed?"

"Maybe just a little," he replied. "In that mixed bag way that you're disappointed when storm clouds blow over without bringing on the storm."

"Can I join you?"

Their attention darted to the doorway as Miguel stepped out to the patio.

"Of course," Emma replied. "Pull up a chair."

"Actually . . ." He hesitated when his eyes met Jackson's. "I was hoping to speak with Jackson."

"Oh." Emma started to get up, but Jackson touched her arm.

"No, you don't have to leave."

"I think I do," she said warmly, and her smile caressed his face before she headed inside.

Miguel took her place on the iron bench, and he swung one leg casually over the other. "How are you, Jackson?"

"I'm all right, Miguel. How about yourself?"

Several beats of silence nudged Jackson to turn toward Miguel.

"You've been avoiding me."

Jackson swallowed hard as he thought

about denying it. But something in his throat wouldn't let him. Finally, he sighed. "I'm sorry about that."

"Have I offended you in some way?"

"No," he said, and turned and faced forward again.

"Talk to me, Jackson. We used to be pretty tight. At least, I thought we were. But after Desiree —"

"It was a hard time for me," he interrupted.

"I know it was. But every time I reached out to help you through it, you rejected my help. And now I feel like it's become a real wall between us."

"No," Jackson said, shaking his head. "Not a wall."

"You can be straight with me." Jackson felt the weight of the words close in on him a little. "What's changed?"

He cleared his throat, then he leaned back against the cold metal scrollwork.

"I guess —" He paused and cleared his throat again. "Well. Losing Desi was quite a blow for me, Miguel."

"I know it had to be."

"I never thought I'd find someone like her. And nobody else thought I would either." He chuckled. "I was all about business and more business."

"I remember," Miguel added softly.

"But she was the first and only woman I've ever loved in my life. Losing her was like cutting out a chunk of me."

Miguel gave Jackson's shoulder a couple of firm pats, then Jackson turned toward him and looked him squarely in the eye. "Having someone tell me that God had a plan in that kind of thing, Miguel . . . well, that was something I just couldn't hear."

Miguel nodded thoughtfully. "And now?"

"I still can't hear it, even now. In fact, I'm not sure I'll ever be able to hear it."

"I don't think that's true," Miguel stated. "Do you want to know why?"

Jackson sighed. "Sure."

"Because the God that I was talking about lives inside you. He always has. And even though things happen that we can never understand, that we can't reason out or make sense of, He is still there. Your mind is battling against your spirit right now, but deep inside I believe you know the truth."

Jackson inched forward slightly to the edge of the slatted wooden bench.

"There's a saying in Latin," Miguel continued. "*Vocatus atque non vocatus dues aderit.* It means, 'Bidden or not bidden, God is present.' "

Jackson sighed. This was what he had been

avoiding all along: a sermon from the gospel according to Miguel.

"Whether you call upon Him, or whether you don't, God knows the pain in your heart, Jackson. He understands that losing Desiree was worse than a knife cutting straight into you. When you cry, He cries with you, and He wants desperately to heal those wounds if you'll just allow Him to do that."

"Miguel," he said, and it pained him as he prepared the words. "No one has what I need to heal my wounds. Desiree is not coming back, and as long as she's gone, there is no healing balm strong enough, no words comforting enough, and no quotations relevant enough to fill this huge empty hole that was left in me when I was robbed of my wife. Does that make sense to you?"

As he leaned toward this young pastor and clenched his teeth tight, feeling the muscle along his jaw jumping, Jackson thought for a moment that he could see his own reflection in Miguel's reaction.

"Yes," he said softly. And then with an unexpected boldness, he continued. "I understand that this is the way you feel. But feeling a certain way doesn't make it true. And there actually is a healing balm strong enough to heal you, Jackson."

"Please just leave my spirit alone," he snapped, then he inched forward again on the bench. "Move along."

"I can do that," Miguel replied. "And I will. If you'll just do me one favor."

Jackson looked into his eyes and saw what was coming before the words were uttered.

"Just let me pray with you one time."

Jackson sighed, and Miguel quickly bowed his head and placed his hand on Jackson's shoulder. "Lord Jesus, only You can fully know the pain and suffering Jackson has endured since the loss of his wife, and only You can comprehend the amount of grace that is needed to heal his heart." Jackson felt something buckle inside of him. He hadn't thought about Desiree's unwavering and, truth be told, irritating faith in God for a very long time. Suddenly, it came barreling back to his memory with a powerful thud.

"Don't turn your back on God," she'd said to him from her hospital bed, so frail that he could hardly hear the words. "Let Jesus heal you, Jackson. Don't harden your heart. He'll bring you out of this toward someone new to love."

Jackson shook the memory from his head. The soft *beep-beep-beep* of the monitors behind her bed lingered now, years later, and he rubbed his temple in an attempt to silence the horrible sound.

"I ask You now for a supernatural healing of Jackson's heart and spirit, Lord Jesus. Point the way to a road of hope, and bring joy back into —"

"Enough," Jackson muttered, bringing Miguel's prayer to an immediate halt. "I'm sorry, Miguel," he said, pushing to his feet. "But . . . enough."

Jackson felt dazed as he plodded toward the French doors. That one step back into the house felt like a wall to climb, and he made his way through the dining room, down the hall, and into the parlor, where he folded into a chair by the window.

"Jackson?"

He heard Emma's voice, but he couldn't even raise his head. Rubbing his temples with both hands, he managed, "Not now, Emma."

"Can I get you anyth—"

"Not now."

He hadn't meant to snap at her that way, but his filters were out of whack at the moment. Remorseful, he looked up with the intention of apologizing, but Emma was nowhere to be seen. Jackson was alone in the parlor; more alone than he'd have thought he knew how to be.

■ ■ ■ ■

Emma found herself remembering a pillow fight she'd had at a slumber party in the 9th grade. One of the feathers from Jenny Jacoby's pillow had floated right into Emma's eye and, no matter how many times she tried to pull it out, she just couldn't manage to get hold of the thing.

That's how sleep was treating her now.

She'd flopped over onto one side, and then to the other, and again to her back. She'd tried propping her head with an extra pillow, and she'd even pushed all the pillows away and had lain out flat. Deep breathing. Counting puppies. Eyes closed, eyes open, fists balled, fists relaxed, arm at her side, arm over her head.

Nothing!

She finally gave up on sleep and surrendered to wide awake, padding through the dark into the living room and sinking into the easy chair. Just about the time that she decided a cup of chamomile tea might do the trick, Emma was distracted by the sudden memory of Jackson's behavior earlier in the evening.

When he and Miguel had finished their talk, Jackson had stumbled into the house like a man under the influence. He was disheveled and pale and hadn't looked a single person in the eye as he wandered past them into the living room, his expression pained and heartbreaking.

A blush of heat sparked on her neck as she remembered the way she'd stomped outside and demanded that Miguel tell her what he'd said to Jackson.

"He'll be fine," Miguel had stated with assurance, but he'd been wearing a similar pained expression. "He just needs some time to process."

"Process what?" she'd asked. "Is there anything I can do for him?"

"Not tonight."

Emma raked her fingers through her hair and pulled it back into a ponytail, securing it with the cloth band on the table beside her. She closed her eyes and rubbed her face as she recalled the steady burn she'd seen in Jackson's eyes, then she folded her arm on the chair and dropped her head on it, staring out the window.

For a moment, she tried to imagine what it must be like to love someone so completely, and then have them stolen from your life. Emma's heart ached a little, and a thin glaze of tears rose in her eyes and just stood there, distorting the street lamp blazing from outside the window.

Emma hadn't done much praying in recent years, or given much acknowledgement to God at all, for that matter. But just then, under the cover of darkness in her apartment, she suddenly felt a desire to pray.

She blinked, and the tears cascaded down her face in streams. She wiped her eyes with the sleeve of her knit pajama top, and then sniffed back another wave.

Help him, Jesus.

It was all she could manage, but it was heartfelt.

"Please help him, Jesus," she said aloud. "He's so lost."

She recalled how raspy his voice had been when he'd snapped at her. "Not now, Emma." She'd backed out of the living room as if she'd been confronted by a lion. And then the anger had risen up in her, an unjustified, inexplicable anger that she'd meant to take out on Miguel for upsetting him. Until she'd seen that Miguel was hurting as much as Jackson had been.

The anger was gone now, the pocket where it had been earlier now filled and overflowing with heartache instead.

"He's hurting so badly," she said, her eyes clamped shut and her face buried in her hands. "He needs to be comforted and encouraged. Please don't let him hurt like this. I can't bear to see that kind of pain in him. He doesn't deserve it. He's a good man, Lord."

Emma stopped herself, opened her eyes and sat there frozen.

She hadn't acknowledged His *Lordship* in her life for a very long time. Or had she ever? But in that moment, as she cried out to God on Jackson's behalf, she'd instinctively called Him "Lord." And it stunned her.

"I'm so sorry," she muttered. "Forgive me."

In the hour that followed those few simple words, Emma had cried so hard that her ribs ached. She wasn't clear whether she was crying for Jackson or for herself, or maybe for the both of them, but when she blew her nose and plodded off to bed, she was completely spent. Once she climbed under the covers and rested her head on the pillow, sleep overtook her.

Jackson had taken to enjoying his midmorning coffee at one particular table. He liked it there in the empty restaurant, the sun streaming through the window and filtered by the chiffon curtain, just the distant hum of conversation or laughter between Emma and Fee in their nearby kitchen.

This particular morning, he'd brought along the full pot from his office and settled at his favorite table while they were whipping up some cake samples in Emma's kitchen. He remembered hearing about two afternoon meetings with potential wedding bookings. The aroma of apples and cinnamon floated its way up his nostrils, and he hoped a sample of the finished product would find its way to his office as often happened. He'd gained at least five pounds since Emma Rae Travis had come into his life, but his taste buds blocked all paths toward caring.

He didn't hear the lobby door open, but the click of heels that followed alerted him to an arrival. Disappointment pinched at him. He'd hoped to have a little more peace and quiet; just a few more minutes, anyway.

Just as Jackson downed the last of his coffee, he was startled to find an older woman standing regally in the doorway, decked out in a mint green evening gown, long white gloves, *and a tiara.*

"May I help you?"

"What is your name?" the woman asked him, planted in her spot.

Jackson got up from his chair and replied,

"Jackson Drake. I own The Tanglewood. Can I help you find someone?"

She didn't reply. The woman simply tilted her head slightly, allowing an overhead sunbeam to ignite her gray hair until it looked like a shiny silver helmet beneath a dazzling crown of fire.

"Are you here to book a wedding?"

The woman chuckled at that, and her eyes sparkled. "My, no. Unless you're asking."

It was Jackson's turn to laugh.

"Are you meeting someone?"

"Yes. I'm meeting someone," she said as she looked around her. "But I think I'm early. Can I wait with you?"

"Of course," he replied, and he walked toward her and offered his arm. "I'm having coffee. Would you like some?"

"Oh, I love coffee," she told him as they ambled into the restaurant.

Jackson held her chair for her, then grabbed a clean cup from behind the bar and set it down before her.

"Do you need cream and sugar?" he asked as he filled her cup.

"I like it black."

"So do I," he said with a grin.

"You own this hotel," she said, as if just catching up to the information. "And your name is . . . What's your name again?"

"Jackson Drake."

"That's a very nice name. Like a hero in a romance novel."

Jackson chuckled. "I'm nothing like that at all," he assured her.

"Well, you're handsome enough," she declared, and when she smiled back at him, her wrinkles formed perfect arches around both sides of her face.

He estimated she was in her eighties, at least, and he wondered why she was dressed in full grand ballroom garb at ten-thirty on a Friday morning.

"I interrupted you, didn't I?" she asked.

"No. Not at all."

"You were deep in thought when I first saw you. Looking like a man who's lost something and you can't remember where."

Jackson felt a squeeze around his heart. "I know where," he told her. "I just don't stand a chance of getting it back." And he instantly wondered why on earth he'd shared such a thing with a total stranger.

"I know that feeling," she remarked. "I have that feeling much of the time."

Jackson smiled at her.

"You know what someone told me recently, though?"

"What's that?"

"When a door closes, God will always

open a window."

He nodded. "That's very positive thinking. Nothing wrong with that."

"I think I read this in the Scriptures," she revealed, scrunching up her face and flexing her index finger, as if trying to remember was almost painful. "Do not remember the former things . . . Behold, I will do a new thing. . . . I will even make a road in the wilderness and rivers in the desert."

Jackson shifted in his chair, but smiled politely.

"So when we can't find the thing that we lost, there's hope that God will bring something new to replace it," she explained. "I think I believe that. Do you, Jackson?"

The familiarity with which she'd called him by name and the sparkle in her once-vibrant blue eyes captured him for a moment. He tilted his shoulder upward in a shrug. "I'm not sure."

"Oh, but you must believe it, boy. If God went to the trouble of getting it into the Bible, then there must be some real meat to it, you know?"

Jackson narrowed his eyes and regarded her for one long moment. "Who was it that you were meeting, ma'am?"

She seemed rather lost, and she didn't reply. Instead, she looked around the room, focusing on things in spurts. First the window, then the table, then the painting on the far wall. When she looked back at Jackson, her expression was sad and somewhat forlorn.

"I'm sorry," she asked with a timid lilt. "Do I know you?"

He reached across the table and took her trembling hand. "Jackson Drake."

"That's a nice name," she told him again. "Did you want to dance?"

He patted her hand tenderly, realizing that there was much more going on with this woman than eccentricity. "Do you know where you live?" he asked her.

She thought about it for a moment and was just about to answer when Emma appeared in the doorway.

"Aunt Sophie?"

Sophie reeled in her chair and ignited with a joyous smile. "Emma Rae! You've come to see me! I knew you would, darlin'!"

"Aunt Soph, what are you doing here?" Emma asked, and her eyes met Jackson's for a frozen moment before she made her way to the table and sat down beside the woman. "I've missed you so much."

Sophie sank into Emma's embrace, her tiara poking Emma's jaw and neck.

"Did Mother drive you here, Aunt

Sophie?" she asked. Then, looking to Jackson, "Is my mother here?"

Jackson shook his head and then shrugged. "Your aunt just walked in the front door."

"Alone?" she mouthed, and he nodded.

Sophie reached across the table and patted Jackson's face with her satin-gloved hand. "This darling man has been keeping me company while I waited for you. I knew you'd come, Emma Rae."

"Of course I did," Emma said in a soothing voice, and Jackson looked on as she kissed her aunt's cheek several times and rubbed her shoulder. "You know I always want to see you."

Five Ways to Give Special Consideration to Your Elderly Guests When Planning Your Wedding

1. When choosing the venue, be sure to take mobility into consideration. For instance:

   - Are the restrooms and main rooms accessible for people with wheelchairs, canes, or walkers?
   - If you're planning an outdoor wedding, you may want to choose a level surface rather than the top of a hill, and consider assigning escorts to your elderly guests to assist them.

2. Plan reception seating for elderly guests away from the loudspeakers and closer to the restroom facilities.
3. Consider reserving the closest parking places for your elderly guests.
4. Ask the DJ to include some classics in the reception music choices, such as Frank Sinatra, Etta James, and Duke Ellington.
5. Consider how to pay tribute to your older guests. For instance:

   - If your grandparents are in attendance, include them in one of the spotlight dances.

- Perhaps ask them for their favorite or special song, and plan a bride-and-groom dance to that selection.
- Include the success of their marriages in one of the champagne toasts at the reception.

13

Emma pushed the tray to the center of the table and leaned in toward it while Fee poured coffee, and Jackson and Sophie looked on.

"The bride says that she and the groom love cake, but neither of them likes frosting," she told them. "The groom even spent his life having birthday *fruit pies* and birthday *parfaits* to celebrate instead of cake because of his aversion to sweet icing. So here's what I've come up with for them to sample."

Large slices of three unique cakes were placed on bone china plates, with several ornate forks in a pile next to them. Sophie's tiara now leaned against the edge of the tray.

"This one is an apple cake layered with vanilla custard and streusel filling," she told them. "It's topped with a brown sugar and cinnamon crumble."

Jackson was first to grab a fork. Turning it

on its side, he sliced off a bite and handed the fork to Sophie.

"Oooooh, darlin'!" she exclaimed when she tasted it. "This is the best one."

Emma chuckled. "You haven't tasted the others yet, Aunt Sophie."

"Oh, I see."

Jackson nodded emphatically after taking a bite for himself. "She's right. This one's the best," he stated with a grin.

"I think so too," Sophie stated, nodding.

"The second one," Emma declared, "is an orange-pistachio cake with a champagne-and-chocolate ribbon running through it. It will be stacked in fluted layers, and lightly sprinkled with powdered sugar."

"Ohhh!" Jackson groaned. "Emma, this is *fan-TAS-tic.*"

"Oooooh, this one's the best," Sophie decided.

"She's right. This one. Best."

"Well, wait a minute!" Emma cackled. "There's one more."

"I'm not sure my heart can take it," Jackson teased. "These are phenomenal." He took a sip of coffee. "I'm just cleansing the palate."

"Good idea," said Sophie, and she followed suit, but she swished the coffee around in her mouth before swallowing.

Fee gave Emma a quick poke in the ribs with her elbow. "This next one's actually the best," she told them.

"The third cake is a very simple yellow cake with thin layers, filled with alternating types of fruit cream. They're very subtle."

"There's banana cream," Fee said, looking like a scientist as she used the handle of a fork like a pointer, "and raspberry cream, and then blueberry."

"It's drizzled with a champagne-amaretto glaze," Emma said.

Jackson held his fork in his mouth for several seconds after inserting it, then closed his eyes and began to make an odd purring sound from deep within his throat.

"He likes it," Fee told her, and Emma watched him carefully.

"Looks like."

"I prefer the other one," Sophie announced. "I don't like amaretto."

"No?" Emma asked. She sat down beside her aunt and squeezed her hand. "I never knew that."

"Mama used to sneak it when she thought nobody was looking. The alcohol, not the cake."

Emma giggled. "This is different, Aunt Sophie. This is the flavor of amaretto without the alcohol."

"Oh." Sophie paused to consider the point, and then shook her head. "No. I like the pistachio best of all. I'd like that for my birthday cake."

"You got it."

Jackson finally pulled the fork from his mouth, but he did it slowly, between pressed lips. When he opened his eyes, he shook his head and groaned again. "Mmm-mmmmmm. That one's my favorite."

"Are you given to drinking, Jackson?" Sophie asked him seriously.

"Not at all, Sophie. But I really like this cake."

"I like the pistachio."

"That one's good too."

He dug his fork into the champagne-amaretto cake for another chunk. "I don't know how you make these things without eating them," he told Emma. "I'd be in a coma several times a year if I were you. I have no willpower when it comes to sweets."

"I taste them," she admitted. "But never more than a bite or two."

"And only after a full meal," Fee added. "She tolerates sugar better when it's combined with protein."

"My nurse," Emma said with a grin, nodding toward Fee.

"You're a nurse, Fee?" Sophie asked,

wide-eyed. "Do you scare your patients when you dress like that?"

Jackson and Emma both snickered as Fee responded by forming her lips into a wordless round O. Before she could answer, their conversation was halted in its tracks as Avery rushed through the doorway toward them.

"Sophie!" she cried. "What were you thinking?"

"Have you met my sister?" she asked Jackson.

"I have. Hello, Mrs. Travis. Why don't you join us for coffee? Everything is just fine here."

Avery's expression melted down a few notches as Jackson held her eyes.

"Yes," she said at last, then she sat down in the empty chair at the foot of the table, Sophie to her right and Jackson to her left. "Coffee would be lovely."

Fee produced another cup and filled it while Avery sat there watching her sister sip her own coffee.

"Sophie," Jackson piped up. "Have you seen our courtyard?"

"Do you have one?"

"We do. Would you like to go for a stroll with me and see it?"

"That would be nice. Will you all excuse

us? My friend Jackson would like me to walk with him."

Emma marveled at Jackson's gentle way with her aunt, and she watched them amble arm-in-arm until they reached the lobby, turning left through the glass doors to the courtyard.

"How on earth!" Avery exclaimed the moment they were out of earshot.

"I'll go start the clean-up in the kitchen," Fee said before leaving them.

Emma nodded, then she turned her attention to Avery. "I don't know. She just showed up here this morning. I found her having coffee with Jackson."

"And that ridiculous outfit she's wearing! Where did she find that?"

"No clue."

"So much for keeping her safe in an assisted-living facility," Avery said on a sigh.

"I'm sure they have these challenges all the time, Mother. We'll just go and speak with the administration staff, tell them they'll have to keep a closer watch on her, that's all."

Avery lowered her head into her hands, and Emma got up, scraped the chair Jackson had occupied toward her, and sat down on it. She placed her arms gently around her mother's shoulders and pulled her into an embrace.

"I just love the crazy old bird so much," Avery said, and Emma gawked in surprise for an instant. Then they both began to laugh at the uncharacteristic comment out of Emma's very proper mother. "Well, she's such a handful."

"But as lovable as they come," Emma reminded her.

"Yes. Yes, she is."

"So I come out of the kitchen to find Aunt Sophie sitting there at a table with my boss, and she's dressed in a ball gown and a tiara!"

Gavin chortled at Emma's description, drawing the attention of all the other diners at Morton's Steakhouse. "I'll bet your mother delivered a full-sized cow when she saw that."

"She's got her work cut out for her," Emma reminded him. "Taking care of Aunt Sophie isn't going to be easy."

"It wasn't easy when she had all her faculties. This is going to be downright impossible." The waiter stepped up to the table, and Gavin diverted his attention momentarily. "I'd like a Grey Goose martini, dirty with bleu cheese olives. What about you, Princess?"

"I'd like a sparkling water with a lime twist," she told the waiter. "And his dirty martini? Can you turn that into the same?"

Gavin clucked an objection that didn't take shape before the waiter nodded. "Two sparkling waters with a twist."

"You take all the fun out of a place like this, Emmy."

"Good. The less fun you have now, the longer you'll be around."

"A longer time to have no fun at all."

"Just the way God intended."

"Bah!" he grumbled. "Well, I'm having a steak for my supper. Not a darn thing you can do about it. Hear me?"

"I can live with that," she said, glancing over the menu. "What do you say to some steamed asparagus, and some spinach and button mushrooms?"

"I say bring it on, as long as it's on the plate next to a pound of steak and a potato swimming in butter."

"You're impossible."

Gavin hesitated before he smiled. "And you are beautiful, Princess. It's good to see you."

"You too, Dad."

"I like this new clan you've stumbled into too."

"The Drakes." She nodded. "They're

pretty great."

"You and this Jackson Drake. Anything going on there that you want to tell your old man about?"

"He's my boss."

"And?"

"And *he's my boss,*" she said, narrowing her eyes and shaking her head.

"You like him."

"I do. He's a very nice man, and he's given me a fantastic opportunity."

"That's it?"

"That's it."

"Then when are you going to find a *very nice man* of your own, huh?"

"I don't know. Why don't you give me some tips?" she suggested as the waiter delivered their drinks. "Are there any very nice *women* on your horizon, Dad? Isn't it time you found one of those for yourself?"

Gavin glared at her for a moment, and then broke into a grin. "Fair enough."

"Now why don't you hand over those cigars you have hidden in your pocket so we can get that out of the way and enjoy our dinner." He didn't move a muscle to comply. "Come on, Dad. You know how stubborn I can be. Do you want to spend all our time tonight battling?"

Without a word, he produced three fat

cigars from his pocket and placed them on the table between them.

"Thank you. Now tell me about your retirement plans," she said as she wrapped the cigars in a linen napkin.

"What are you doing? Don't do that."

"Waiter?" she said as a uniformed server passed the table. "Would you dispose of this and bring me a new napkin, please?"

"Certainly."

"Ahhhh," Gavin groaned, and he could hardly yank his eyes away from the disappearance of his cigars. "That was uncalled for."

"So you . . . retiring. Explain this to me in a language I can understand."

He moaned softly, glanced longingly in the direction of the waiter's exit, and then sighed. "How did I raise such a cruel young woman?" he asked, punctuated by another grumbly sigh. In another instant, he brightened. "Oh, that's right. That would be your mother's influence."

"Dad," she chastised. "Don't do that."

"I have to. We're divorced. It's what we do."

"Speaking of you and Mother . . ."

"Must we?"

"Aside from a couple of random digs, you two didn't make any horrible scenes to embarrass me or yourselves the other night. What's up with that?"

Gavin grimaced. "What'd we do, let you down?"

"Not at all," she enunciated. "It was just so unusual. What's going on with the two of you?"

"We've had a lot of space between us," he remarked. "If we'd only limited seeing one another to every few years while we were married, we'd still have wedded bliss."

Emma groaned.

"Don't analyze us, Emmy. It will only make you crazy."

They matched one another with crooked, quirky little smiles, then in stereo: "Too late."

Two steak dinners later, they'd covered every subject under the sun that related to Emma; however, Gavin wasn't doing much talking about his own life.

Eerily evasive, she thought as she watched him hand the waiter the leather folder with his credit card poking out of it.

"So. Dad."

"Nothing good ever came from a beginning like that," he quipped.

"When we talked on the phone, you said you'd sold Travis Development. What led you to do that?"

"Old age."
"Dad, you're hardly a senior citizen."
"I'm sorry to have to break this to you," he retorted, "but I turn seventy next month. That's senior."
"Seventy? Really?" Emotion clouded Emma's thoughts. She didn't think of her father in numeric terms. The realization was rather staggering.
"I should have sold TD a long time ago, Princess. The right buyer came along at just the right time, and I decided not to wait any longer."
Emma stroked his hand. "Now what? Will you stay in D.C.?"
"For a while."
"Any chance of getting you to come back to Atlanta?"
Gavin narrowed his eyes and arched his brow. "I never say never."
"Really?" The excitement bubbled up inside her, and then reality dawned. "In the same city with Mother?"
In his best Old West cowboy voice, he said, "Hombre, this town ain't big enough for the both of us."
"Dad."
"You really don't think we can coexist in the same city, Emmy?"
"Well . . ." She shrugged.

"How about the same county?"
"Mm, I don't know."
"State?"
"Maybe."
Gavin chuckled and drained his coffee cup. "If there's no dessert or cigars in my immediate future —"
"Which there isn't," Emma cut in.
"— then what do you say we *am-scray,* Princess?"
"Sounds good."
It was another mild evening in Atlanta and, after kissing her father good-bye in front of the restaurant, Emma was on her way home with the window cracked about an inch and classic oldies on the radio. She cranked up the volume in an effort to disguise her somewhat tone-deaf rendition of "Ain't No Mountain High Enough," and slipped under a yellow light at the intersection.
Georgia 400 was unusually open, and the ride back to Roswell was brake-light-free. Twenty minutes later, she pulled into the space behind her apartment building with #6 painted on it in neon orange. She turned off the engine, propped open the door, and then just sat there with her head back, listening to the melodic semi-silence of the evening.

The soft hum of distant traffic was overlaid with the harmony of Mr. and Mrs. Eggleston's late-day conversation wafting through the back door they almost always left propped open. A slight metallic tap-tap-tap from somewhere far away added the conjunct movement of the song, and the rhythm of the breeze through crisp autumn tree branches created perfect triad chords. Her little Roswell neighborhood composed the soundtrack of her life on nights like this one, and Emma was prone to being mesmerized by the music.

"Emma."

The timbre of Jackson's voice fit so melodically into the song that she almost missed it.

"Emma Rae."

She snapped her neck to the side and came centimeters away from letting out a scream when she found herself face-to-face with Jackson, folded down toward her, his arm draped over the side of the open door.

"I didn't mean to startle you," he assured her.

"What are you doing here?" she asked, her heart pounding against her hand.

"We have a little problem."

When he stepped away from the car, Emma looked past him and saw her aunt

Sophie, dressed in a terrycloth bathrobe and mismatched slippers, propped on the top step near her neighbor's back door, bathed in the yellow glow of the porch light and waving at her.

"Good morning, Emma Rae," she called out. "How would you like your eggs?"

Unique Wedding Themes for the Discriminating Bride

1. A sunrise wedding, with an elegant brunch reception.
2. A "white diamond" wedding theme, with everything in white and crystal.
3. A murder mystery weekend with a *surprise wedding* thrown in for the guests.
4. A secret location for the wedding, with a "treasure hunt" that morning that leads the guests to the venue by various clues.
5. A vintage wedding, held in an English garden with high tea, parasols, and lace gloves.
6. A "Roaring 20s" wedding that includes feather boas, flapper dresses, and long pearl necklaces.
7. A theme park wedding location where, instead of a reception, guests ride roller coasters and play arcade games afterward.
8. An eco-friendly wedding where, instead of gifts, the guests donate to the couple's favorite environmental charity, the flowers are wild, and the candles are made of soy.
9. An Asian theme, with edible orchids topping the cake, traditional dishes and chopsticks for the reception, and Oriental fans as centerpieces.
10. Bring the outdoors in with an *"au*

naturel"-themed wedding, decorating with stones, vines, twigs, and pinecones. Use rustic containers and pillar candles for unique ambiance, or baskets of fresh herbs as a centerpiece.

14

"I think you two should consider doing something different. Not the traditional sort of fare. Something truly unique."

"Aunt Sophie," Emma said as she unfolded the quilt and tucked it under Sophie's chin, "what are you talking about?"

"Your wedding!" the woman exclaimed, and the quilt slipped right out of Emma's hands.

"My . . . what?"

Sophie inched down and tilted her head into the fluffed pillow beneath it, closing her eyes as she smiled. "You make such a lovely couple."

Emma shifted on the edge of the bed and looked back at Jackson where he stood in the doorway of her guest room. His expression was blank as he returned the stare for a moment, then he turned around. She heard the padded thump of his shoes on the hall rug as he walked away.

"Aunt Sophie," she whispered. "Jackson and I are not a couple. He's my boss."

Emma flicked off the lamp next to the bed, and a stream of warm light illuminated Sophie's cheek from the hallway.

"Don't be silly," Sophie replied. "You have nothing to be afraid of, Emma Rae. You'll be just the wife Jackson needs. You'll see."

Emma's pulse fluttered within her, and her wide eyes ached.

"Sleep well," she said, then she placed a gentle kiss on Sophie's cheek.

Just as she reached the doorway, her aunt whispered to her. "Do you know what I was thinking, Emma?"

"What's that?" she replied from the doorway.

"Wouldn't it be funny if I caught the bouquet?"

Emma sighed. "That would be funny."

"Does Jackson have an uncle who can sing?"

"I . . . don't know." Her cheek twitched as she tried to connect the dots.

"If he does, and I catch the bridal bouquet, make sure to tell Jackson to aim the garter at him. I'd like a man who can sing. Nobody in our family can carry a tune even if it's in a paper sack with a handle."

That was the truth, but Emma didn't say

it out loud. "Good night, Aunt Sophie."

"Good night, dear."

Emma flicked off the hall light as she passed through. The living room was dark, the only light at all coming in through the window from outside and from the dim overhead in the kitchen.

Jackson's silhouette reminded Emma of her father the way he fit perfectly into the Ercol Bergere easy chair.

"Coffee?" she softly asked him.

"No. Thanks."

She was almost on her tiptoes as she moved to the sofa and sat down on the edge.

"I called your mother," he told her. "She's going to call the facility and let them know that Sophie is safe for the night."

"How —"

"I found her number in your cell phone. I hope you don't mind."

"Mind?" She chuckled and slid back into the couch, kicked off her shoes, and folded into the padded arm. "You've been so amazing, Jackson. I can never repay you for your kindness to my aunt."

"She makes it very easy to be kind. She's a wonderful woman."

"Underneath all the crazy."

"No. Right on top of it," he corrected.

Emma dipped her chin down atop her

folded arm and smiled at him. "She thinks we're engaged, you know."

"That's very generous of her."

She tilted her head. "What do you mean?"

"When she first showed up at the hotel tonight, she thanked me for asking her to marry me. Now it looks like she's handing me over to you."

Emma chuckled. "I guess she thinks we're a better match, then."

"Astute."

Her eyes darted up again, and she watched Jackson carefully, although his gaze didn't return to hers.

"You're sure you don't want any coffee?"

He nodded. "Do you mind if I make myself some tea?"

"Sure. Go ahead."

Emma rose from the couch and padded off toward the kitchen in bare feet, and she filled the stainless-steel kettle with water. When she turned back again to ignite the stove, she thumped into Jackson.

"Oh! Sorry. I didn't know you were —"

He didn't let her finish. He just wrapped his arms around her waist and pulled her into him, angling his face and pressing his lips against hers. She was so surprised that she drew in a long, deep breath through her nose and then just held it there as the warmth of his kiss began to settle on her. Aware of a ticklish tingle to her lips, she pursed them a little more, pressing in.

Suddenly the kettle that had been in her hand clanged to the floor. She jumped slightly at the noise, but neither of them was deterred. After a moment, Emma's knees felt weak, and she slipped her arms around Jackson's neck and leaned into him. Wiggling her toes against the bamboo flooring, she realized she could feel a crazy vibration all the way from her lips to her frosted pink toenails. She pushed away the notion of hopping up into his arms to continue the evolution of this very appealing development, instead allowing him to pull away gently. It was a natural ending, but one she wasn't ready to face.

When their lips had parted, Emma fell back against the green granite counter and held on to it with both hands. Her heart pounding, her breathing shallow, her head beginning to spin the way it did sometimes when her blood sugar dropped.

"I probably shouldn't have —"

She silenced him mid-word with the wave of her hand. With her eyes closed, she shook her head from side to side. "Can you please not ruin this moment by saying what a mistake you just made? Can we please just enjoy it?"

When she opened her eyes again, Jackson was grinning.

"I was just going to say that I probably shouldn't have surprised you," he said, then he nodded toward the stream of water on the floor from the overturned kettle.

"Oh." She stared at it, feeling as if she'd been glued to the spot by its contents. "Right."

Jackson reached past her and produced a towel and leaned down to mop up some of the water while Emma grabbed the kettle and set it on the counter behind her. She kept her back to Jackson and clung to the edge of the counter with her eyes clamped shut.

Don't do it, she warned herself internally. *Do NOT do it.*

But everything inside of her pushed and nudged and poked at her. All she wanted was to spin around, dive back into his arms, and kick that kiss up a notch from where they'd left off.

Emma flew into the kitchen, leaving the door flapping behind her and squealing to a halt.

Fee glanced up from kneading the batch

of ivory fondant. "Hey, girl. Where've you been?"

"I had to take my aunt back to Sandy Springs," she replied, contorting her lips into what her mother used to call a "dried apricot imitation."

"Again? What's up with —"

"Fiona. Stop talking," she snapped. "It's my turn right now."

Fee looked up again, this time meeting her urgency in the gap between them. "What's wrong?"

Emma shifted from one foot to the other, then bit the corner of her lip.

"Em. What is it? Something happened?"

"Yes."

"Something bad?"

"Yes." Then she reconsidered. "No."

"Which is it?"

"I'm not sure."

Fee rinsed her hands, and was drying them as she stalked right up to Emma and stared her down. "Spill."

Just as Emma started to speak, the kitchen door whooshed open and Norma walked in. Emma made a sort of whoosh of her own as she drew in a breath and snapped her mouth shut.

"Emma, do you have time to meet with someone?"

"I . . . uh . . . yes, of course. Who is it?"

"A potential wedding customer and her mother. The bride has a very specific theme in mind, and I think it might help her to have your input on designing her cake. We're in the salon."

The salon.

It used to be a simple storage room, converted into a consultation room. Now it was *The Salon.*

"Give me five minutes?"

"Thank you."

Norma left the kitchen, and Emma waited a solid ten seconds before she even flinched. Then she turned toward Fee, invading every inch of her personal space.

"Aunt Sophie came to the hotel last night," she said softly, but at warp speed. "Jackson brought her to my place. I put her to bed in the guest room, I went into the kitchen to make some tea, I turned around and he was *rightupinmyfacethisclose,* and then he kissed me, Fee. It was fantastic, I couldn't sleep thinking about it, and now I'm afraid to run into him for fear that I'll humiliate myself and plaster him against the wall and lay another one on him. I'm going to go do a consult now, thanks for listening."

Fee didn't have time to speak a single

word before Emma spun around and exited the kitchen, leaving her friend in the dust of her confession. As she turned the corner and set her hand on the knob of the door, she heard Fee hoot with laughter from behind her in the kitchen.

"Emma Rae Travis," Norma said as she entered the room. "Meet Vivian Rochester, and her daughter Rachelle Rochester. Rachelle is going to be a spring bride."

"Congratulations," Emma said, her smile quivering slightly.

They all sat down, gathered around the desk where half a dozen magazine clippings were scattered. Rachelle pointed to them and tapped the desk with a nervous little rhythm.

"It's going to be a small ceremony," she offered. "Fifty people or less. And we'd like to have it at sunrise on the roof of the hotel, and then bring them all down to the courtyard for a reception."

"Sunrise in the spring," Emma considered.

"Early May."

"So around . . . what is that? . . . seven o'clock in the morning?"

"Something like that," Norma confirmed. "They'd like a simple brunch afterward, perhaps some quiche, fresh fruit, maybe an omelet station."

"We'd like a wedding cake," Rachelle interjected, "but nothing traditional; something a little more lighthearted, and of course appropriate for such an early time."

"Emma is one of the region's premiere cake designers," Norma told them. "She won the Passionate Palate Award just this year for her amazing crème brûlée wedding cake."

"We read about that in *The Journal*," Vivian told them.

"I just knew you'd come up with something unique," Rachelle said with obvious hope brimming in her expressive dark eyes.

"What do you think about not having a cake?" Emma suggested.

"No cake?" Rachelle's disappointment spilled over.

"What I mean is instead of a cake, we could customize some cupcakes and set them up on a stand to make it take the shape of a wedding cake."

Rachelle gasped, and she turned to her mother with a smile that cracked with happy inspiration. "A cupcake wedding cake! I've seen pictures of those."

"We could choose several different spring flowers perhaps, and design and place them so that they resemble your bridal bouquet."

Emma glanced from the bride to her mother and back again. "Or we could —"

"I love that idea!" Rachelle cried. "Mother, I love that idea." Before Vivian could respond, Rachelle snatched one of the clippings from the desk and thrust it toward Emma. "This is what my bouquet will look like. They're lilacs and hyacinth. Do you think you could do something with these?"

"My assistant makes a beautiful hyacinth out of sugar," Emma told her. "We can match the colors, and we'll work on creating something for the lilacs."

Fee poked her head into the room at just that moment and, as soon as she caught Emma's eye, she stated, "Sorry to interrupt. You have an important call."

"You go ahead, Emma," Norma said. "We'll finish up here, and then Emma will call you, probably in February, to talk about the cake in more detail."

"Thank you so much," Rachelle said, shaking Emma's hand until her arm hurt.

"It's going to be beautiful," Emma reassured her. "And having a sunrise wedding is very unique and symbolic of a new beginning. I love the idea."

"Thank you again."

Emma hurried around the corner, with

expectations of hearing that Sophie had stowed away on a cruise ship or grabbed a flight to Bora Bora. She crossed the kitchen and skirted around her desk. But when she went to pick up the phone, she noticed that none of the lights were illuminated.

"They hung up," she told Fee, who was standing in the doorway.

"There was no one on the phone."

"What do you mean?"

"I lied."

"Why?"

"He kissed you? Sit down because I want every detail."

Susannah set a fresh cup of coffee down on the desk before quietly slipping back out again, leaving Jackson to continue his very important work.

At least he thought it probably looked quite important. But that spreadsheet had been up on his laptop screen for hours and, with his back to the door and his face toward the credenza, he probably appeared to be completely engrossed in the figures entered there. But the truth was . . . Jackson couldn't have cared less about that spreadsheet!

He turned around and picked up the coffee and took a sip. Susannah never failed him. Every morning for the last however many years, she'd brought him two or three cups of perfectly blended black coffee. She was a genius about coffee. Not to mention the other thirteen thousand things she did for him every day. He couldn't help wondering if such a genius also knew that he'd been sitting in his office for the last hour or more with his thoughts as far away from business as they could possibly be.

Those lips of Emma's haunted him. All the way through the night, into the morning, and up to that very moment, he'd thought of little else. Not just her lips either, if he admitted the whole truth. The way she'd dropped that water kettle to the floor, dove toward him and tossed her arms around his neck like a tightening noose of velvet! The feelings those actions resurrected in him had become almost foreign to him now, after the years without Desi in his arms. But there he'd been, his arms wrapped around Emma, their lips locked, their hearts pounding.

Jackson leaned back in his chair and closed his eyes. He could almost taste the heat of it again; he nearly felt her pulse hammering against him. It had been such a long, *long* time since those paralyzed reactions had been awakened. If it hadn't been such an amazing feeling, he might actually sense a little guilt over it. He couldn't help wondering what Desiree would think of him kissing another woman.

Not just another woman, he corrected himself. *Emma.*

What was it about her?

Jackson swiveled his chair around to face his desk. He could hear Susannah's fingers tapping on the keyboard on the other side of the doorway as he drank his coffee and sat there in silence. He wished he could talk to her about what he was feeling. Or talk to somebody, anyway.

His nephew Miguel tripped across his thoughts just then, and he was suddenly right back there on Norma's veranda, the night that Emma's parents came to town.

". . . only You can fully know the pain and suffering he's endured since the loss of his wife, and only You can comprehend the amount of grace that is needed to heal his heart."

Jackson recalled the heartfelt prayers of the young Latino man of God who had married his niece. He also remembered how those prayers had brought to mind his late wife's advice.

"Let Jesus heal you, Jackson," Desiree had said. "Don't harden your heart. He'll bring you out of this toward someone new to love."

He let those words pedal around inside of him for a few minutes, then suppressed an inward groan.

Love?

Jackson didn't love Emma. It was just basic animal attraction.

Love. Bah!

He'd already loved the woman he was meant to love. And now she was gone. He wasn't going to replace her. Desi was irreplaceable.

But he had to admit one thing, if only to himself.

Adorable Emma Rae Travis sure can kiss.

The Secret to Emma Rae Travis's Award-Winning Crème Brûlée Wedding Cake

1. Emma's special sour cream cake recipe is used for the layers.
2. Sugar syrup is created out of butter, dark brown sugar, and water.
3. The syrup is spread into the bottom of the cake pans, and the sour cream cake batter is carefully spooned over it before baking.
4. After baking, the pans are set atop wire racks for 15 minutes before the first layer is inverted onto the cake board.
5. Layers are stacked with a special creamy vanilla and caramel filling.
6. Each layer is inverted with the syrup side down.
7. After the cake is constructed, it is frosted with a special icing made of whole egg butter cream and sugar syrup.
8. The cake must be refrigerated overnight before further decorating is attempted.

15

Emma hadn't seen much of Jackson for the first few days of that week. They were in the countdown toward Friday's reception launching The Tanglewood to Atlanta's upper crust as a premiere wedding and event destination hotel. As NASA might say, it was *T-minus one day and counting.*

She took the stairs up to the fourth floor, pausing at each level to breathe deeply and compose herself in preparation for the meeting to come. She wondered how Jackson would react to her now, or if he would have any reaction at all. And more importantly, how would she feel when she saw him again for the first significant space of time following that unbelievable kiss?

She'd spent far too much time drowning in the memory, lingering over the details of his soft lips, his strong arms, and his perfect height. He was just the right height for kissing a five-foot-eight-inch woman. It all fit together just the way it was supposed to.

On the landing of the third floor, Emma giggled at the memory of kissing Danny Mahoney back in high school. They were exactly the same height, and so they came at one another like bookends. Noses pressed against noses, smacking arms as they fumbled for a comfortable embrace. It was like roller derby kissing.

Stop thinking about kisses, she warned herself. *This is a very important business meeting. Get yourself together.*

Several more deep breaths outside the office door . . .

Okay. I'm ready.

One step inside Susannah's office, and the whirlwind of activity nearly blew her right back out into the hallway.

". . . hasn't gotten the final menu to me yet, but I have the first draft from last week."

"We need a final menu. Get him on the phone."

"There are still twenty-seven outstanding invitations with no responses yet."

"Susannah, we'll put you on that. Can you call those people and try to get a head count?"

"Will do."

"What time will the florist arrive?"

"Tomorrow morning at eleven."

"Oh, no. You'd better call them. We need them earlier than that."

Susannah, Madeline, Georgiann, Norma, and Jackson buzzed between the two offices, each of them carrying paperwork — Madeline's on a clipboard — making notes and checking off items from several different lists.

"Oh, good!" Madeline exclaimed when she spotted Emma standing in the doorway like a deer caught in the headlights of a bus full of hunters. "Emma's here."

"I've made your tea already," Susannah told her, shuffling her along into Jackson's office. "We need to get started."

"This isn't started?"

Susannah didn't respond, but her snicker and the pat to Emma's arm answered for her.

"Good morning," Jackson said when she entered, but he didn't look at her so it could have been a general greeting to signal the start of the meeting. "Does everyone have Susannah's agenda?"

Emma looked around, and everyone seemed to be holding a copy of it except her.

"I don't . . . No, I don't seem to —"

"Here. Have mine," Norma said, and she handed over a single sheet of paper jammed with more words than white space.

"Why don't we start with the decorations," Jackson said. "Georgiann?"

"Florist will be changed to ten," she responded with confidence. "The cleaners finished this morning. The linens have arrived. The china has been inventoried. We've added two hundred strands of lights to the courtyard and the ballroom and placed every available tea light in every available crystal holder."

"Staffing?"

"Check!" Georgiann piped up. "Five bartenders, seventeen servers, and nine more to bus and wash dishes. Six valets, four housekeeping, and three desk clerks, including Philip."

Emma glanced at Norma, who whispered, "Manager."

"Silent auction update, George."

"There's going to be an auction?" Emma whispered.

"To benefit the Ovarian Cancer Research Fund," Norma replied. "In memory of Desiree."

"— celebrity donations, and some gallery pieces. Oh, and the Atlanta Falcons have donated a sideline experience package where someone will get to watch a game from the sidelines at the Georgia Dome."

"What?" Emma asked. "I'm sorry, what was that?"

Without hesitation, Jackson moved on. "Music."

Emma wondered if she stood a snowball's chance of scoring that package. She loved the Falcons almost as much as she loved cake.

"He arrives tomorrow morning."

"And his room is ready?"

"A suite on the top floor."

"Whose room?" Emma whispered as she leaned over toward Norma.

"Ben Colson."

Emma blinked hard, and then opened her eyes wide. "Ben Colson?"

All eyes turned toward her, and Norma asked, "You didn't know? Your mother was kind enough to —"

"Wait. My mother knows Ben Colson?"

"She knows his mama," Georgiann cooed. "Isn't that wonderful?"

"Ben Colson is to Atlanta what Harry Connick, Jr. is to New Orleans," Emma exclaimed. "He's performing at the opening of The Tanglewood?"

"That reminds me!" Norma cut in. "When does the stage building begin?"

"Two o'clock," Susannah answered, and Norma pointed to something on Madeline's clipboard, which her sister immediately checked off.

Emma was still pondering the fact that her mother knew the very soulful, pop-jazz singer when she looked up to find that Jackson was staring her down with an expectant fire in his eyes.

"I'm sorry. What?"

"The cake. How is that progressing?"

"Oh!" Emma shook her head. "I'm sorry. It's all baked and filled and frosted, and sitting in the refrigerator. We'll add the finishing touches tomorrow morning."

"This is the same cake that won you the award?" he asked her.

"Crème brûlée," Madeline stated with confidence. "It's a masterpiece, Jackson. Stop worrying."

"I'm not worried," he replied. "Just going down the list."

"Does anyone not have their dress yet?" Georgiann asked.

"I've had mine for weeks," Madeline answered.

"I'm all set," Norma added.

"Me too," said Susannah.

All eyes turned to Emma again, and she giggled. "I'll be wearing what all the finest bakers wear."

Her answer didn't seem to compute.

"Topped off with the sweetest little chef's hat you've ever seen."

She wondered why she was the only one smiling.

"Oh, no, *sugah.* You'll be dining with everyone else tomorrow. You'll wear something elegant, Emma."

Emma's foot began to tap. All on its own. She had no control over it, and she glanced down at her leg as if it wasn't the one she came in with.

"I'm sure you have something lovely in your closet," Madeline said with a smile. "Jackson, did you pick up your tuxedo from the cleaners?"

Tuxedo?

"I'm taking care of that today," Susannah informed them.

The tap in her foot moved all the way up her leg, and Emma used both hands to press down her knee.

"You know," she interrupted. "I'm really honored to be included in the whole affair, but I'm just *the baker.* I mean, I baked the dessert, and I'll serve it —"

"Oh, no!" Georgiann cut her off. "You won't be serving tomorrow night, darlin'. Your mama and daddy will be in attendance, and all of us will be here as guests."

"You're not just an employee," Norma

chimed in. "You're part of the family here, Emma. Tell her, Jackson."

Emma raised her eyes slowly. When they met Jackson's, she flinched.

"You'll be acting as one of the hostesses, Emma. No hiding in the kitchen."

She swallowed, and then nodded. "Thank you."

"And I'd like Fee to attend as well?"

Emma wondered if they all heard the thud that followed.

"Cool. Can I bring a date?"

Emma stared at Fee for several thick and foggy seconds.

"You mean, *you want to come?*"

"Of course."

"Knowing that you have to dress up?"

"Sure. What's the problem?"

Emma started to answer, and then scratched her head instead.

"I like a good party," Fee informed her. "Are you afraid I'll embarrass you?"

"N-no."

"I won't wear full Goth, Em."

"I know."

"It will be fun. I mean, we've been with this almost from the beginning. Don't you want to share in the whole unveiling deal?"

"I . . . yes."

"So what's got your soufflé in a pancake?"

Emma wasn't exactly sure. She'd expected Fee to be appalled and worried right along with her. Not having that was . . . disconcerting.

"I guess I thought you'd be in a panic too."

"What's to panic about?"

"Oh, I don't know. My parents *both attending.* Having to find a *dress.*" Emma dropped to the chair behind her desk and stared straight ahead. "I haven't worn shoes with heels in five years, Fee."

"It's like riding a bike."

"No. It's really not." She fixed her eyes on Fee and asked, "When was the last time you wore shoes without rubber padding on the bottom?"

"I do have a life outside of working with you, you know."

Emma considered that. "You do?"

"I actually go out into the world on a regular basis," she revealed. "I eat at relatively nice restaurants, frequent some museums, even attend a play or two."

"You go to plays?"

"Okay, you're starting to frost my cookies, Em."

"I'm sorry. I just . . ." Emma scratched her head again before she bit her lip and asked, "Do you have a dress I can borrow to wear to this thing?"

"No," Fee told her without pause. "But I know where we can get you something. Come on."

Fee grabbed Emma by the wrist and tugged.

"Wait! Let me get my purse!"

Less than half an hour later, the two of them had closed the distance between The Tanglewood in Roswell and a small vintage store in Alpharetta.

"Hey, girl!"

The sales clerk seemed to know Fee well, and the black eyeliner and ruby red lipstick she was wearing made Emma a little nervous about what kind of dress she was likely to find here.

"This is Emma," Fee announced. "She needs something unique, pronto."

"We're all about unique here. You know that."

"But it has to speak to her style."

The woman with the nametag that read *Arielle* looked Emma up and down as if deciding whether to accept her for consignment.

"What is your style?" she asked at last.

Emma turned to Fee.

"We want something that says *sweet.* Princess-like. Belle of the ball."

"We do?" Emma asked under her breath.

"And we want it to say, 'I'm fabulous, so you better be willing to do the work to find that out.' "

Emma laughed out loud at that.

Arielle began to nod. "Ooookay. I'm getting the vibe. I can see that."

"Oh, and when it comes to the shoes, we want to go easy on the height," Fee added. "She's been off the stilts for a long time."

"Let's find the dress first," she suggested. "We'll worry about the details after that."

Emma just stood there while Arielle and Fee started pulling dresses from the racks. When each of them had several in their arms, they shuffled her off to a dressing room. There was so much fabric on the hangers they flipped over the wall hooks that she could hardly fit in the tiny cubicle along with them.

The first was a copper number with thick ruffled straps and a slit from floor to thigh. Although it was somewhat entertaining to try on, Emma had no intention of wearing it out in public.

The second dress might have been the one, if not for the fact that it was made for a pixie with four inches less length in the leg than Emma had. And of course there was that questionable flower on the shoulder.

Dresses three, four, and five were just too hideous to model beyond the confines of the dressing room, and Emma refused to step out and prove it. She just tossed them over the top of the door.

"Em, come on. Let us see."

"You can see the next one," she promised, pulling a pale lavender dress from the hook. "This one looks pretty."

"Which one is it?" Fee called from the other side, and just the top of her head bobbed up as she stood on her tiptoes.

"Wait. I'll show you in a second."

She used the wall of the dressing room to support her elbow as she contorted to grapple with two long purple ribbons as long as the whole dress. The full-length mirror was partially obstructed by the billowing skirt of one of the three remaining dresses, so she pushed open the door and stepped out.

"I can't figure out," she groaned, tossing one of the ribbons over her shoulder and pulling on the other one, "what to do with these things."

"Here. Turn around."

She did as she was told while Fee and Arielle straightened the thick ribbon.

"It laces. Like this," Arielle said, and when they were finished, she crossed the ribbons and extended them around to the front, tying them into a bow at Emma's waist.

Fee gasped. "Emma. That . . . is . . . wow."

Emma looked at Arielle. "It really is."

One of the few customers in the store stopped what she was doing at a nearby rack and nodded enthusiastically.

"Gorgeous," she mouthed.

Fee took Emma's arm and nudged her toward the mirror. "You look like a ballerina."

Emma shifted her weight to one leg and considered her reflection. A simple, high-necked bodice with three thin spaghetti straps on each shoulder; a low back with criss-crossed ribbon laced from top to bottom; and a full skirt overlaid with shimmering beaded tulle.

"But it's autumn," she told them. "I can't wear this."

Arielle didn't say a word. She just scurried across the store and reappeared a few seconds later with a deep purple velvet cropped jacket with a loose rhinestone chain at the closure.

"Try this."

The smooth silk lining glided over her arms, and the minute Emma caught sight of her reflection she knew this was what she would be wearing to the reception.

"It's amazing," Fee told her.

"Perfect," Arielle added.

"If you're not going to buy that, I want it," the customer chimed in.

"Sorry," Fee said softly. "But she's buying it."

Emma grinned at her friend through the mirror's reflection and nodded. Fee immediately stepped up behind her and wrapped her arms around Emma's shoulders.

"And there will be no smooth, straight ponytail either," she told Emma's reflection. "And no horn-rimmed glasses on a chain, or clear strawberry lip balm. There will be curls and makeup and jewelry and pouty little lips."

"It's tea-length," she replied. "Everyone else will be wearing full-length, don't you think?"

"Em. You'll knock his socks off."

Emma started to object, set Fee straight, tell her that Jackson Drake had no bearing on her anticipation of the party they would be attending. But the look in Fee's eye and the lopsided grin she was wearing silenced Emma. It wasn't even worth the effort to deny it.

I can't wait for Jackson to see me in this dress!

Welcome to the Gala Opening
of
The Tanglewood Inn

<u>Your Menu</u>
Award-Winning Chef
Anton Morelli
Celebrates Southern Cuisine

Starters

Proscuitto-wrapped Figs with
gorgonzola and balsamic
Fried Green Tomatoes with buttermilk
bleu cheese
Heirloom Tomato Salad with hearts of
palm, candied pecans,
and citrus vinaigrette

Entrée Choices

Roasted prime rib of beef
Grilled salmon with pear vinegar
Shrimp & lobster cheddar grits
Petite ravioli with butternut squash
Shitake mushrooms &
caramelized shallots
Sautéed greens with shallots & Pancetta
White asparagus with pistachio
vinaigrette
Candied cranberries with walnuts

Your Dessert

From this year's recipient of

The Passionate Palate Award

Emma Rae Travis

Crème Brûlée Cake

Your Entertainment

Grammy Award-Winning Performer

Ben Colson

16

Jackson's sisters had organized the evening down to the most minute of details. From the ruby red carpet unfolded from curb to lobby door to the metallic gold "T" embroidered on each linen napkin, they had created just the elegant atmosphere they'd been chattering about for weeks on end. The staff moved about the hotel, inside and out, with the ease of longtime employees, from uniformed servers to red-vested valets to the desk clerk manager in suit and tie. Every flower in the English Rose ballroom was perfectly placed, every crystal glass smudge-free, and every bulb of the thousands of twinkling white lights beamed to its fullest potential.

"Desi's dream," he said quietly to Norma as they surveyed the room. "It's come true tonight."

"It wasn't just Desiree's dream, once upon a time," she pointed out. "I remember a time when it was your dream too."

"Mine. No. It was always her."

Jackson felt a bit like a doorman standing at the door in his penguin suit, greeting guests as they arrived: the deputy mayor and his wife; two members of the city council; several representatives from the Chamber of Commerce. It was just the kind of guest list Georgiann had insisted upon, right down to the members of Atlanta's social elite; in particular, one Avery Buffington Travis, dressed in a designer that Georgiann knew at first glance, and curiously arriving on the arm of her ex-husband, Gavin Travis.

Jackson wondered how Emma would react to the sight.

He casually looked around for her, first in the ballroom, then the atrium, then down the hall toward the restaurant. "Have you seen Emma?" he asked Madeline.

"She's in the kitchen, I think."

Jackson greeted them and then excused himself from Ned and Judith Gallagher, and headed straight for Emma's kitchen. The spicy aroma coming from Anton Morelli's preparations made his mouth water as he shoved open the adjacent swinging door and peered inside.

"Oh!" Fee exclaimed, pushing out of the

arms of her young friend with messy hair and a slightly rumpled suit. "Hey, boss."

"I was looking for Emma."

"She's next door."

Jackson smiled at Fee in her long scarlet gown with the black ribbon choker. "You look quite beautiful, Fee."

"Really?" she asked with a wide grin. "Thanks, boss. You're a Dapper Dan yourself. Have you met Peter Riggs?"

"The photographer?"

The young man moved forward and extended his hand. "Good to meet you, Mr. Drake."

"You too."

Jackson walked over to Morelli's kitchen and nudged open the door to find the chef himself feeding Emma a bite of something with a meat fork.

"Mmm," she purred. "That is delicious, Chef Morelli."

"I thought I told you no hiding in the kitchen," Jackson teased.

When Emma turned around to face him, Jackson was reminded of his days as the high school quarterback. He was suddenly sacked, the breath knocked right out of his lungs.

She grinned at him and shook her wavy curls away from her beautiful face. "Wait until you taste this, Jackson. It's heaven on earth."

Jackson tried to smile, but he was fairly certain that it came off as a smirk.

"You look . . ."

When he didn't finish, Anton took over for him. "EX-quisite!" he shouted, and then kissed two fingers and lifted them upward.

"Thank you," she replied on a giggle. "Both."

She was a vision in purple velvet over lavender shimmer, light nylons clinging to tiny, tapered ankles, and elaborate three-inch heels with rhinestone straps. She was nearly as tall as he was in those shoes!

Her normally silky straight hair was thick with s-shaped waves, combed back with a thin rhinestone headband, and dark amethyst earrings dangled from earlobe to shoulder. As she walked toward him, Jackson felt a rush of heat move over him, and the palms of his hands began to sweat.

"See you out there," Emma called back to Anton, and he gave them a rolling wave.

"That tux is lucky to be wearing you," she told Jackson. "You look like the top of a wedding cake."

"I think I'm supposed to."

As they rounded the corner, Avery and Gavin were there to greet them.

"Please behave yourselves tonight," Emma whispered when she saw them standing there together.

"You are a vision, Princess," Gavin told his daughter.

"Isn't she though," Jackson muttered.

"Honey, you look so pretty," Avery added. "I didn't know you had it in you anymore to dress up like this."

"I had help," she replied. "It kind of took a village."

"Well, the village should be rewarded. You look exquisite."

Jackson concurred, sans words.

"Jackson, this young lady rebelled against every social grace I ever tried to inflict upon her. As soon as she was old enough to choose her own wardrobe, she couldn't get enough of plain trousers and dark blazers, blue jeans and tennis shoes."

He didn't tell them how great he thought she looked in her casual clothes as well.

"Jackson, there you are," Georgiann said as she hurried toward him and snagged his arm. "It's time to welcome everyone." As they headed toward the lobby, Georgiann tossed another greeting to Avery over her shoulder. "So happy you came."

His sister reminded Jackson of a street sweeper, albeit a very well-dressed one, as she made contact with every stray guest along the way.

"We're gathering in the ballroom. So glad you're here. Come along to the ballroom."

Jackson paused at the doorway. The lights had been dimmed, the guests were mingling, the candles were all lit.

"You ladies really did a masterful job, George."

Georgiann took less than ten seconds to beam, and then she resumed her master sweep. With one hand pressed against his back, she led Jackson forward toward the stage.

"There's a microphone set up. Go welcome your guests."

Jackson cleared his throat as he took the three steps. A bluish spotlight found him almost immediately, and someone handed him the microphone.

"Good evening." An impulse of applause greeted him, and Jackson thanked them with surprised sincerity. "I'm so happy you all could be with us tonight to celebrate the opening of the new and improved Tanglewood Inn."

He glanced around the room, then found his sisters and Susannah standing in a small swarm at the edge of the stage.

"The place looks pretty good, doesn't it?"

he asked the crowd with a grin, and they erupted into applause. "Well, believe me, it didn't get this way by my hands. I've been fortunate enough to have some women around me with magnificent taste and astounding commitment to bringing this dream to life. Please join me in thanking a group of stunning women — my sisters, Georgiann Markinson, in charge of staffing the place, and putting together that amazing auction in the other room to benefit ovarian cancer research; Madeline Winston, our wedding coordinator; and Norma Blanchette, event planner extraordinaire. We also have my assistant Susannah Littlefield, and the very beautiful baker Emma Rae Travis. And what chef Anton Morelli lacks in beauty, he makes up for with talent. This group of people has been instrumental in putting this place, and this night, together in honor of my late wife, Desiree."

Applause thundered, and Jackson's chest constricted with emotion.

"Desiree used to work here, as many of you may know. Somehow, she caught a vision of converting a perfectly fine boutique hotel into a spectacular wedding and event destination. Once she caught hold of that picture," he added, shaking his head as he remembered, "there was just no going back.

She spent countless hours cutting out magazine photos, and making notes about how she would do it. She left me with a sort of blueprint, actually. And tonight, everyone in this room plays a part in seeing Desi's dream come true. From the bottom of my heart, I thank you."

Jackson let the applause die down before announcing, "Dinner is about to be served. And afterward, you'll be dazzled by Emma Travis's award-winning dessert, and the musical stylings of Mr. Ben Colson. Enjoy! And welcome to The Tanglewood Inn."

Initially, Jackson had thought Madeline's idea of each of them hosting a different table was a good one. It would be a nice way to mingle with the guests during dinner, answer any questions they might have, network a bit with the members of their community. But as soon as he sat down at his table, and saw Emma making her way to another one at the other side of the room, Jackson began to rethink that choice. He'd have preferred to have dinner with Emma at his side. In fact, he considered a complete overhaul of the plan that involved him walking over there and sitting down in the empty chair beside her.

The thought had no sooner materialized than a sandy-haired stranger in an expensive

Armani suit appeared out of nowhere and snagged that chair. Jackson craned to see if the chair on the other side of her was open. To his disappointment, he saw that it was occupied by his niece Janelle. On the other side of her sat her husband, Miguel.

Georgiann had managed a perfect score: flanked on one side by Avery and Gavin Travis, and the deputy mayor and his wife seated on the other.

"Is seating arranged? Or can anyone sit here?"

Jackson glanced up to find an attractive redhead standing with her hand on the back of the chair beside him. He rose and held out the chair for her. "Please. Join me."

"The best seat in the house," she said as she sat down. "I'm sitting next to the Man of the Hour."

"Oh, I'm sorry," Jackson teased. "Ben Colson is somewhere else. I can't sing, but I'll try to be interesting. How's that?"

"Deal," she beamed. She extended her hand toward him once Jackson sat down. "Christina Valentine, Channel 12 news."

"Good to meet you, Christina. Do you know the others at our table?"

Emma struggled to rid herself of the movie montage flashbacks flipping through her head. Growing up as Avery Travis's daughter hadn't left much room for being a klutz at the dinner table, but most of Emma's finer clothes ended up with a splatter stain of some kind on them just the same.

"Do you have a hole in your chin?" her mother asked so often that her ears tingled with the instant replay, even now.

I know this is a wacky time to start praying again. But please don't let me slop anything on this dress. A large, supernatural bib would be greatly appreciated.

"Gravy?"

"No thanks."

Stephen West touched her arm. "No. I mean, would you pass it?"

"Oh!" Emma tried to smile. "Sorry."

She cringed as she reached for the gravy boat, hoping the sleeve of her jacket didn't come back with some of her salmon hanging from it.

Victory.

She handed Stephen the gravy, and he thanked her with a warm smile. Emma wasn't sure she'd ever seen teeth as white as Stephen's.

"The food is spectacular," he commented, filling a ridge cut across his potatoes.

"Chef Morelli is a genius. You should see

what he's planning to do with simple barbecue."

"Barbecue!" he exclaimed. "I wouldn't think of Morelli as a barbecue kind of guy."

"Oh, he's not. Definitely not," Emma chuckled. "We have a wedding coming up that is sort of sports themed. He's adapting."

"A sports-themed wedding."

"Baseball. Atlanta Braves, to be precise."

"Romantic." Stephen curled his upper lip and shook his head. "Not."

"I guess it is for the couple who met at a Braves game."

Stephen considered that, and then shook his head again. "Not."

Emma flaked another bite of salmon with her fork and popped it into her mouth.

"So, what do you do, Stephen?"

"I own the staffing company the hotel worked with," he replied. "For the housekeeping staff, the waiters, that kind of thing."

"Oh! You're that West," she said with a nod. "Georgiann said you were really great."

"Did she? Nice to know. Thank you."

With her fork in midair and her wandering thoughts jumping from the Falcons sideline package on the auction table, Emma just happened to glance toward the door, and she did a double take.

"Uh oh."

"What is it?" Stephen asked.

Emma dropped her fork, pushed back her chair and popped to her feet. "Excuse me." Before he could reply, she was on her way across the ballroom toward the door where her Aunt Sophie was standing in her mint green ball gown, white satin gloves and crooked tiara. As she got closer, Emma realized Sophie was also wearing white terry-cloth bed slippers.

Jackson must have seen her too because he appeared at Emma's side just a few yards away from the door, and they both hurried toward Sophie without actually running.

"Aunt Sophie!" Emma hugged her and then kissed her on the cheek. "How did you get here?"

"I took a taxicab," Sophie stated. "Just like last time."

Emma and Jackson looked at one another.

"A taxicab," Emma declared. It was clearly a revelation for them both.

"Sophie, you look exquisite," Jackson told her. Offering his arm to Sophie, he turned to Emma and said, "Get your mother."

Emma nodded and turned to scan the room.

"Ten o'clock," Jackson directed. "At

George's table."

Emma scurried off in that direction and sighed when she caught sight of her mother.

"Emma, darling. Are you enjoying yourself?"

"I really am," she said, her smile just a little too wide to be genuine. "Mother, could I see you for a moment?"

"Now? We've just started —"

"I know, I'm sorry. But there's someone here you're really going to want to see."

Avery regarded her daughter's concrete smile for several beats, and then she returned it with a slightly more normal one. "Of course. I hope you'll all excuse me for a moment."

The instant they stepped away from the table, Emma linked her arm with her mother's and whispered, "Aunt Sophie is here."

"What?" Avery replied softly, the elegant just-right smile still pasted to her face.

"And get this. She took a taxi."

"Where did she —"

"I have no idea. But she's here."

"Oh, good grief," Avery said as soon as she caught sight of her sister. "Jackson, I just could not be more sorry."

Jackson shook his head. "No need at all. Sophie has just been charming me with stories about growing up in Savannah."

"Sophie," Avery enunciated. "What are you doing here?"

"I saw the announcement about the party on the evening news," she told them. "I don't remember getting my invitation, but I knew I had to be here to help Jackson and Emma Rae celebrate their wedding."

"Oh no, Darling, it's not a wedding. It's just a party to mark the opening of the hotel."

"Don't be silly, sister."

Sophie was already holding Jackson's hand, and she took Emma's with her other. "Isn't Emma Rae the most beautiful bride you've ever seen? I wish you'd have told me about your dress, sweet pea. My bridal veil would have been perfect. It's made out of real Chantilly lace from Paris. Our grandmother wore it for her wedding too."

"That's such a sweet thought, Aunt Sophie." Emma covered Sophie's hand between both of hers and kissed her. "But honestly, this isn't my wedding. It's a party for Jackson's hotel opening."

Sophie looked at Jackson and cocked her head to the side. "Jackson. You own a hotel?"

CREATING DELICATE SUGAR ROSES

- For small, detailed rosebuds, it is best to use gum paste or sugar paste, colored in green (for the leaves) and pink (or whatever color you want your roses to be).
- Prepare a flat Styrofoam holder for the roses.
- Create foundational cones that are slightly smaller than the petals you'll be using.
- Insert a toothpick into the bottom of the cone, and poke the cone into the holder so that it stands upright. You can do this 24–48 hours ahead so that the cone will dry completely.
- Roll out the colored sugar paste and cut out three petals.
- Using a dog-bone tool, bend the edge of the petal so that it takes on a realistic curve. If you're making a volume of roses, place the petals in a plastic container so they don't dry out.
- Brush the cone with a layer of sugar glue, and wrap a petal around it tightly, covering the pointed end.
- Brush with sugar glue again, and wrap two more petals into place.
- Use your fingers to create a flutter shape in the petals and allow them to dry for 30–45 minutes.

- While drying, cut out three more petals and repeat the sugar glue treatment.
- Place the next layer of petals so that they overlap.
- Brush with sugar glue and dry completely.

17

"I appreciate this so much."

Emma removed the tiara from Sophie's head and set it on the nightstand next to the bed. Stroking her aunt's silken hair, she asked Fee and Peter, "Are you sure you don't mind?"

"Not at all," Fee replied. "Go downstairs and present the cake. We'll be quiet as church mice while Sophie sleeps."

"Thank you." Emma squeezed Fee's hand. "I shouldn't be more than an hour."

Standing in the doorway, Emma took one last look at her aunt. The green taffeta dress looked oddly out of place poking out from beneath the quilted bedspread, loosely grasped with satin-gloved hands.

"Sleeping Beauty," she commented, and Fee grinned.

The moment the elevator doors opened on the lobby level, Avery was there to meet her.

"She's fine, Mother. Already asleep."

"Emma Rae, I'm so sorry. I hope this hasn't ruined your party."

"No worries. Fee and Peter will watch over her until after the cake is served. Then I'll stay in her room overnight, and we'll take her back in the morning." The two of them walked side by side down the carpeted hallway leading to the ballroom. "But you really have to talk to the administration, Mother. She can't just come and go as she pleases."

"I know."

"We might have to think about moving her —"

"Oh, I'd hate to do that. She's already made friends, Emma. You should see her when she's there. She's at peace."

"But not peaceful enough to stay on the premises, Mother."

They reached the ballroom entrance, and Avery hesitated. Pressing two fingers to her temple, she closed her eyes. When she opened them again, they were misted with a glaze of emotion.

"It's going to be all right," Emma promised, taking her hand. "We'll make adjustments. Everything will be fine."

"She's my big sister," Avery remarked. "It's difficult to see her this way."

"I know. But she's still the same Sophie inside."

Avery lifted a tired smile and gave a fragile stroke to the bend of one of Emma's wavy curls. "You look so pretty tonight, sweetheart."

"Thank you. But you're the most beautiful woman in that room." Emma grinned. "In any room."

"Well, now you've just gone crazy," Avery teased.

"I'll have them serve you a warm dinner."

"I couldn't eat."

"You have to eat, Mother."

Avery raised a perfect arched brow, then she smoothed her hair as if it might be out of place. "Role reversal doesn't suit us, Emma Rae."

Emma chuckled. "Then don't make me do it."

"Where did you two get off to?" Gavin asked them as he stalked toward them.

"Aunt Sophie's here."

He stopped in his tracks and heaved a sigh as he scratched his head. "Well, Nell's silver bells."

"It's fine now. She's upstairs in a room."

"Alone?"

"No. Fee is with her."

Gavin angled his head toward Avery and

cinched up his mouth into an odd little grimace. "Can I do anything?"

"Not by all prior proof to the contrary. And really, Gavin . . . why start now?"

Gavin and Emma stood by and watched her as Avery floated across the ballroom toward her table.

"Funny. I didn't even see that one barreling toward me," he said.

"Yeah. She's sneaky like that."

Emma poked her head inside the door to the kitchen with a wary smile.

"Is it safe to enter?" she asked Pearl, Anton's sous chef.

"At your own risk," she replied, wrinkling her nose and grinning from ear to ear.

"I missed most of dinner," Emma announced. "And I'm ravenous."

"Well, we can't have that. Let me get you a plate."

Pearl's salt-and-pepper hair, mostly salt, seemed to push against her white chef's cap in an overt desire to break free, and her very blue eyes shimmered with a blend of amusement and wonder.

"Oooh, you look pretty. Is the dress new?"

"Thanks. Well, it's new to me. Fee took me to one of her secret consignment locations."

Emma scraped a stool across the floor and sat down at the center island where Pearl smoothed a linen napkin into a makeshift placemat. With meticulous care, she set out flatware and presented a plate of salmon with all the accoutrements, including a sprig of parsley atop the potatoes.

"How do you think it all went tonight?" Emma asked her as Pearl poured cold water into a crystal goblet.

"With Anton?" Emma nodded. "He was . . . *Anton Morelli.*"

Emma chuckled. "How long have you been working with him?"

"Eleven years. He took me right out of cooking school and put me to work in his kitchen. I've gone from cleaning vegetables and doing prep work to full-on eye-of-the-storm assistance." Pearl leaned on the counter and smiled at Emma. "He's a genius, you know."

Emma did know. With her mouth full, she nodded and waved her fork. "Mm-hmm."

Pearl folded both arms on the counter and leaned forward. The pride in her indigo eyes was unmistakable and, for the first time since she'd first met Pearl, realization crept over Emma.

"There's something going on with you and Chef Morelli, isn't there?"

Pearl's gaze sharpened as it darted straight for Emma. "What do you mean?"

"I know that look," she said, pointing with her fork. "You have a thing for him."

Pearl hesitated, then shifted, angling her head as her lips tilted into a timid grin. "Do you really want to talk about employees who have a thing for their bosses?"

Emma's pulse fluttered.

"I mean, if you want to go there —"

"No. You're right. It's none of my business."

"Mm-hm." It was fragmented and sharp, but pregnant with meaning.

"Is there any more cake?"

"You can't have cake," Pearl clucked. "Anton told me you're diabetic."

"I just want a taste. That's why I made sure to eat something first. Ooh, you know, I want to try and make it into the auction room and place a bid on —"

All thoughts of cake and football snapped right out of her mind as the kitchen door blew open and Fee stood there looking like she'd just escaped a hurricane.

"What's wrong?"

"Sophie," she panted. "She ditched me."

Emma sprang to her feet. "What do you mean she ditched you?"

"I was watching television. I heard the

door, but I thought it was Pete coming back with ice. Then when he did come back a minute later, we realized Sophie was gone. What do we do?"

"We find her!" Emma cried as she rushed toward the door. With an offhanded wave across her shoulder, she added, "Thanks, Pearl."

Before Pearl could respond, Emma was down the hall and scurrying through the lobby. At the door of the ballroom, she waited for Fee to reach her and whispered, "Let's find my mother and bring her right back here." The two of them flew inside and darted off in separate directions.

Emma scanned the room.

"Where is she, where is she?" she muttered.

Jackson caught her eye from the dance floor. He was holding that woman from the news in a loose embrace. Emma bit her lip and tilted her head, and Jackson excused himself from his partner and headed straight for her.

"What's wrong?"

"Aunt Sophie. She's on the loose again."

"I thought Fee had this covered."

"So did she."

Jackson quickly looked around the room. "Where's your mom?"

"I was just trying to figure that out."

"Okay," he said, and he rubbed her shoulder. "I did see her earlier. Come with me."

Emma hesitated, but only for a moment. Ben Colson's silky voice drew her attention to the stage for an instant. A soft blue backlight lent a vintage vibe to his rendition of "Smoke Gets in Your Eyes." Wishing she had a few minutes to enjoy the bluesy performance, Emma hurried off to catch up with Jackson.

". . . seen Mrs. Travis?"

"No, sir."

She hadn't come to a full stop before Jackson moved on from the valet and headed toward the empty restaurant at the far end of the lobby. Georgiann was seated at one of the tables, one of her stocking feet stretched out over its abandoned shoe.

"This'll teach me to wear a new pair of shoes without breaking them in," she said on a chuckle as they reached her. "It's a lovely affair, Jackson. Just lovely."

"Have you seen Avery Travis, George?"

"Yes, a few minutes ago," she told him. "She was out in the courtyard."

Jackson touched Emma's arm and led her to the lobby again. "If you see her before we do," he tossed back toward his sister, "tell her we're looking for her?"

"Y-yes," Georgiann called after them, bewildered. "Yes, I will."

Emma pushed past Jackson through the doors and out to the brick courtyard. A dozen or more guests milled around, some of them holding glasses and some of them seated at the wrought-iron bistro tables. Emma thought that it looked like a scene from a movie with all of them dressed in elegant costume, a million tiny white lights twinkling in the trees overhead.

"I don't see her, Jackson. What are we going to do?"

"Don't panic," he assured her as they stood there, side by side, scrutinizing every face before them. "Sophie will probably turn up in the ballroom. That's where all the action is. We'll go back there and wait for her."

It was as good a plan as they had at their disposal, so Emma decided to follow Jackson's inclination until something better came along. One more circle to check back in the restaurant, and then . . .

They both noticed it at the same moment, and Jackson and Emma stopped in their tracks. The door to the consultation room was cracked slightly, and a beam of light streamed out from inside. Jackson reached it first, but the moment he pulled the door open and peered inside, he closed it again and turned toward Emma. The look on his face was one of amused alarm, mixed with . . .

The taste of a bad lemon, Emma decided.

"Is it Aunt Sophie?"

"No." He stated it with a firm resolution that further piqued Emma's interest.

"What is it, Jackson?"

He reached for her but missed when she sidestepped him and pushed open the door.

Time froze and a shower of prickly needles poked at her. Without further thought, Emma opened her mouth and allowed the scream that rose up from the very pit of her stomach to catapult over her throat and straight out her mouth. In the very next instant, Jackson stood behind her, bracing her against him, and he covered her mouth with his large hand.

He hadn't silenced her fast enough, however, and her parents reacted to her scream, fumbling out of the embrace in which she'd caught them, sputtering a forced end to their very passionate kiss.

"What are you DOING?!" she bellowed into the palm of Jackson's hand. "Are you out of your MINDS?"

Avery swiftly pulled the handkerchief from Gavin's pocket and shoved it toward him, nodding at the smear of lipstick around his mouth.

Dabbing at it while he spoke, Gavin stammered, “Th-there you are, P-Princess. We . . . your mother and I, that is . . . we were wondering where you’d gotten off to.”

Jackson slowly eased his hand away, bracing Emma’s shoulder with a firm grip.

“Try counting to ten,” he whispered, his breath tickling her ear.

Emma’s eyes were so wide and round that they stung. “There isn’t a number in the world big enough for me to count down. What are you two *doing?*”

“Well,” her father said on a chuckle. “We’re smooching, Emmy.”

“Gavin!” Avery gasped, smacking his arm with the back of her hand.

Emma turned around, her parents behind her. Swallowing hard and wondering if she was about to lose her dinner, she muttered, “Aunt Sophie is missing. We need to find her.”

As she walked away from them, she heard her mother and Jackson whispering.

Good, Mother. Involve my boss in your breakdown.

She shook her head as she ambled back toward the ballroom, and Fee stepped into stride beside her.

"Did you find her?"
"No."
"Are you all right?"
"No."
"Em, really. I am so, so sorry."
Emma stopped in her tracks, and Fee nearly ran right into her.
"If you had seen what I've just seen . . ."
"What?" Fee cried. "What did you see?"
"I mean, my eyes!" she exclaimed. "They may be scarred for life, Fee."
"You're freaking me out."
"You don't know what it IS to be freaked out. Not until you've seen your divorced parents, feeling each other up and sucking face in a closet."
Fee's entire face scrunched up into a balled fist. "Ew."
Emma nodded knowingly, then shook her head again. "It was tragic."
"Are they . . ." She leaned in toward Emma and whispered, ". . . getting back together?"
Emma considered the thought and then shuddered.
"Watch your language, Bianchi. Even in a whisper, that comes off obscene."

The Year's Most Unique Wedding Favors

1. Acrylic heart coasters, engraved with poetic quotes about love.
2. Scented candles in the shape of a wedding dress.
3. "Love is Brewing" gift boxes with flavored teas and tea accessories.
4. A gift box with petit fours in the flavors of the wedding cake.
5. Cookies made to look like the wedding invitation.
6. Place cards set in beautiful, ornate take-away picture frames.
7. "Mint to Be" boxes of take-home mints, chocolates, and almonds.
8. Beach-themed bucket filled with chocolate starfish and seashells.
9. Bottle of wine or champagne with label commemorating the wedding.
10. "Perfect Blend" packets of flavored coffee with personalized labels.

18

Six of the servers stood by the lobby door in two perfectly straight rows, handing out favor boxes to the guests as they made their way outside. Norma had outdone herself with the idea of wedding-type favors made out of fold-out cardboard boxes in the shape of a horse-drawn carriage, filled with tulle-and-ribbon bags of fragrant wildflowers, Jordan almonds, and gourmet chocolates bearing the ornate gold T that served as The Tanglewood's logo.

"Jackson, it was a beautiful party," Christina Valentine said as he helped her slip into her evening coat. "I just wish we could have spent a little more time together."

She snapped her bright red locks out of the collar of her coat and struck what he assumed was her best model pose.

"I'm glad you enjoyed yourself," he told her. "Drive safely."

The disappointed drop in her gleaming

white smile wasn't lost on Jackson, but women like Christina Valentine just didn't interest him. Too much makeup, too much hair, and far too much effort to keep it all up. He'd always been drawn to a simpler type, like Desiree. Her natural beauty was attractive, yes; but it was her quiet confidence that set her apart from the other women he'd known.

Jackson's attention was nudged toward Emma, as if his jaw was attached to an invisible hook on a long string. It had been quite a night for her, and yet there she stood, so beautiful and gracious as guests complimented her wizardry in the kitchen.

"I wouldn't have believed the hype if I hadn't tasted that cake for myself," the deputy mayor assured her. "You have quite a talent, Miss Travis."

"Thank you so much. I'm glad you enjoyed yourself."

Her smile betrayed not one trace of the worry Jackson knew had consumed her. Sophie was still M.I.A., the sight of Gavin and Avery Travis locking lips was no doubt burned into their daughter's memory, and yet Emma was just as sweet and cordial as if she had not a care in the world.

Her gaze clicked with his for several beats before she looked away and smiled at the next in the line of departing partygoers. Strange how vacant it left him when she broke away. Jackson's odd and unexpected connection with Emma was palpable, even across the width of a hotel lobby teeming with people.

"Best of luck with this venture," Bob Harding said as he shook Jackson's hand. "I think you have a winner here."

"Let's hope," he returned, and he patted Bob's back as he passed through the door.

When he looked back again, he noticed Fee at Emma's side, and the two of them were deep in animated conversation, punctuated by Fee pointing toward the far end of the lobby. Once again, Emma's eyes met Jackson's. He could almost hear the click of it, like a gear set into place. One nod from her, and the two of them took off across the lobby, meeting up at the front desk, and turning the corner in perfect unison.

"Exciting night," Jackson commented.

"I've tried having dinner twice now, and failed both times," she told him as they scurried down the hallway. "And I don't think I heard Ben Colson finish one entire song."

"But on the bright side, you got to see your parents making out."

He felt certain from the look in her eye

that Emma was just about to shoot something scathing in his direction, but then she jumped.

"There she is!" she cried out, and Jackson looked up just in time to see the mint-green hem of an evening gown disappear on the landing of the ornate staircase.

Emma and Jackson hurried toward the stairs and began the ascent. Just as they reached the landing, they both jumped, and Emma squealed, as a flutter of wildflowers cascaded out of nowhere over top of them.

"Wheeeeeeeee," Sophie cried from above them and tossed another handful of the flowers into the air before they floated down over them.

"Aunt Sophie," Emma said on a sigh.

"Have a wonderful honeymoon!" her aunt exclaimed, tossing one last scoop of wildflowers at them. "The wedding was just beautiful!"

Jackson brushed the flowers from his shoulders and out of his hair as Emma closed the gap between them and her aunt.

"I haven't had a Jordan almond in years," Sophie told her as she plucked one out of the tulle bag in her hand and happily plopped it into her mouth. Then she lifted one of the chocolates and held it out to Emma. "What does the T stand for? I thought your new name was Drake."

"Can I speak with you?"

Emma regarded her mother for a moment, then she touched her arm. "Just take Aunt Sophie and we'll talk tomorrow."

Avery frowned. "I can explain."

Emma hugged her mother and kissed her cheek. "Please don't. I don't think I could bear the details."

"But sweetheart —"

"Really, Mother, let's leave this on a need-to-know basis and —" Gavin walked up beside her and the two of them finished in stereo. "— I don't need to know."

Emma gave her father a tired smile.

"Let's give Emmy a day or two to get over it, and then we'll talk."

"You say that like I might survive what I've seen tonight."

Gavin kissed her forehead. "Love you, Princess."

Emma folded her arms and stood planted in her spot, watching as her father wrapped his own coat around Sophie's shoulders before walking her and Avery out of the hotel.

"You have quite an *in-trestin'* family," Madeline said, appearing beside Emma.

"Yeah. Interesting." Grinning at Madeline,

she suggested, "That's what we should call them from now on. *Interesting.*"

Madeline chuckled. "Good night, Emma."

Emma wasn't sure what to do with herself, so she just stood there and massaged her forehead with the fingertips of both hands.

"Ms. Travis?" She looked up to find one of the hotel desk clerks standing before her. "Mr. Drake called the front desk to ask if you would join him in the ballroom for a few minutes."

"Any idea why?"

"None. Sorry."

"I'm pretty sure all of my family members have vacated," she commented. "What could it be?"

She didn't wait for the reply. She just touched his arm and muttered a quick "Thanks" before heading off in the direction of the ballroom. When she reached it, most of the lights had been turned out; only the first row of tables was illuminated, and the blue spot on the stage highlighted a lone piano. Jackson and Ben Colson were talking at the front of the empty room. Jackson leaned against the stage.

"You wanted to see me?" she asked as she approached them.

"Emma, have you met Ben?"

"I haven't had the pleasure," she said,

shaking his hand. "But I'm a big fan of your music."

"I appreciate that," he replied, and she couldn't help but notice what a picture-perfect man he was. The way he tilted his head and smiled, he looked like any one of his album covers. "Do you have a favorite song?"

"A favorite . . . Pardon?"

"Jackson tells me you didn't get to hear one song all the way through tonight. We thought you might like to, now."

Emma glanced at Jackson, then back to Ben. "Really?"

"What's your pleasure?"

"Oh, I just love the classics from your second album. Anything. Really, anything would be great."

Ben nodded, then he rounded the stage and climbed the stairs.

Jackson smiled at her sweetly, and she shook her head. "Thank you, Jackson. Really. What a nice thing to do."

On the first note from the piano, Jackson offered his hand. "Dance with me?"

Emma's heart thumped against her throat and she hesitated only a moment before taking Jackson's hand and moving into his arms. As Ben Colson serenaded them with "The Way You Look Tonight," Emma leaned into Jackson and they swayed in perfect sync to the music.

It felt so good there in his arms, and she had the sensation of finally landing somewhere that she'd been struggling to reach for such a very long time. Emma nuzzled her face into his shoulder and closed her eyes, breathing in a deep whiff of the faint spicy wood and citrus that was becoming familiar to her now.

The music came to a gentle end, but the two of them remained in one another's arms, swaying softly to the silent song in the very large room. After almost a full minute, Colson's smooth voice began to fill the room again, this time with his bluesy rendition of Van Morrison's "Crazy Love." Then came the piano notes to accompany him, and Jackson and Emma still hadn't missed a single beat. Emma's eyes were still closed as she imagined that they were dancing somewhere all alone, on a bridge or a mountaintop, and the music lulled them through a pouring rain that washed away everything else on earth except the two of them. Jackson's arms around her felt like a satin cloak, and the thump of his heartbeat set the back-beat for Ben Colson's beautiful song.

When Emma opened her eyes again, the

stage was empty and the blue spotlight had vanished. With her face still pressed against Jackson's shoulder, Pearl smiled at her as she moved several plates from a large tray to a table set with lit candles and shimmering glassware.

"Want to try this again?" she asked, and Emma grinned.

Jackson gently eased back from her and then kissed her forehead. "I asked Pearl to bring us whatever was left over."

Keeping his hold on Emma's hand, he led her toward the table and held out her chair.

"Pearl," Emma said. "Thank you so much."

When she noticed two small plates on the table, one with a normal-sized slice of crème brûlée wedding cake and the other with a tiny fraction of a slice, Emma laughed right out loud.

"It's a masterpiece," Pearl told her. "You should at least get to taste it."

Pearl gave them a funny little wave that seemed almost like a salute, and then she disappeared through the door behind the stage.

"This is perfect," Emma said, and Jackson smiled.

They barely spoke another word as they devoured the dinners set before them. The glances they shared were sporadic at first, and then more rhythmic, and then finally their eyes remained locked without the possibility of breaking away.

"You really look beautiful tonight," Jackson said at last.

"So do you."

When the words settled in, they both grinned, and Emma dropped her head as the flush of embarrassment warmed her face and neck. "I mean handsome," she clarified. "You look really handsome in your tux."

"That's a relief."

"Oh, don't get me wrong," she teased. "You're pretty too."

Jackson groaned, and they both began to laugh.

"Pretty as a picture," she sang. "Like a life-sized Ken doll."

"That's enough out of you," he warned her. "Or I'm eating your square of cake."

Emma quickly snatched the plate with the miniscule serving on it and held it close. "Keep your hands off that cake! I've been dreaming about this one tiny bite for days on end. And it's mine, I tell you. All mine."

Jackson raised his hands in surrender and laughed. "Okay, okay. It's all yours."

"You bet it is."

"Can I get you some coffee with that?" he asked and then broke into a grin. "Maybe hazelnut?"

"Hazelnut!" she gasped, putting on her best Jackson Drake imitation. "Are you obsessed with hazelnut or something? Hazelnut this, and hazelnut that. I just want a plain cup of coffee. Black and strong. Do you hear me? No hazelnut!"

Jackson's laughter was rich, and it resonated deep within her. Emma leaned back and enjoyed it until Jackson handed her a clean fork.

"Take a deep breath," he told her. "And then enjoy yourself."

The serving Pearl had brought her amounted to no more than three bites, and she sliced off a portion with her fork and gently wrapped her lips around it. The sweetness of the cake engulfed her, and she leaned forward on her elbow, the fork still in her mouth as she moaned.

"I know," Jackson said, nodding. "It's amazing."

"Mm-hmm."

"You're sure you don't want coffee?"

"Uh-uh."

"Milk?"

"Shhh," she said as she filled her fork a second time. "Don't blow the moment. I don't get that many of them."

"Okay," he whispered. "I'm not even here."

Emma looked into Jackson's eyes and grinned. She didn't know which was sweeter: the cake or the man sitting across from her.

On the third bite, she decided it was the cake. But that was up for debate later. She didn't want to think about anything else just then. After all, she had plenty of time to consider Jackson's attributes . . . after she picked at the crumbs left on her plate.

Colson Strikes Right Note for New Tanglewood Inn

Atlanta, Ga. — Last night, in the historic corner of Atlanta known as Roswell, new hotel owner Jackson Drake introduced his new destination event facility to a list of uber-stylish guests gathered from Atlanta's governing offices and social register.

Locals will recall that Drake purchased The Tanglewood Inn earlier this year when it went on the auction block again for the second time in five years.

At the invitation-only opening night gala, 150 guests dined on gourmet cuisine from the kitchen of renowned chef Anton Morelli and a decadent crème brûlée cake from award-winning baker and Georgia native Emma Travis. For those in attendance who wanted to kick up their heels on the dance floor, Drake provided no ordinary DJ or dance band. Grammy-award-winning artist Ben Colson performed original music as well as such classics as "A Wink and a Smile," "Crazy Love," "At Last," and "Over the Rainbow." Colson also served as The Tanglewood Inn's first hotel guest, saying that his suite "easily rivals some of the finest European boutique hotels."

The party season begins for this new event venue next month. "We've booked a baseball-themed wedding, a traditional Victorian affair, and a murder mystery party to celebrate the twentieth wedding anniversary of Georgia senator Virgil Franchese and his wife, Patricia," says proprietor Jackson Drake. "I've assembled one of the finest staffs a new business owner could dream up, and we have high hopes for The Tanglewood."

"In this economic climate," says party guest, district attorney Zachary Dillon, "this was a risky move for Drake. But if tonight is any indication of his future, I'd say we have a permanent fixture for some pretty spectacular social events here in Roswell."

Morelli's, the 100-seat onsite restaurant, is open to the public from 5 p.m. until 11 p.m. Sunday through Thursday beginning next week, and an English tea room operated by baker Emma Travis will take reservations for Tuesday and Wednesday afternoons from 1:00 p.m. until 4:30 p.m. Wedding and party planning can be facilitated by calling Madeline Winston at 770-TANGLEWOOD.

19

Emma grabbed her travel mug and bag from the seat and hurried from her car across the parking lot. There was no more pulling into the circular drive out front, hugging the curb and taking less than twenty steps into the hotel. Now The Tanglewood was open for business. Excitement buzzed through her at the thought as she jogged across the lot and took the sidewalk to the back entrance into the restaurant.

The door to Anton's kitchen was propped open. "Morning!" she called to Pearl as she passed.

"G'morning, Emma."

She pushed the second door open and strode across her own kitchen and into her office. She took a sip of hot tea as she flipped on the computer. She produced the small glucose monitor from her bag before she stowed it in the bottom drawer.

No e-mails from Jackson, she thought when

her inbox popped up. *That's unusual.*

It took a few quick seconds to poke her finger, apply a drop of blood to the strip, and insert it into the monitor.

117. A little higher than normal for this time of day, but Emma attributed it to emotions. The truth was that she'd been hoping for a call from Jackson on Sunday, and she'd checked her personal e-mail from home at least a dozen times over the course of the day. When communication never came, she was up before the alarm on Monday. And for someone whose normal driving speed had been compared to a stagecoach or a fast cow, Emma felt a bit out of her element reminding herself to slow down and pay attention to the stoplights on the drive over to the hotel.

Disappointment twittered around her ribcage like a fizzy drink. After his overtures on Saturday night, with the dinner and two dances to Ben Colson's songs, she'd begun to imagine something might actually happen between her and Jackson Drake.

Emma sighed, and she zipped the monitor back inside its case, dropped it into the drawer, and, with a click of the mouse, began to review her calendar.

10:30 a.m. — Status meeting for the next month with Norma

12:00 — Lunch with Connie Edison, the hotel's publicist, to discuss the tea room

1:30 — Cake consultation with Beverly Branson regarding her summer wedding

2:30 — Consultation with Callie Beckinsale

Emma's stomach knotted. She hadn't thought much about Callie and Danny's upcoming wedding except for the occasional mention of the sports-themed wedding being the first held at The Tanglewood.

Norma would be going over the final details, she reminded herself. All that would be required of Emma would be a simple update on the plans for her baseball mitt wedding cake.

"You're in early," Pearl remarked, curled around the door with just her head inside.

"Yeah, I thought I'd get a jump on the week."

"Do you want tea?"

"No, thanks. I brought some from home," she said and held up her travel mug from Starbuck's.

Pearl hesitated. "How about some protein? Have you had any this morning?"

"Yes."

"Well, are you doing okay?"

Emma glanced up at her. "Sure. Why?"

"Saturday night looked pretty intense. I

just wondered how the rest of your weekend went."

Emma wiggled her fingers at Pearl, who crossed the kitchen and sat down in the chair flanking her desk before Emma could say, "Come on in."

"It was quite the romantic scene," Pearl said. "I mean, he made like he was just trying to be nice and make sure you got something to eat. But it looked like a lot more when you two were on that dance floor."

"It felt like a lot more too," she admitted. "But I don't think it was."

"Why do you say that?"

"Well, because that's all there was. We had a dance, a great dinner, some nice conversation, and then we called it a night. He didn't call me yesterday, there's nothing from him in my inbox —"

"Emma, how old are you?" Pearl interrupted.

"Thirty-four. Why?"

"Well, I'm fifty-seven. And men don't get any different between your age and mine. He's in *After Care.*"

"After Care? What's that?"

"It's like surgery, Emma. The operation is the hard part where they slice into their own egos and, in a weak moment, they let you know that they're attracted. Then there is the light of day. That's the stage that follows his moment of weakness, where he goes home to recuperate and has time to really think about what he's done. He starts to ask himself questions like, 'Do I really want to get involved with someone right now?' and 'What expectations is she going to start having now that I've let her know I'm interested?' "

Emma giggled, but Pearl regarded her seriously with one arched eyebrow. "This is a fundamental time, Emma Rae. What you do right now will determine how long he'll make you wait every time he's in after care."

"Every time! How many times is he going to do this?"

"Depends on the guy. But for Jackson . . . he seems like a pretty good guy, so I'd say . . . four or five."

Emma deflated and sank back into her leather chair.

"Anton is in Phase Nine. Or is it Ten?"

"Nine! Good grief."

"Which one is this for Jackson?"

"Second. There was a night where we had a takeout dinner at my house, and the next morning when he gave me a ride to work you'd have thought he ate nails for breakfast."

"Yep. Phase One."

"And then there was Saturday night, with no phone call or e-mail since."

"The good news is that you're probably halfway through it," Pearl promised. "You just take it easy. Don't seek him out unless you have to. Don't let him know you've even noticed that he didn't call. And whatever you do, don't get all melty when he finally does come around."

"Melty!" Fee exclaimed from the doorway, and Emma scowled.

"I'm not melty."

The diamond stud Fee wore in her nose on Saturday night was now replaced by a thin silver hoop, and her raven hair was pulled into two loose braids.

"Is our boss making you all melty? What happened that I don't know?"

"Oh, it was quite the after-hours scene," Pearl told her softly. "Dinner. Dancing to a private Ben Colson concert."

"Really!"

"And of course now he hasn't called her."

"I'm in the room, you know," Emma reminded them.

"Ah," Fee nodded. "After Care."

Pearl darted toward Emma and nodded. "Yep. Phase Two."

"You know about After Care too?" Emma

asked Fee.

"Oh sure. All guys do it," she said with a nod. "It's kind of like buyer's remorse. Just a couple more episodes to go with Jackson, I'm guessing," and Pearl nodded at her too.

Jackson poured another cup of coffee and turned off the burner. It was his third of the morning . . . or was it the fourth?

He hit #1 on the speed dial of his cell phone, then plopped down into the supple tan leather recliner and took a swig from the large blue mug.

"Jackson Drake's office. Susannah speaking."

"Hey, Suzi. How was your weekend?"

"My what?"

Jackson laughed. "Okay, so how was your Sunday?"

"I don't know. I slept through most of it."

"Wish I could say the same."

"No?"

He decided not to expound. "Listen, kiddo, I'm not coming into the office today."

"Are you all right?" The slight alarm in Susannah's tone gave Jackson a warm sort of feeling.

"Fine. I have some personal business I need to tend to. Can you hold down the fort?"

"I've been holding down your fort for more years than I can count, Jackson. I think I can manage it another day."

"Are the Hens in yet?"

"Norma and Madeline are here. Georgiann has an appointment this morning."

"Okay, good. Can you reschedule Connie this afternoon?"

"Sure. Anything else I need to know?"

"Not that I can think of, but I'll call you if something comes to me."

"I know you will," she replied with a lighthearted chuckle. "Have a good day, Jackson."

"You too. See you tomorrow."

Jackson couldn't remember the last time he'd played hooky. It was his second day in the same gray sweatpants and navy blue T-shirt, and the empty pizza box from last night's dinner was still propped open on the coffee table. He scratched his stubbly cheek and realized he hadn't shaved since Saturday, and when he propped up his feet on the recliner, he noticed that his big toe was just about to poke through the white sock on his left foot.

He grabbed the remote from the floor beside his chair and snapped on the television. Dozens of cable channels from which to choose, and not a thing of interest anywhere in sight. He wondered what people watched when they were home during the day, and then he landed on a riveting scene where a blonde bombshell accused her cat-eyed mother of sleeping with her fiancé.

"Okay. Enough of that." He flipped off the television and stared out the window for several minutes.

It hadn't happened to him so quickly in a very long time, but in those couple of minutes Jackson found himself drowning in thoughts and memories of Desiree. He fought back the pinch of emotion that tweaked his throat and sighed. Surrendering to it, he tossed down the footrest, got up, and stalked across the hardwood floor toward the master bedroom.

There it was, tucked into the back corner of the walk-in closet. The large box with the flaps sealed down, the one that contained the photos and journals and greeting cards; the box that neatly concealed all that Desiree had left behind.

Jackson peeled back the tape and opened the box. There on the top was their wedding photo. They'd bought that pewter filigree frame on their honeymoon in Maui. He lifted it out of the box with care, holding it with both hands and looking into the crystal blue eyes of his smiling blonde bride.

She was such a beauty; so fragile and thoughtful and funny.

Not funny like Emma. Now that girl is hysterical. Very different from Desi, and yet —

He almost heard the needle scratch across the record of his thoughts. There he was again, comparing Emma Travis to his sweet Desiree.

What is the matter with me?

It wasn't just Desiree that made his thoughts leap over to Emma. In fact, there didn't seem to be a thing on earth that didn't remind him of something about her. He saw a random red Mini Cooper on the road last week, and another car driving about 30 miles per hour under the speed limit, and then there was that arbitrary bakery truck on the interstate. They'd all pelted him into ridiculous reflections about Emma Rae Travis!

But Desiree? Wasn't his life with her sacred? What kind of man let thoughts of his dead wife inspire meditation on another (live) woman? There was something rather demented about it, and Jackson was having none of it.

He poked the framed photograph back into the box and dragged the thing back to its spot in the closet beneath his suits and next to his gym shoes. Then he plunked down on the edge of the bed and tried to excavate the picture of his dance with Emma from the front of his mind.

She'd fit so perfectly into his arms, as if she'd been custom-fitted to take her place there. Her head rested lightly against his chest, and he could almost smell her hair again now. Sweet vanilla and berries.

In his mind's eye, he shoved her away from him and vowed once again to stop thinking of her in terms like those. He wished he hadn't kissed her. He wished he hadn't taken her into his arms for that dance. He wished —

So many things.

He couldn't help but wonder what Emma thought was going to happen now. He'd allowed her to draw expectations, to imagine he was ready to open his life to someone at this point.

The next thing I know, my award-winning baker is going to start thinking like a woman and want me to step up onto the top of one of those wedding cakes of hers. I've got to put a stop to this here and now before there's collateral damage.

Now he had his head together. Now he was thinking like a reasonably intelligent man. What had he been thinking? Kissing

Emma Travis? Romancing her?

It may have taken him two days, but Jackson now felt like he was back in the game. Falling backward onto the bed, he laughed out loud and then groaned.

A minute later, he leapt to his feet and grabbed his favorite pair of Nikes. A couple of hours at the gym, and he'd be as good as new.

Traditional White Layer Cake

Ingredients:

2 cups sifted cake flour
1/2 teaspoon salt
1 1/2 cups softened butter
1 1/2 cups granulated sugar
2 eggs
1 teaspoon baking soda
1 cup buttermilk

Sift or mix the flour and salt together.

In separate bowl, blend butter and sugar. Then add eggs and mix well.

Dissolve baking soda in buttermilk.

To the butter, sugar, and eggs, add a portion of the flour mixture, then the buttermilk mixture, then the rest of the flour mixture. Mix well in between.

Pour into greased and floured pan(s).

Bake at 325 degrees for approximately 30 minutes, or until a toothpick comes out of the cake clean.

Always cool completely before frosting.

20

A current of electricity buzzed through Emma's arm as she twisted the knob and stepped into the consultation room. She wondered where Jackson was hiding these days, now that the room had a steady flow of traffic.

"Oh, good." Madeline grinned as Emma entered. "Your timing just couldn't be *bettah.* Emma Rae Travis, meet Beverly Branson, The Tanglewood's first *summah* bride."

"It's a pleasure."

"Emma will work with you to design the perfect wedding cake, Miss Branson. I'll be in touch to confirm the details we've worked out today." Madeline smoothed the front of her robin's egg blue dress, looking every part the mature Southern hostess as she rose from her chair and shook Beverly's hand. "Here's my business card. If you have any questions at all, please feel free to call upon me at any time."

"Thank you so much."

Emma took Madeline's place at the table and smiled at Beverly. "Madeline told me you were planning an intimate wedding, with an English garden theme."

"Yes. My grandparents are both from England." Beverly's bright red hair formed a halo of curls around her round face, and her hazel eyes danced as she spoke of her family. "My gram is a very proper lady from Sussex, and she loved to tell me stories about tea parties in beautiful English rose gardens. I'd love to recreate that for my wedding."

"It sounds lovely."

"We thought we'd have the ceremony in the courtyard, around one in the afternoon. And then we could have a traditional English high tea for the guests at the reception: finger sandwiches and scones with Devonshire cream. Madeline said you'd work out a menu with me."

"That's my department," Emma said with a grin. "Do you know what you have in mind for the cake?"

"Something elegant," she replied thoughtfully. "Rather traditional. Lots of roses."

"And your colors?"

Emma's meeting ran long and, by the time she said good-bye to Beverly Branson in the lobby, she had to scurry into the courtyard where Madeline's run-through with Callie Beckinsale was almost certainly winding down.

She pushed through the glass doors and hurried toward them.

"I'm so sorry. That last consultation was more involved than I'd expected."

"Emma Rae Travis."

It had been twenty years since Emma had heard her name come from those lips, with just that precise Southern inflection.

"Danny!" she exclaimed, and then stopped in her tracks, hand to thumping heart.

His crystal blue eyes still shimmered, and his square jaw still set slightly off center when he smiled. He ran a suntanned hand through his wavy blonde hair, and the sixteen-year-old heart still beating within Emma started to pound.

"You haven't changed," he seemed to sing. "Not one bit."

He moved toward her without warning and swept her into his arms for a colossal embrace, rocking her from side to side with the rhythm of her name.

"Emma — Rae — Travis."

"Hi, Danny," she said when he let her go.

"I couldn't believe it when Callie told me who was bakin' the cake for our weddin'."

Danny shook his head at her and clicked his tongue. "Emma Rae Travis. You've hardly changed one iota since high school."

"You either."

"It's just the most amazing coincidence," Callie said as she got up from the table and joined them. "I mean, really! What are the odds?"

Her wide, starch-white smile and Southern charm didn't deflect the trace of disappointment in Callie's voice, and Emma didn't blame her a bit. How many brides want their fiancé's first love to be involved in their wedding plans?

"Emma Rae Travis."

Okay. You can stop saying my name now.

"I just can't get over it."

Why don't you try?

"So," Emma said, locking arms with Callie and leading her back toward the table. "Not long now, huh? You two will be married before you know it."

Callie beamed. "I know. I can hardly believe it."

"I'm going to leave you in Emma Rae's capable hands," Madeline said as she excused herself. "I think everything is in order, don't you?"

"Yes," Callie replied, bobbing her head and pumping Madeline's hand with enthusiasm. "Thank you so much for everything."

"I'll see you on the big day," Madeline told her. "You call me any time if you have any questions or concerns, you hear me?"

"Yes. Thank you again."

Emma and Callie sat down at the bistro table, but Danny just stood there over them, his hands on his denim-clad hips, shaking his head.

Please don't say my na—

"Emma Rae Travis."

She gave an inward groan and then disguised it with a wide smile. "Would you like to see the final sketch of the wedding cake Callie's chosen?"

Danny sat down at last, and Emma pushed the pad toward him. He picked it up and stared at the drawing. "You can do this with a cake?"

"Sure can."

"How? I don't understand. I mean, what's the process?"

"Dan, what's it matter how it's done?" Callie asked him. "That's what Emma does."

"Yeah, I know, but . . . Have you done *this particular cake* before?"

"This is a one-of-a-kind cake, Danny. It's going to be created just for you and Callie."

"But how?"

Emma's foot started tapping just an instant before Callie drummed her fingers on the tabletop.

"Dan."

"Funny, you baking cakes and all," he pointed out. "Bein' a diabetic."

"Yeah," she nodded. "That is funny."

"But you can do this," he clarified, holding up the sketch pad, "with a cake?"

"Yes. I can. It's baked and filled, and then sculpted."

"Honey," Callie chimed. "Emma has won awards for her cakes."

Danny scratched his head. "Really. Awards?"

Emma nodded, lifting one shoulder into a shrug.

"But not with this *particular* cake, right?"

The sixteen-year-old inside Emma got up and walked out of the building just then. Never to be seen or heard from again.

"Ooo-kay," she said with a sigh. "So this is your cake. It will be ready for your reception. And I think that's about it. Callie, do you have any more questions for me?"

"No. Thank you."

"Good to see you again, Danny." When he headed toward her with plans for a hug in his eyes, Emma grabbed his hand and shook it. "I wish you and Callie all the very best in your life together."

Now, don't let the door hit you in the —

"Great Scott. Am I having a senior moment?"

Emma noticed her father standing at the entrance of the courtyard, his arms folded across his chest as he stared Danny down.

"Hey, Mr. Travis. Long time, no see."

"Yes."

Emma could read her father's mind, and she was marginally happy that he didn't complete the thought.

"Dad, this is Danny's fiancée, Callie Beckinsale."

Gavin shook her hand and then kissed it. "My condolences, child."

Callie giggled.

"Do you have some time for your old man?" he asked Emma, and she nodded.

"We were just finishing up."

The timing couldn't have been better had they planned it, but as the revelation dawned on Emma that she was going from one uncomfortable conversation to another, her expression soured. By the time Danny and Callie finally headed out the door and Emma fetched a cup of tea for herself and some coffee for her father, the full impact of the coming discussion sat on her chest like a gorilla with a glandular problem.

"What's up, Dad?" she asked, although she really didn't want to hear his answer.

"I think you know."

Emma shrugged. "You want to apologize for traumatizing me? Embarrassing Jackson on the opening night of his hotel?"

"Oh, I think you've been far more traumatized than that," he pointed out. "And as for Jackson, he handled the whole thing just dandy. It was you standing there screaming like a girl and —"

"I am a girl, Dad."

"— calling attention to it that embarrassed him, I suspect."

"What were you thinking, Dad?"

"I was thinking that my wife looked staggering that night, and I wanted to kiss her."

"Ex-wife."

"Well. That's the thing."

Emma's blood pressure whooshed, and her heart plummeted to the pit of her stomach as she waited.

"Princess, your mother and I never did actually . . . officially . . . *divorce.*"

"What are you talking about? You've been apart for years."

"Apart, yes. But not as apart as you think."

"Do I even want to know what that means?"

"Probably not."

"Please tell me you're joking."

Gavin leaned back into the chair and sighed. "I love your mother, Emmy. Always have. But she's not as mild mannered as she likes to let on."

"You just bring the worst out in her. With everyone else, she's —"

"Mother Teresa. I know."

"Well, I wouldn't go that far."

"Nice to know you haven't lost all perspective."

Emma chuckled, then she reached across the table and touched her father's hand. "Give it to me straight, Daddy. What don't I want to know?"

"Your mother and I have been married for forty years next month."

"Straight?" she asked, miming out a long, straight road with her hand.

"One after the other."

Emma fell back against her chair. "Huh. Really?"

"Really."

"Why didn't you ever tell me?"

"Your mother didn't want to disappoint you."

"By telling me that my parents were still happily married?"

"I don't think anyone said anything about being happy."

"She thought I'd be less disappointed if I went on thinking you were divorced."

Gavin shrugged. "You did seem to embrace the idea, Princess."

"That's only because you seemed to hate one another so much."

"Now, there's one thing I've never felt toward your mother, Emmy. I love that woman as much as the day is long."

Emma gasped and cocked her head. "You do?"

"I do."

Emma considered that for a very long moment.

"Does she know?"

Gavin laughed. "Yes. I think she does."

"And she loves you?"

"Passionately."

Several more beats ticked by as Emma thought it over.

"Well, no wonder."

"No wonder, what?"

"No wonder I'm so messed up."

"Oh, that's messed up."

"I know."

"And you think I'm psych."

"Not anymore."

Emma and Fee sat on opposite sides of the desk in Emma's office, staring at one another and occasionally shaking their heads.

"Seriously. Messed up."

"Oh, yeah."

"What's messed up?" Pearl asked from the doorway.

"Emma's parents."

"Why?"

"They're married," Fee told her. "Can you believe that?"

Pearl's expression told them that she was making every effort but just couldn't catch up to the conversation.

"Oh!" Fee exclaimed. "Pearl! I heard Anton fired you last night!"

"What?" Emma gasped.

"It's true," she replied, smiling back at them.

"So what are you doing here?"

"Prep work for the dinner crowd. We've got a full house tonight for the opening."

"But he fired you?" Emma enunciated.

"Oh, it's nothing. He fires me all the time. It's foreplay."

"I beg your pardon?"

"He's leading up to taking another stab."

Emma grimaced. "This is what I have to look forward to?"

"With Jackson? Not at all. He's much more balanced than Anton."

"Are you sure?"

Pearl chuckled. "Yes. I'm sure. Anton fires me, then I come back to work and act like nothing's happened. That goes on for a couple of days, and then he asks me to dinner or to go with him to a food show. We have a wonderful time, and then he withdraws again."

"That seems like a lot of work."

"Oh, it is. But he's worth the effort."

Fee and Emma exchanged glances, and they both shrugged.

"Well, to me, anyway."

"I feel like a freak for having such a normal relationship with Peter," Fee pointed out. "We just hang out and tell each other what we're thinking. It's very low drama."

"Wait," Emma said, shaking her head. "You're the conventional one in the room?"

"I know. It's shocking."

Norma stepped into the kitchen and ambled up behind Pearl in the doorway. "Can I have a word with you, Pearl?"

"Sure. What's up?"

"Anton's temper."

Pearl nodded knowingly.

"Any chance you could go in there and talk him down?"

"Absolutely."

Pearl turned back toward Emma and Fee,

straightened her clothes and stood erect with a mock-serious expression as she told them, “Cover me, ladies. I’m goin’ in.”

Devonshire Cream

for serving with scones or fresh berries

Beat a 3-ounce package of softened cream cheese on high.

While mixing, add 2 teaspoons of sugar, 1/2 teaspoon vanilla extract, and a pinch of salt.

Gradually add 1/3 cup whipping cream and mix until stiff.

Store in the refrigerator overnight.

21

"They were waiting in line Monday for the opening of the restaurant," Norma said, "and the manager told me we had nearly a full house last night."

Jackson leaned back into the leather desk chair, and it groaned under the pressure. He raked a hand through his hair and smiled at her. "Morelli is a very big personality, but what he brings to the table far exceeds the challenges."

"That's my thinking too."

"Do you have any information on the hotel side of things?"

"I do," she replied, and then flipped through the stack of paperwork in her hands. "We had twenty-three rooms occupied on Monday night, and eighty-one last night."

"Eighty-one?"

"George was able to send me that group in town for the food and beverage convention. Even with the group discount, they're getting us off to an amazing start. And they'll be here through Friday."

"Do we have anything else coming up?"

"A full house at the end of the month with the home improvement show, and I'm working on something with the Atlanta Symphony."

"Outstanding, Norm. Weddings?"

"Madeline's doing a last-week's-status kind of thing now every Monday. It should be sitting in your inbox."

"That works. What's our first wedding?"

"Beckinsale-Mahoney."

"The baseball couple."

Norma nodded. "I just hope the wedding takes place. The groom turned out to be an ex-boyfriend of Emma's."

"She mentioned that."

"Well, he was here yesterday, and Maddie said he was falling all over himself to talk to Emma, right in front of the poor little bride."

Jackson grimaced. "Class act."

"He even came back this morning with an armful of roses."

"Roses," he exclaimed. "You weren't kidding when you said the wedding might not happen?"

"The boy is smitten all over again. But

who can blame him, really. Emma is such a little doll."

Jackson leaned forward, wondering about Emma's reaction to her first love coming back into her life. "Are we through here?"

"I think so. Do you have anything for me?"

"No," he replied. "You're doing a great job, Norm. I'll catch up with you later."

Jackson stalked through Susannah's office and down the hall. He decided not to wait for the elevator and took the stairs instead.

"Good morning, Mr. Drake."

Jackson nodded to the desk clerk and strode through the lobby and into Emma's kitchen, where she and Fee were bellied up to either side of the island, kneading balls of different-colored dough.

"Hello, Jackson."

Her nose and cheeks were dusted with flour, and her silky hair was pulled back into a folded ponytail with ends poking out in several different directions. Her glasses hung around her neck on a knotted chain, and her apron was splotched with bright colors of dye.

"Do you need me for something?"

"Uh, no." He didn't really have a reason for the visit. Not one he could confess, anyway. "I just hadn't seen you in a few days, so I thought I'd stop in and see how things are going."

"Just dandy," she replied, and then she turned her attention toward Fee. "Can you pull the cake, Fee? We can get the fondant over the first couple of layers, anyway."

"You got it."

Fee freed her hands from the dough then went to the sink to wash them.

Jackson glanced around the kitchen, and peered through the doorway to Emma's office.

"So where are they?" he asked.

"Where's what?"

"The roses. I heard there were quite a few of them delivered this morning."

Emma looked up and stared at him intently. He was just about to fidget beneath her gaze when she broke it and returned her attention to the bowl before her. She grabbed the ball of dough and threw it against the floured surface of the island.

"I gave them to Lucille so she could put them out at the front desk."

She pushed at the dough until it flattened, and then she dusted the rolling pin with flour and began to roll it out.

"Mm-hmm." Jackson nodded. "Nice. Do we still have a baseball-themed wedding to look forward to?"

"I think so."

"You think so?"

"Well, I can't really speak for Callie or Danny, but it was just a momentary lapse. He got caught up in the whole nostalgia thing."

"But you shot him down," he stated, hoping that she had just told him that she had.

"Well. Yes. I mean, it's been twenty years since then."

"So the whole *nostalgia thing;* you didn't get lost in it along with him?"

"Maybe for a minute," she said as she rolled and rolled the dough. "But in the end, no."

Emma pulled her hands from the fondant and let them flounder in midair above it. Jackson saw the disappointment in Emma's green eyes, and it pinched at him.

"I showed him the sketch of his wedding cake." She shrugged, as if she could push the memory from her shoulder and let it drop to the floor. "He couldn't seem to wrap his brain around the idea that I could make it, that I could . . . do something extraordinary."

When she looked up at him, she tried to smile, but it was lost before it ever reached her eyes. Then she shrugged and took hold of the rolling pin and started pressing the dough again.

"His loss."

Emma glanced upward and gave him a grateful shadow of a smile.

Jackson couldn't imagine someone missing how really spectacular Emma Travis could be, but something deep within him whispered that he was happy Danny Mahoney lacked that ability.

"Well. Carry on," he said and turned on his heels and left the kitchen.

Emma had been hiking the Vickery Creek Trail for years. After the climb over a series of short ridges, she normally slowed her pace down the section of wooden stairs, allowing her the opportunity to read the signs along the way that told the historic story of Roswell Mill. Today, however, those signs were a blur as she flew past them, her running shoes thump-thump-thumping in her ears. She couldn't even manage to enjoy the spectacular scenery that had kept her coming back to this trail whenever her mind needed a good cleansing.

Unfortunately, despite the best efforts of rushing river waters, rustling tree leaves, and the crisp, grassy scent tickling her nose, Emma was lost in thoughts of Jackson Drake. After nearly two hours on the trail, she'd thought of little else.

She jogged down the incline toward her parked car, then stopped to catch her breath. Several more cars had joined hers in the lot, and it wasn't until he waved and called out her name that she recognized one of the hikers as Miguel Ramos. Holding his hand was a petite blonde with her hair pulled back into a tight ponytail.

"Fancy meeting you here," Miguel said as they approached. "How are you, Emma?"

"Good," she replied, and she returned the blonde's friendly smile.

"This is my wife, Rosalie."

"Georgiann's daughter?" Emma clarified.

"Yes."

"It's so great to meet you. I adore your mother."

"She's easy to adore," Rosalie beamed. "I tried to meet you at Uncle Jack's opening night party, but you were on the move that night."

"Yes, that was quite a night."

"It seemed like a big success."

"I think it was." Emma glanced at Miguel and asked him, "Do you two hike here often?"

"Rosalie does. I don't get out here as often as I'd like."

"There's Mindy and Art," his wife pointed out. "I'll let you two chat for a few minutes while I go and say hello. It was great to meet you at last, Emma."

"You too."

Miguel nodded toward an open wooden bench overlooking the river, and Emma followed his lead toward it.

"How are things going for you, Emma?" he asked once they sat down.

"Just fine," she replied, rubbing her throbbing calf. "How about you?"

When he didn't reply, Emma looked up and found Miguel gazing at her with an understanding glimmer in his eye that, for some reason, made her want to immediately burst into tears. She fought the inclination, darting her attention out to the water before them.

"People are talking over at The Tanglewood," he said softly. "Everyone seems to think you and Jackson are getting very close."

Emma tapped her feet and grabbed hold of the bench seat with both hands. Shrugging, she answered, "You know how gossip is, Miguel. They're making something out of nothing."

Miguel nodded. "It got me to thinking how difficult it would be for anyone in that position. Getting close to Jackson isn't an easy thing to do in recent years."

She glanced at him for a moment, and then looked away again.

"He's wrestling with a lot of demons since the loss of his wife."

"Understandable," she remarked.

"But then I guess we all have our issues to battle, don't we?"

Emma nodded, lifting her face into the breeze. She didn't realize quite how large the gap of silence had become until Miguel bridged it.

"Would you like me to pray for you, Emma?"

Once again, her eyes darted toward him, but this time he held her gaze.

"Prayer is a remarkable thing."

"Oh, well, I haven't really done much of it lately," she told him. "I did say a prayer for Jackson recently, though."

"Did you?"

"He just seemed to need it."

"I understand." Miguel touched her arm. "That's the way you appear to me right now. Like you could use a prayer or two."

Emma chuckled. "I wouldn't know where to start."

Miguel reached out and took her hand with a tentative smile. "I'll start. You just chime in if you feel led."

He waited for her response, then translated her halfhearted shrug as an agreement. He closed his eyes and bowed his head.

"Lord Jesus, I feel compelled in this beautiful environment to thank You for Your creation. The river and the trees and the canopy of blue; it's all so inspiring, and we thank You for the gift."

Emma dropped her head but, instead of closing her eyes, she just focused very hard on the knotted lace of her shoe.

After several minutes, Miguel walked her to her car, rubbed her arm, and closed the door behind her without another word. Something about the stillness was attractive to her, and Emma flipped off the radio as soon as she turned over the engine, and drove home in silence. Her ears sort of ached in the silence, but she even shushed the music of her own thoughts to take in a little more of the quiet she hadn't really known she'd been craving.

When she reached home, she parked and turned off the ignition. With no inclination to move a muscle, she sat in her car for nearly fifteen minutes. In his prayer, Miguel had spoken of God whispering comfort into her waiting ears, and Emma wondered if that might be just what was going on. Her heartbeat had slowed considerably since she'd headed off for the Vickery Creek Trail several hours prior, and she didn't sense even a trace of that bitter anxiety that had driven her there.

"If that's You," she whispered, then she looked around to make sure no one saw her alone in her car, seeming to talk to herself. "Thanks."

Emma cranked the door handle and hurried toward her front door.

Once inside, she turned away from the beckoning red blink announcing voicemail on her cell phone, which she'd purposely left behind earlier in the day. Instead, she opted for hanging up her jacket, grabbing a bottle of water from the fridge and an apple from the bowl on the counter. As she plopped into her chair by the window, Emma groaned and picked up the phone.

"You. Have. Four. New. Messages."

"Hey, girl. Peter and I are going to that gallery opening I mentioned this morning. If you're interested, give me a shout and we'll swing by and pick you up. If not, and you're just a big bore, I'll see you in the morning at ten."

A big bore was just what Emma felt like being, and she wasn't going anywhere. She leaned back into the chair and took a bite out of her apple to prove it.

"Emma Rae, this is your mother. Call me

directly, please."

She knew that tone. Translated, it meant, *You have ignored me long enough, and I know your father has spoken to you, so you'd better call me or I'll show up at your door unannounced and make you talk to me.*

Another big bite from the Gala apple announced that she wasn't going to be coerced into anything just then.

"Hello, Princess. Better call your mother."

Emma chuckled, wondering if her mother was in the room holding a letter opener to her father's throat until he made that plea on her behalf.

After the next beep, a moment of silence followed. Then a slight clearing of the throat.

"Uh. Hi."

Emma's hand froze, the apple just inches from her lips, her eyes wide and glazed as she waited for Jackson's next syllable.

"I, uh . . . No. Never mind. Well. Actually, I wondered if you wanted to . . . The thing is, my buddies have season tickets. When the guy who has the seats next to theirs can't make it to a game, well, so . . . I have these tickets for Sunday. I don't know if this even interests you, but I remembered seeing you in a Falcon jersey one day at the hotel and, you know, if you want to —"

Beeep.

"What!" Emma cried, pulling the phone from her ear and staring at it. "If I want to, what? Jackson, what?"

She played it through one more time, frustrated when the message ended at the exact same spot.

"Crud."

She pressed the seven key to erase it, and then hit number four on her speed dial, tapping her foot frantically until Jackson answered.

"Jackson Drake."

"Hi. Jackson. It's Emma. I got your message. Well, part of it. My voicemail cut you off halfway through."

He made a sort of grunty noise, and Emma waited for him to follow it up.

"I didn't know if any of it came through."

"Oh. It did. At least as far as you talking about my Falcons jersey."

"Right."

"Number 2," she told him with a sway to her head. "Matt Ryan."

"You are a fan then."

"Yes."

Again, she waited. But this time, nothing.

"So were you inviting me to a game?"

"If you want the ticket."

"Would I be going with you, Jackson? Or

are you offering me a ticket to go on my own?"

"I could pick you up. We could go together. Or not."

This was fast becoming the most uncomfortable telephone conversation of Emma's life, and she dropped her head backward and closed her eyes.

"Well, here's a thought," she said. "Why don't you decide about that and get back to me. Good-bye, Jackson."

Items to Keep on Hand When Covering a Sculpted Cake with Fondant

1. PIZZA CUTTER — This tool is much easier to handle than a knife when cutting away excess fondant from the base of the cake.
2. ROLLING PIN — This tool is not only needed to roll out the fondant to about a quarter of an inch; it is also very handy in applying the fondant to the sculpted cake.
3. SMOOTHING TOOL — This tool looks like the one used to apply spackle to a damaged wall.
4. SCULPTING TOOLS — At first glance, this set looks very much like miniature gardening tools; however, they are used to form, shape, and imprint the fondant once it is placed and smoothed.

22

The cake had been filled, layered, and sculpted into the perfect shape of a baseball glove before going into the freezer overnight. Fee made sure it was crumb-coated and went to work on creating the little bride and groom for the top while Emma applied a thin layer of butter cream to the cake board and set the glove into place.

She rolled the brown fondant around the pin and had just begun to unroll it over the cake when the kitchen door popped open and Jackson stepped inside.

"Can I talk to you?"

"Not right now, unless it's an emergency. Can I see you after we get this cake together?"

Jackson stood there in the doorway, his head angled so that he could see what she was doing. "Is that your boyfriend's cake?"

Emma glared at him without moving a muscle.

"Ex-boyfriend," she clarified. "Yes."

"That's . . . amazing."

"Jackson?"

He lurched upright. "Sorry. I'll talk to you later, then?"

"Yes."

When he didn't turn to leave, she straightened and stared at him until he did.

Returning her attention to the glove, she draped it in the fondant, and shaped it with both hands, smoothing it out beneath her touch.

"That's going to look smokin'," Fee commented from a stool at the far side of the island. "So, what's going on between you and Boss Man?"

"What do you mean?"

"Come on, Em. The tension was so thick you could spread it between layers."

"Make yourself useful, Fiona. Hand me the smoothie."

Fee slid the tool toward her and took her place across from Emma.

"He's jealous, I think."

"The roses from Baseball Boy?"

"Yes."

"Ha! Good."

"So he called me yesterday and invited me to the Falcons game on Sunday."

"Very good."

"But he botched it so badly that I didn't know if he was tossing a ticket at me before he ran, or if he was actually asking me out."

"Typical."

"The thing is," she said as she rolled the cutter around the edges, slicing away the excess fondant around the base of the glove, "I don't even know if I want him to ask me out. I mean, he's still so in love with his late wife, Fee. I don't know how I could ever compete with that."

"Yeah, but . . . she's dead, Em."

"Not breathing, maybe. But she *is not dead.* Not to him, anyway."

Fee reached across the counter and took the cutter out of Emma's hand. "Look, it's like this. Are you warm for the guy? Does he have what it takes to float your boat?"

"I don't know," she stated, and then she sighed. "Yes. He really does."

"Do you have stuff in common?"

She nodded.

"Can you look down the lane and see him standing there?"

Emma tipped her head to the side and smiled. "Way down there, at the very end of the lane. Yes, he could be there."

"Then what are you waiting for? Grab a taxi and go."

"I can't."

"Why?"

"There's construction going on down the lane. Road closed."

The *phloop!* of the kitchen door sounded again, and both of them fell instantly silent as Jackson walked back in.

"The thing is," he said to her, looking very much like a rod was tucked up his jacket to hold him upright, "I have these tickets. Falcons-Redskins, on Sunday. Would you like to go?"

"I would," she replied.

"I'll pick you up at your place around eleven. We'll be joining some of my buddies for tailgating prior to the game, so come hungry. There's a lot of food."

"Food is good."

"All right then. I'll see you on Sunday."

"Sunday."

The moment Jackson disappeared behind the flopping door, Fee appeared at Emma's side, but they both faced the door in silence until its last *phloop.*

Raising two fists before her, Fee grinned from ear to ear as Emma tapped them with her own. Then came the palm slaps, first two and then another two, a quick couple of hip bumps, and then raspy whispers —

"Hoo-yeah!"

■ ■ ■ ■

Emma bounded out her front door and trotted down the stairs toward Jackson where he stood leaning against his car.

"I was headed up to get you," he told her.

"No need. I saw you pull up."

Her silky hair was twisted at the back and pushed upward with a big clip, flopping back down over it in a perfect, bouncy curve. She wore a black and red leather Falcons bracelet on her left wrist, and the oversized bright red Falcons jersey was knotted at the hip of washed-out Levi jeans with a rip under the left knee. Jackson wondered if she bought them that way or created it herself with some scissors or a dull knife.

As he held the car door for her, he noticed a sprinkling of freckles dotting her nose and cheeks and, when she grinned at him, her lips shimmered with a pale pink glaze. He closed the door and rounded the car, thinking that she could easily pass for a college student, and hoping he didn't look like her perverted older professor in his Dockers and black Henley.

When they reached the Georgia Dome, Jackson went ahead and parked in the first spot he could find. It was about half a mile out, but he knew precisely where to go to find his friends. He and Emma walked side by side for most of the way, but then she slipped her arm through his and angled her face up toward him. The whole scene felt strangely familiar to him, from the sideways pirate smile with which she charmed him to the intimate loop of her arm through his.

They made their way to Decker Stanton's SUV. Like every game Sunday, Decker and Joe had likely arrived at the break of day to claim their spots near the grass. There were lawn chairs lined up, a grill was set up behind Decker's Yukon, and a long folding table stood at the back of Joe Ridgeway's F-150 next to the grill.

"Glad you could join us," Decker called to them as he tended the burgers and dogs on the grill.

"Traffic," Jackson called back to them. "I want you all to meet Emma Rae Travis. She works for me at the hotel."

"Hey, Emma Rae. Welcome to The Bullpen."

Emma smiled and waved at him.

"That's Decker Stanton," Jackson told her. "And this is his wife over here, Felicity."

"Hey, girl," Felicity said in that cool way she had about her.

"Roger Strang and Deanna Brody over here. And that's Joe and Connie Ridgeway. Everyone, this is Emma."

After the circle of greetings made it around, Emma strolled over to the table and offered to help them set out the food. Joe took the opportunity to elbow Jackson in the ribs.

"I'm sorry," he joked. "After two seasons of stagging it, you show up with a chick in tow after never even mentioning her?"

"First of all, Emma is no *chick*."

Joe raised his hands in surrender and laughed.

"Second, I'm mentioning her now."

"So she works with you over at the hotel. What's she do for you there?"

"She bakes wedding cakes."

After overhearing Jackson's comment, Connie hurried toward Emma. "You're the one who took the award for your wedding cakes!" she exclaimed in a high-pitched Southern drawl. "I read all about you in the newspaper. Why on earth would you go to work for Jackson Drake?"

They all laughed, and Emma tossed Jackson a toothy grin. "I'll let you know when I figure that out."

Joe leaned in close and whispered, "She's a keeper, man."

Jackson hadn't really thought of this as a *trial date* until that moment, but then he had to ask himself whether the swelling pride pushing against his chest betrayed a trace of it. Had he brought Emma along just to see how she fared when tossed into the lion's den with his friends?

Emma's laughter chimed like a church bell in the distance, and he watched as she casually chatted with Felicity. Standing there together, they looked like opposites in the same set of bookends; Felicity with her dark African-American skin and wild, natural curls, and Emma, her pale skin flushed, and her hair smooth and silky and twisted away from her face. Each of them was extraordinarily beautiful in her own way, but as different as two women could be.

In fact, Emma stood out that way the entire day; completely different from the other women, but so much a part of their group after such a short amount of time. After they'd eaten and visited, Emma helped Felicity, Joe, and Connie clean up the table, and Deanna stopped at Jackson's chair and rubbed his shoulder lightly before leaning down and softly telling him, "I like her, Jackson."

He didn't quite know what to say to that, so he just smiled at her, and Deanna sauntered away with Roger to carry the trash to one of the nearby receptacles.

It was more of the same as the eight of them made their way to the Dome and found their seats. The conversation was casual, and Emma was very much a part of it, never once giving off the air of being the new kid on their block.

She watched the game with sharp, attentive focus, cheering in all the right places, groaning at every misstep. Emma was as much a *Falcaholic* as the rest of the thousands crowded into the Dome to watch their team wipe the floor with the Washington Redskins.

Ryan had a short throw that turned into a forty-yard touchdown play, and a ten-yarder to Tony Gonzalez that gave the Falcons a 14-7 lead at halftime. Emma spontaneously exploded from her seat, joining Decker, Felicity, and Roger in one of their Falcon happy dances that looked like a hybrid version of that chicken dance people sometimes did at weddings.

Desi couldn't have cared less about football, or any other sport for that matter.

The comparison jolted him, and Jackson leaned back in the uncomfortable seat with a sigh. Why was he always comparing Emma to Desiree? Would a time ever come when he was ready to start a relationship that didn't hinge on memories of Desiree?

The Falcons took the game, 28-14, and the jubilation of the crowd seemed to carry them along out of the stadium. Emma chattered with Felicity most of the way, and the two women embraced warmly when they said their good-byes in front of the Yukon.

"I'll call you next week," he heard Felicity promise, and Emma was still waving at them halfway down the parking lot aisle.

"That was so much fun!" Emma exclaimed when they were finally out of sight. "Thank you so much for inviting me, Jackson. I really liked your friends."

"I'd say they really liked you too."

"I'm going to have Felicity over to the tea room next week. She's awesome."

Her enthusiasm was almost contagious, and Jackson wrapped an arm around Emma's shoulder and pulled her close to him as they walked. After a moment, she slipped her arm around his waist and leaned into him slightly. Once again, it was a moment of familiarity, as if they'd walked a hundred streets, just like this.

Emma was much taller than Desiree, and she fit into the fold of his embrace in a much different way. Still, there was something natural and relaxed about the easy manner they had when they were together.

When they reached his car, Jackson pulled open the passenger door for Emma. Instead of passing, she moved directly in front of him and stopped. When he looked down at her, he felt the click of their gazes locking together, and Emma slipped her arms around his neck and tugged him toward her.

"Thank you, Jackson," she whispered, extending her neck until her lips reached his.

The kiss was tender and provocative, lingering just long enough to show him she meant business, but not long enough to make promises she wasn't going to keep.

"I had such a great time," she said, still close enough that he could feel the warmth of her breath as it caressed his face.

"I did, too, Emma. I hope we can do it again."

"I'd really like that."

She slipped into the passenger seat, and Jackson closed the door before jogging around the car. He hadn't realized it had gotten so cold out, but his skin was now tingling from it. Once he started the car, he flipped on the heat.

"It should warm up in a minute."

The drive back to Roswell was filled with conversation about the game and his friends, about the symphony group coming into the hotel the following month, and a murder mystery weekend being planned by the couples ministry of one of Atlanta's biggest churches.

"Maddie feels like we can make it a regular event for them every year," he told her.

"That might help bring in other church groups as well."

"Maybe. They're incorporating a Sunday service into the plot, and they're going to use Miguel."

"Is he okay with that?" she asked. "I mean, the whole murder thing."

"Oh, I'm sure he'll weave a spiritual message in there somewhere. It's one of the things Miguel does best."

"Yes," she commented with a knowing nod. "He certainly does."

They both fell silent, and Jackson couldn't help replaying his conversation with Miguel the night of the dinner at Norma's.

There's a saying in Latin, Miguel had said to him. *It means, "Bidden or not bidden, God is present."*

God had not been bidden by Jackson very much in recent memory. But according to Miguel, He was there anyway, watching over him, waiting to commune.

Jackson glanced over at Emma, and she chose that exact moment to look up at him as well. There was a certain shimmer in her eyes that drew him in for an instant, and then she unleashed one of those immaculate smiles on him.

I'm done for, he thought. *I don't stand a chance against that smile.*

Welcome to Morelli's
at The Tanglewood Inn

Award-Winning Chef
Anton Morelli

Your Dessert Menu
From the Award-Winning Kitchen
of
Emma Rae Travis

Key Lime Pie
The *pink flamingo* of Southern desserts
Tangy lime filling topped with whipped cream in a sweet graham cracker crust

Caramel Pecan Pie
A new twist on a Georgian specialty
Traditional pecan pie laced with sweet caramel and toasted coconut

Champagne Pistachio Cake
All your favorite flavors in one slice of heaven
Orange-pistachio cake with a ribbon of champagne and chocolate, sprinkled with powdered sugar

Praline Cheesecake
Straight from the recipes of old Southern living
Creamy cheesecake in a praline-and-graham cracker crust with a crunchy praline topping

Chocolate Revelation
For the discriminating chocolate lover . . . Brace yourself!
Six layers of chocolate cake filled with chocolate custard mousse and frosted with chocolate fudge

Apple Raspberry Cobbler
Tart tradition . . . with a twist
Granny Smith apple cobbler with whole raspberries, served warm with a scoop of vanilla ice cream

23

"Engaged."

It was her third time repeating it.

"Really," Emma stated, and she leaned back in the chair behind her desk and sighed. "You're sure?"

"I know it's been a short time," Fee reasoned, "but we're both as sure as we can be. Pete and I belong together."

"And he proposed."

"Dude. Take a breath. This is *good news.*"

Emma looked up at Fee and realized in that one instant that she'd never seen her friend so happy. Beneath the layer of pale foundation and black-black eyeliner, to the side of the nose ring and the choker of barbed wire, how could she have missed the beaming smile that Peter Riggs had brought to Fee's face?

"You're happy, Fiona?"

"Well, don't tell everyone," Fee grimaced. "But yeah. I'm pretty close to ecstatic."

Emma sighed again, then she stood up and rounded her desk and grabbed her friend with such vehemence that Fee stumbled slightly.

"Whoa," she said on a chuckle as Emma engulfed her with both arms. "Dude."

"You're very brave," Emma told her.

"Nah. Just captured."

Emma hugged her again, and then kissed her cheek several times.

"Somebody win the lottery?" Pearl asked from the doorway.

"I guess Fee did," Emma replied. She kissed her friend one more time before letting go of her. "She's getting married."

"Married! Peter?"

"Yup." Fee beamed.

"Married, really? How many phases did it take him?"

"Just two."

"Two!"

Emma sat down again, and Pearl sank into the chair on the other side of the desk.

"I've got cobblers in the oven," Fee told them, pointing toward the kitchen. Then she leaned down to make awkward eye contact with Emma. "You all right?"

"Fine," she replied with a sigh. "Go."

"Congrats," Pearl said, prompting Emma to straighten.

"Right! Congratulations."

Once Fee went to work in the kitchen, Pearl and Emma made eye contact.

"Huhh," Pearl snorted with a raised brow.

"You said it."

"Anything new with you and Jackson?"

"We had a date," Emma revealed.

"Oh, how was it?"

"Next to perfect."

"Oooh!"

"That was Sunday. I haven't heard from him since."

"Eww," Pearl soured. "Four days."

"Yeah. What about you and Anton?"

"We're coasting."

Emma shrugged one shoulder and nodded. "Better than After Care."

"I guess."

Once Pearl vacated her office, Emma closed the door and tried to focus on her sketch pad. She'd been working on the English rose wedding cake for Beverly Branson all morning. It should have been quick and simple, but she just couldn't get the sketches right, and she'd promised to fax them over before the end of the day.

Hoping for a little inspiration, she clicked on Beverly's e-mail from the previous morning.

"I've attached a photo of the beautiful

vintage hair sticks I'll be using in an up-do on my wedding day. I thought you could match the roses on the cake to these."

She opened the attachment and admired the exquisite detail. Just about the time that inspiration poked its head around the corner, Emma's office door opened and another corner with another head weighed in.

"Good morning, darling."

"Mother."

"You're trapped," Avery stated, closing the door behind her and taking the chair across from Emma. "You have to talk to me now."

Emma groaned softly and tossed her pencil down onto the half-finished sketch before her.

"I'm really busy, Mother."

"And you'll be very busy after I leave. But for this moment, right now, I need your attention."

Emma crossed her arms and leaned back in the chair. "All right."

"We've never gone this long without speaking, Emma Rae." Avery pressed the impeccable Chanel skirt with her hands, a sure sign that she was uneasy in this role of pursuer.

"I know," Emma told her. "And I'm sorry."

"I don't really think it's fair of you, either," she continued. "I mean, you're clearly still speaking to your father, and he was in that room too. It wasn't just me all alone in there. Although I suppose if I had been all alone, this wouldn't be an issue at all, would it?"

Emma smiled. Avery Travis had probably been flustered three, maybe four, times in her entire life.

With a sigh, she said, "I guess I expect more from you than I do from Dad."

Avery pressed her lips together and blinked — a long-standing expression meaning, "Go on."

"You've always been the more clear-headed, sensible one of the two of you, Mother. You know that you're like gasoline and a match, and yet you let him break you down. And now to find out that, after all these years, my parents are actually *still married* —"

"What!"

"Yes, Mother. Dad told me your dirty little secret."

"I hardly think —"

"How could you have kept that from me? As your only daughter, you didn't think I had a right to know?"

"Emma Rae, I never once told you that

your father and I had divorced."

"But you never corrected me when I said it."

The flame in her eyes drifted to embers. "True."

"I just don't understand why or how . . . I mean, what are you thinking?"

"Emma Rae," she said softly, "I love your father. I always have. As infuriating and maddening as he can be, and please do not mock me when I tell you this, for some reason I've always believed in our marriage."

Emma refrained from comment by biting the corner of her lip.

"I know. I can only imagine what you're thinking. But it's true."

"It's kind of hard to believe, the way you two go at it, Mother."

"Yes. I can see that." Avery sighed and examined the backs of her hands as they sat primly in her lap. "Your father has a bit of trouble with trust, Emma Rae. He's moody, and . . . and he can be *very grumpy* . . . and he expects the worst out of people . . . everyone except you. And for the rest of us, that can be a difficult obstacle to struggle against every day of your life."

"So, where do you stand?" Emma asked her. "I mean, are you together, are you apart, are you somewhere in between?"

"We're reassessing."

Emma sighed. "What does that mean?"

"It means I still want to be married to your father, may the Lord help me. So we've entered into a form of . . . well, into . . ."

"Mother, what?"

"Counseling."

"Counseling," she repeated. "Marriage counseling?"

"Sort of."

"Sort of marriage counseling. What is that?"

"Actually, we're seeing Reverend Ramos."

"Miguel?"

"Yes. He's been quite helpful, Emma Rae."

"You and my father are seeing a *reverend?*"

"We are."

"Does he *pray with you?*"

"Sometimes. But mostly, he listens, and he asks questions that provoke discussion between us. And you know better than anyone that getting your father to talk about his feelings is nothing short of miraculous."

Emma realized that her jaw was hanging open, and she shook her head and leaned back against the chair and closed her eyes for a moment. She tried to imagine Gavin and Avery Travis joining hands with Miguel Ramos and letting him pray for their *marriage.*

She could hardly even think it. In her head, they'd been long divorced. Now to find out that they had a marriage was —

Well, she didn't know what it was!

"You've spent more of your marriage apart than together, Mother."

"We've been together more than you know."

"Why doesn't that surprise me?"

Avery revealed a tentative smile. "I'm sorry, Emma Rae. We should have handled this differently, all the way around. But remember when your father came to Atlanta and moved back in with us?"

"That was the happiest time of my life."

"Until your high school graduation, when he withdrew again and went back to Washington."

Emma noticed a glaze of tears in her mother's dark eyes, and she reached across the desk toward her. It took a few seconds, but Avery surrendered her hands and clasped them with Emma's.

After Care, she realized in that instant. *My father is in Phase, like, 236 of After Care.*

For the first time since she'd found them in that clutch in the consultation room,

Emma remembered that her mother was probably the strongest woman she'd ever known.

"How do you hang on to your hope?" she asked her.

"Sometimes, by a thread," Avery admitted. "But if I didn't know *that I know that I know* that your father is the man God intended for me, I'd have snipped the thread and moved on a long time ago."

Now it was Emma's turn to tear up.

"Oh, Mother," she sniffed, squeezing Avery's hand. "God has a lousy sense of humor."

"Look who you're telling."

Fee jacked herself up to the counter and sat there, kicking her feet.

"Baseball cake presented," she announced as Emma sprinkled powdered sugar over three champagne pistachio cakes.

"So Danny and Callie are safely married?" Emma asked her.

"Looks like it."

"Thank God. Jackson would have throttled me if I broke up the hotel's first wedding couple."

Fee laughed as she hopped down to help Emma move the cakes from the center island.

"Listen," she said when they were through, "I was wondering about something. You know, speaking of weddings. Don't let this blow your mind or anything, but I was kind of hoping you'd be my maid of honor."

Emma turned slowly toward Fee and smiled. "Really?"

"I know, you probably didn't expect me to go with tradition, but there are some things you just can't sacrifice, you know? And having your best friend standing up there next to you when you make the biggest commitment of your life, well —"

Emma sliced Fee's words right in two with her embrace. "Of course I'll be your maid of honor, Fiona. I'd love that."

"Oh, good," she replied, and the words were muffled against Emma's shoulder. "Thanks."

Thrusting Fee away from her, and clamping her by the shoulders, Emma exclaimed, "Have you started shopping for the dress?"

Fee shook her head.

"I want in on that, okay? The dress and the cake are the best part!"

"Speaking of the cake, we kind of really want a crème brûlée."

"Really?" Emma grinned from one ear to the other. "I'd love that. When's the date?"

"We haven't decided on that yet. We're

talking about spring or summer, but there's no rush really. I'll let you know."

Emma regarded her friend with interest. Something was off. But what was it?

"Emma Rae?"

She looked up to find Danny standing in the doorway in blue jeans and tennis shoes, with a tuxedo jacket with tails.

"Danny. Congratulations."

"Yeah, I just stopped in to —" He glanced at Fee. "Can I talk to you alone?"

Fee got the message and grinned. "Don't have to hit me over the head with a baseball bat."

"Thanks," Danny tossed at her as Fee made her way past him, out of the kitchen.

"Sure thing. Em, I'll see you out front in ten?"

Emma nodded, grateful for the boundary.

"So that cake," Danny commented. "It was out of hand."

"You liked it?"

"I can't believe you can do that with cake, Emma Rae."

"Well, I've been designing cakes for a long time."

"Listen," he broached, and then hesitated, pressing the toe of his shoe into the corner of a checkerboard square on the floor. "Seeing you again . . ."

"Can I just stop you right there, Danny? I have something I need to say to you."

"Yeah. Okay. Sure."

"You are the luckiest guy on the planet. Callie adores you, and the two of you are going to make a really good life together."

"Well —"

"But only if you get one thing straight in your head, Dan."

He looked up at her with embers of curiosity burning the blue of his eyes into a deep indigo.

"Men have a tendency to get distracted," she told him. "They have something good in their hands, but they wonder if that shiny thing over there might be better, so they make excuses and they let themselves drift away from where they're supposed to be. It's kind of like when we went down to Clearwater on spring break. Do you remember that?"

"Y-y-yeah."

"You were out there in the Gulf on that big inner tube, remember? And you fell asleep for just a few short minutes, and by the time you woke up again you'd drifted so far away that we had to get a boat and go out and tow you back. Do you remember that?"

"Yeah. Good thing you were paying attention to how long I was out there."

"Well, that's kind of how life is. You can be floating along, and then get distracted by something else for just a few minutes and, before you know it, you're so far from shore that you might never get back." Emma narrowed her eyes and asked him, "Do you see what I'm saying?"

"Kinda."

"Don't get distracted, Danny. Focus on Callie, and stay focused on her."

"Yeah, okay."

"You and I are different people now. I'm not the one for you. I probably never was. You've found the person you're supposed to be with, so man up and make it work. Okay?"

"Well, yeah," he said on a sigh. "I was only just gonna tell you that it was cool to see you again. Once I thought about it, it kinda made me appreciate Callie even more."

"Oh." Emma bit her lip and smiled. "That's great. Hold that thought, and you two will be really happy."

Danny snickered. "Whadja think? I was gonna go all ape over you again? Nah, I'm over that. Callie's my bride now. You take care, Emma Rae. You'll find somebody eventually."

As he trotted through the kitchen door,

Emma gave an inward groan.

All that sage advice built up inside of me, and I wasted it on Danny Mahoney. Not so sage after all, am I?

The Five Most Important Questions to Ask Yourself When Composing Your Wedding Vows

1. When you were a kid, what did you imagine about your future spouse?
2. What does marriage actually mean to you now?
3. What are the three best things about the person you're about to marry?
4. What is your favorite memory of your fiancé?
5. What do you see when you look down the road of your marriage?

24

The instant she saw it in the newspaper, Emma knew what she had to do. And what a stroke of sheer genius it turned out to be too.

My Fair Lady was playing for one afternoon only on the big screen in an old retro theater downtown. It was the first movie Emma ever remembered seeing, and her Aunt Sophie had been the one to take her. She recalled that Sophie knew every word to every song back then, and Emma had seen it again so many times on her small screen at home that she knew them now as well.

When she glanced over at her aunt in the darkness of the refurbished 1920s theater, she saw that Sophie was enrapt. With her hands clasped together under her chin, her blue-gray eyes wide and reflecting the movement on the screen, wonder emanating from her smooth features, the woman looked half her age. *Eliza* floated up the staircase in her dark green jumper with the bright-white petticoat, singing about her evening and how she could have danced all night, and Sophie looked to Emma to be as light in her seat as wind in the trees. As her caretakers tried to prepare *Eliza* for bed, and all she knew for certain was that she could easily have danced all night, Sophie sang out along with her in a full, crystal clear voice. The ladies in the row behind them chuckled as she did.

Emma lost herself a bit as well, stepping directly into Audrey Hepburn's peach-colored suit and curved straw hat with the flower as she sang to Jackson — errr, *Freddy* — about the importance of stepping up to the plate. Words, she shouted from somewhere deep inside, were useless now. If Jackson wanted to create a future with her, words would no longer do him any good at all; he'd have to show her!

Sophie reached out and grabbed Emma's hand as *Eliza* vowed that life would go on without *Professor Henry Higgins,* despite his beliefs to the contrary, and she clutched it to her heart when *Higgins* finally admitted that he'd grown accustomed to *Eliza*'s face. Emma and Sophie left the theater hand-in-hand, and Sophie was luminous.

"Oh, Emma Rae, that was beautiful,

wasn't it? Thank you so very, very much for bringing me. Did you love it as much as I did?"

"I did, Aunt Soph. What do you say we go and have a cappuccino or a cup of tea? Do you think you can make it down to the end of the block?"

"I think I could dance that far on the air," Sophie told her, and she made Emma almost believe her.

Emma drew Sophie's arm through hers, and then tightly covered her hand. They walked slowly, and her aunt's steps were deliberate. When they reached the café at the corner, Emma helped Sophie get seated before she went to the counter and ordered a pot of tea and two cups.

"Do you like cream?" Emma asked once the tea had steeped.

"Please."

She dressed the tea for her aunt, and then moved the cup and saucer from the tray to the table before her.

"Does that *Henry Higgins* remind you of anyone you know?" Sophie asked her before taking a sip.

Emma chuckled. "Yes, Aunt Sophie. He certainly does."

She was astonished that her aunt was so lucid, that she could so astutely recognize

Jackson Drake in the character of —

"I thought you would see it. That Rex Harrison and your father could have been brothers, they look so much alike."

"Wait. Dad?"

"Oh, what that man put your mother through over the years, with his grumbly, growly arrogance."

"Did he?" she asked with a timid yet resolute sigh.

"First he's in, then he's out, and then he's back in again. It's a wonder poor Avery doesn't have whiplash, isn't it?"

As Sophie tended to her tea and crooned a chorus of "I'm an Ordinary Man," Emma couldn't help but picture her father in the part. Lowering her voice several octaves as she impersonated *Henry Higgins,* or perhaps Gavin Travis, musing about what happened to a man's life when he allowed a woman into it, Sophie had Emma in stitches.

Despite feeling a bit like she'd betrayed her father by the fact that he so easily slipped into the suit and guise of *Professor Higgins,* Emma still had to admit that her aunt was on to something.

"I'm going to have a meeting in the restaurant this afternoon," Jackson told Fee and Pearl from the door of the kitchen. "Would one of you mind setting up coffee service for two?"

"Glad to," Pearl replied.

"Fee, by the way, I heard there are congratulations due. Wonderful news about you and Peter."

"Thanks very much."

Jackson started out of the kitchen, then backed up. "Where's Emma?"

"She took the afternoon off," Fee told him. "She's spending it with her aunt."

He took a seat at his favorite table in the empty restaurant, fidgeting with the tablecloth as he wondered why he'd given in to the impulse of calling Miguel over to the hotel for a chat. He was more than capable of working things through on his own, after all.

Of course, if that were true, I'd probably have done it by now.

Pearl delivered a tray to the table and gave Jackson's shoulder a couple of pats.

"If you need a refill, or anything else, just give me a shout."

"Will do. Thanks, Pearl."

He'd just filled his own cup when he spotted Miguel heading toward him across the lobby, so he poured a second one as well.

"Thank you for meeting me, Miguel," he said as he got up, and the two of them shared a congenial handshake.

"I was happy to receive your call."

They sat down and made small talk over the coffee for a few minutes before Miguel asked what he might do for Jackson.

"I'm not entirely sure," he replied in earnest. "I've been thinking a lot about the things you said."

"I talk an awful lot, Jackson. Maybe you could narrow it down for me."

They both chuckled, and Jackson melted down to a serious fragment of a smile.

"I'm having a hard time moving on," he began. "You know, after Desi."

Miguel nodded. "But you're feeling that tug at your heart, the one that tells you it might be time?"

"Yes."

After a thoughtful pause, he asked, "With Emma?"

Jackson's eyes darted to Miguel's as he wondered just how obvious they had been about their growing attraction.

"I've sensed something building there."

Jackson ran his hands through his hair and sighed. "You have? It's that apparent?"

"To anyone paying attention," Miguel confirmed. "And she has feelings for you as well?"

"I'm not sure. I think so."

Miguel's dark eyes softened, and he leaned forward slightly toward him. "And what is it that's holding you back? Your memories, or something specific?"

"I suppose it's the memories," Jackson admitted. "It seems like every time we get close, I find myself comparing her to Desi. It doesn't seem fair to either of them."

"I can assure you that Desiree would not take issue with you moving on at this point, Jackson. I think you know that. But you're right, it's not fair to Emma to hold her up to the light when she doesn't know what you're looking for."

"I know," he said, shaking his head. "I know. But why do I keep doing that? When am I going to let Desi go and feel free to move on?"

Miguel took a draw from his coffee and smiled as he replaced the cup to its saucer. "You know, you probably don't want to hear this, but I'm going to be straightforward with you, Jackson. If you're asking me when you're going to stop thinking about your life with Desiree, my answer to you is that you never will do that."

Jackson raised an eyebrow. "Thank you, Miguel. You've been very helpful."

He chuckled. "Desiree was a very important part of your life. She's not going to be forgotten as you move on. She'll be integrated into your new life. It's a natural process for you to use her as the bar by which you measure others with whom you consider moving forward."

"So you're saying it's not a negative thing? Because it feels that way when it happens."

"I'm sure it does, because the emotions are new. You haven't found your groove with them yet. But new is not negative. New is just . . . *new.* You have to allow yourself to feel whatever you're going to feel, knowing that God has your best interests in His hands."

Jackson sighed. It seemed almost too pat, too perfect an answer. *Just do it. Let go and let God. He's got the whole world in His hands.*

"Does that resonate within you? Does it make sense?"

"I don't know. In some ways, yes. But —"

Jackson fell silent as he watched Gavin stride across the lobby straight for him. He took a deep breath, cleared his throat and rose from his chair.

"Mr. Travis, how are you today?"

"Good," he replied, then he smiled when he saw Miguel. "How are you, son?"

"Very well, sir."

Turning back to Jackson, he added, "I'm looking for my daughter. Is she around?"

"I think she's spending the day with Sophie."

"Ah." Gavin just stood there, as if he wasn't quite sure what to do next.

"We're having some coffee. Would you like to join us?"

He looked from Jackson to Miguel and back again before replying, "Yeah. Thanks."

Jackson grabbed a third cup and filled it before sitting down across from them.

"Are you being counseled, too?" Gavin asked him.

"Pardon me?"

"Miguel," he said with a nod. "He's been counseling Avery and me. I just thought —"

"Oh," Jackson said with a nod. "I guess he is."

"And I've interrupted. I can go, if you two want to —"

"No, no, please. We're just talking. I've been having a hard time letting go and moving forward after the death of my wife."

Gavin and Miguel shared a loaded glance.

"You know," Gavin said, and then he took a sip from his coffee. "I was married before Avery."

"I didn't know that."

"For three years. I was barely twenty-two when my wife was killed in a traffic accident."

Jackson's chest constricted slightly. "I'm so sorry to hear that."

"I had a very hard time moving on myself. When I met Avery, I was in no way prepared for a woman like her." Gavin shook his head and grinned. "She's a handful of woman for a healthy man."

Jackson understood, but he didn't comment.

"You know, I think my daughter has grown quite fond of you, young man."

Lowering his eyes, he admitted, "She's a wonderful woman."

"Yes, she is. And like her mother, she deserves more than someone who's going to make choice after choice to paddle around in the past rather than go ahead and swim over to the other side. If I can be so bold, Jackson, don't be an idiot like I was."

Jackson met Gavin's gaze and held it for a second or two.

"Don't be so afraid of losing someone again that you never take a chance on being *with* someone. Keep your memories, boy. But take them with you. Don't just sit back there and drown in them. And for pity sake, don't use them over and over as an excuse to pull you away from the next good thing you might have in store."

After a moment's thought, Jackson turned

to Miguel. "Are you responsible for this?"

Without a word, Miguel simply pointed upward and smiled.

A moment later, they were interrupted by an unfamiliar man in a very expensive suit approaching their table.

"Good afternoon," he said in what Jackson perceived as a slight French accent. "I am looking for a young lady, please. Emma Travis."

"Emma's away from the hotel this afternoon," Jackson said as he extended his hand. "I'm Jackson Drake. Can I relay a message to her for you?"

"Luc Granville. I would like to steal her."

Jackson chuckled. "I'm sorry. Steal her?"

"*Oui.* Steal her. Steal her away."

Jackson looked to Gavin just as he stood up.

"I'm the girl's father," he declared. "I think you better tell me just what you're talking about."

FUN FACTS ABOUT FRENCH BAKING

- A *pâtisserie* is a French bakery specializing in cakes, pastries, and breads.
- In France, you may only use the word *patisserie* in the name of your business if it is run with a *maître pâtissier* (master pastry chef) on the premises.
- The *pâtissier* is a trained baker who has completed formalized training.
- Often, the *pâtissier* has also served as an apprentice under the tutelage of a *maître pâtissier.*
- American studies in the *pâtisserie* and baking arts include artisan bread production, the creation of chocolate/sugar showpieces, and classic European pastry production.

25

It was five-thirty by the time Emma returned to The Tanglewood. She parked in the back and entered through the rear door of the restaurant. They'd had half a dozen reservations for the tea room that afternoon, and she planned to head straight in to talk to Fee, wondering if everything went well.

A scuffle of raised voices drew her attention and, when she rounded the corner, she saw a group gathered near the entrance. Her father and Jackson appeared to be yelling at a man she didn't know, while Fee tossed around some very animated Italian, apparently directed at Anton as Pearl made every effort to keep him calm.

"What's going on?" she asked, but her question fell on deaf ears.

As she approached, she met Miguel's gaze, and he hurried toward her.

"What's this all about?" she asked him.

"You, I'm afraid."

She looked on curiously, trying to catch hold of some snippet of conversation that made sense to her.

"This is my hotel," Jackson announced to the stranger, "and I'll thank you to leave the premises immediately."

The stranger said something she didn't understand. Was he speaking French?

"Hellooooo," she called out, and the whole group fell silent and all eyes landed on Emma.

Her father was the first to speak. "Princess, there you are. I want you to —"

And then she was lost again beneath the tangle of voices and questions and accusations.

"Did you do this because of me?" she heard Pearl exclaim before tugging at Anton's arm. "You did this, didn't you? Because I talked to you about Jackson and Emma —"

The roaring hum of other voices drowned them out, and Emma couldn't focus in on any one of them.

"Hold it!" she shouted, and they faded once again. Before they could resume the craziness, she insisted, "One at a time, please. Daddy, what are you doing here?"

"I came to see you."

"And Fiona, why are you shouting in Italian?"

"I'm trying to make Anton understand that he can't just call his friend into this hotel and help him drag you away by the hair like some . . . some . . . culinary caveman!"

"Who are you?" she asked the stranger in the very expensive blue suit.

"I am Luc Granville, and I've come to steal you away, Emma Travis!" he announced with *very French* flair.

She immediately wished she hadn't paused to think that over because the cacophony of voices rang out again, and she couldn't understand a single phrase of it. In desperation, she cut through them toward Jackson. Tugging at his hand, she dragged him behind her by the wrist across the kitchen and into her office, where she closed the door.

"What on earth!" she exclaimed as she plopped down in the chair behind her desk. "Who is the French guy, and why does he want to kidnap me?"

Jackson folded into one of the chairs flanking her desk and groaned. "Luc Granville is evidently an old colleague of Morelli's. He has a fleet of bakeries across France, Anton told him you're some sort of pastry genius, and now he's here trying to hire you away from me to start a franchise here in the States." Before she could open her mouth to respond, he quickly wound himself up tighter than a wristwatch. "And if you're thinking of taking him up on his offer, let me remind you that we have a contract. You are exclusive to The Tanglewood for three years and —"

"Jackson, please!" she interjected, raising one hand in the air. "I know we have a contract."

"And while I have you here behind closed doors," he added and then softened, "I'd like to speak to you about our date last weekend."

She eyed him for a long moment.

"Oh. Was that a date, Jackson? I thought it was just two friends going to a football game."

"Well, I sort of thought of it as a date," he remarked.

Emma felt her blood pressure bubble upward toward the top of her head.

"No. That wasn't a date. I know this for certain because, once you dropped me off at my door, I never saw or heard from you again."

"Emma —"

"Now I'm going out there to meet Mr.

Granville. You are free to stay in here, or to come out there, either way. I don't care, as long as you don't continue shouting at me or talking about nonexistent dates."

Ten minutes later, the group of them was gathered in the restaurant, except for Fee, who looked on from the kitchen, and Emma and Luc Granville were seated in her office behind a closed door and too many windows. Fee's scowl cut straight through the glass and pressed in on Emma's forehead until it throbbed.

"You've caused quite a stir, Mr. Granville."

"Luc."

"Luc," she enunciated. "May I ask why you chose to talk to my co-workers and family before you brought your offer to me?"

He grinned at her. "Enthusiasm?"

"Well, thank you. However, I hate to burst your enthusiastic bubble, but I'm under contract to The Tanglewood. I couldn't leave and come to work for you even if I wanted to."

"If you want to come to work for me, Miss Travis," he declared in bumpy English, "I can make this happen."

"Again, thank you. But I really don't want to go anywhere, Luc. I'm afraid you've wasted a lot of time. And generated a lot of grief and lung power."

"I am assured by my friend Anton that Miss Bianchi is more than capable of taking over for you here. And if you will only consider making this very lucrative move —"

"Anton is correct. Miss Bianchi really is more than capable," she told him. "But I don't go anywhere without her, and I'm certainly not going to leave Mr. Drake and his hotel in the lurch. So you can see how that creates a rather insurmountable problem."

"Nothing is insurmountable, Miss Travis. There's more to hear about my offer. You listen five more minutes, and then you decide if the problem is truly insurmountable."

When Emma finally emerged from her kitchen, Fee was on her heels. Emma didn't even make eye contact with Jackson as she passed him; she simply paused in front of Anton, planted a kiss on his cheek and squeezed his hand.

"Il mio tesoro," he said, and they exchanged smiles that looked to Jackson to be almost loving.

"Emma, I think we should talk about —" Jackson began.

"I'm going home," she announced. "And Fee is going with me."

With that, she resumed her staunch mission toward the lobby.

Fee turned back toward them for an instant, then she fumbled to catch up to Emma.

"Emma," he called after her, but the solid brace of her shoulders told him she had no intention of slowing down. Turning back to Anton, Jackson sighed. "Why would you bring this on? Haven't we treated you well here? Haven't we given you everything you've asked for?"

"Sì veramente," Morelli replied stoically. "This has nothing to do with me."

"It has everything to do with you," Jackson corrected him. "You brought this down on me, but why?"

"Una questione del cuore," he answered as if Jackson might know what it meant.

In desperation, he looked to Pearl, and she nodded knowingly and touched his hand. "A matter of the heart, Jackson. Anton feels Emma's heart is no longer safe here."

"Her what? What are you saying?"

"Lei è un uomo molto egoistico," Anton growled, pointing a solid finger at Jackson. Then he turned to Pearl and softened as he

added, *"Sono qui finito."*

The two of them swept out of the room and into Anton's kitchen without so much as a glance back at him.

Jackson took three short steps backward and plopped into the nearest chair. After a moment, Gavin sat down on one side of him and Miguel on the other.

"What just happened here?" he asked them.

"Hah! Schah," Gavin puffed out as he scratched his head.

"Not one clear clue," Miguel added, and the three of them just stared ahead, toward the closed door to Anton Morelli's kitchen.

The door on the other side of it popped open just then, and Luc Granville stepped out of Emma's kitchen. He paused just long enough to straighten his tie and shoot Jackson a fleeting glance, then he sauntered through the lobby and out the front door of the hotel.

Important Translations for the Savvy Hotel Owner

Wedding cake (English)
Torta nuziale (Italian)
Gâteau de noce (French)

Bridal hotel (English)
Hotel nuziale (Italian)
Hôtel de mariée (French)

Gourmet meals (English)
Pasti di buongustaio (Italian)
Repas de gourmet (French)

Happily ever after (English)
Felicemente mai dopo (Italian)
Heureusement jamais après (French)

Bumpy road ahead (English)
Le strada ineguali avanti (Italian)
La route irrégulière en avant (French)

26

"Are you going to say something eventually? Do you need some insulin?"

Emma blinked. She looked over at Fee, perched on the arm of the sofa. "Sorry. I was just processing."

"Dude. I wanna process too."

Emma chuckled. "Sorry."

"So turn on the light. It's dark in here," Fee teased, tapping her temple with her index finger. "What did Granville say to you, and how is this going to play out?"

"Could you sit on a cushion?" Emma asked, cringing. "Maybe a chair?"

Fee slid down the arm of the couch with a plop. Seated at the opposite end of the sofa, she looked at Emma over the bridge of her square glasses. "Spill."

"Okay!" Emma leaned forward and rubbed her hands together. "So it's really all about Jackson."

"I don't get it."

"Anton has been watching us, and I suspect that Pearl has filled him in as well."

"Loose lips."

"Mm," Emma said with a nod. "Well, Luc Granville and Anton have apparently known each other since they were knee-high, and Anton called on his friend for help after he cooked up this whole thing in hopes that Jackson would come to his senses in the face of possibly losing me, face what he's feeling about me, confess his undying love —"

"And you both live happily ever after," Fee finished.

"I guess. Blah blah blah."

"Kind of ironic, coming from someone who's had a decade-long turtle race toward love himself."

Emma giggled. "Very ironic."

"So there's not really an offer on the table from Granville." Fee sighed.

"That's the interesting part."

Her eyes darted toward Emma, and she waited.

"Granville did some research, and now he *really wants me to come to work for him.*"

Fee pressed her lips together and her eyes widened.

"He's offered to buy my three-year contract from Jackson, and double my salary, and pay my expenses to *move to Paris for six months.*”

Emma raised her palm in the air, expecting a high-five slap. When it didn’t come, she lowered her hand and shrugged.

“Well, what do you think of that?”

After a long moment’s thought, Fee cocked her head and sighed. “I think I’d like to know what you think first.”

“Meaning?”

“Meaning . . . Are you going to abandon everything for a trunk full of francs and a view of the Eiffel Tower?”

“Fee —”

“Really!” Fee exclaimed, then popped up from the couch and stood there, at the other end of it. “Is this what you’re telling me, Emma?”

“Fiona.”

“And forget me for a minute. You would do that to Jackson? To his sisters? Just to . . . to tango with . . . with . . . a *Frenchman?!*”

“Settle down, will you? We’re just talking here.”

“Talking about what?” she asked her. “What exactly are we talking about here?”

“We’re talking about a successful French businessman looking at me and seeing someone worth a gazillion American dollars to him. That’s all. I am sharing that excitement with my best friend. This guy looked at me . . . at what we do, Fee, and he thought it was valuable enough to buy out a three-year contract and double my salary! Do you know what that means? Well, I'll tell you. It means that two girls making pastries at The Backstreet Bakery one day are now *on the map* the next day!"

"So you're not thinking about accepting his offer, then?"

Emma stretched out and propped her feet on the sofa and crossed them at the ankle, then folded her arms behind her head and grinned. "Of course not."

Fee picked up Emma's feet and nudged them back to the floor before occupying the space where they'd been on the other end of the couch.

Emma leaned over and took her friend's hand and jiggled it. "Fee. We're building something here. You and me, together. I'm not going anywhere that you aren't going too."

Fee smiled. "Well, you've just saved yourself from a hard sock in the gut."

"Besides, not only wouldn't I ever think of doing that to you, but I couldn't do it to —"

When she paused, Fee laughed.

"Jackson?"

Emma tilted into half a shrug. "I love him, Fee."

Fee straightened. "You love him? Like with sugar sprinkles and chocolate sauce, and the whole big shebang?"

She nodded. "Something awful. I think this is the first time I've said it out loud, but my heart's been screaming from the top of its lungs for weeks now."

"Yeah. I've heard it a few times," Fee admitted. "I think it's like when you shout down into the Grand Canyon. It echoes for all of the rest of the world to hear."

"Yeah?"

"Oh, yeah."

Emma groaned and tossed her head back against the arm of the sofa and flung her feet up into Fee's lap. "What am I gonna do, Fee?"

Fee patted Emma's ankles several times. "You know how those burros take you right down into the canyon?"

Emma grimaced. "Not really. I've never been to the Grand Canyon."

"Well, they offer you all kinds of ways to get your canyon on. In your case, you don't want to take a helicopter ride over Jackson, Em. You want to rent a donkey and go right down in there and get him."

Emma's eyes narrowed, and she gave her

forehead a brisk rub. "English, Fiona."
"You love him, right?"
"Right."
"Does he love you back?"
"Some days, I think he might."
"Well, I know he does."
"Really?"
"And we're just going to go digging into that big old cavern known as Jackson's heart and *excavate!*"
"How?"
"Prayer."
Emma dropped her hands from her face and stared at her friend. "Pardon?"
"What, you don't think prayer works? How do you think you two have gotten this far? Jackson's sisters, Miguel, me, Peter . . . We've all been praying you into this canyon, Em. Now you just grab Jackson, and we'll pray you both right back out to solid ground."
Each of them jumped at the knock on the door, and Fee grabbed Emma's hand.
"Let's start now."
Dragging her hand from Fee's grasp, Emma tripped toward the window and peered outside to see Jackson's car parked at the curb behind Fee's. She twirled around and pulled a face of panic.
"Is it him?" Fee asked, and she nodded.

Emma took in a deep breath before she tugged open the door. Fee slid into her jacket.

"Can I talk to you?" Jackson asked Emma, and she nodded. When he noticed Fee behind her, he hesitated. "I'm interrupting."

"Nah," Fee said, and she eased past him. "We were just talking about the Grand Canyon. Have you ever been, Jackson?"

"When I was a kid," he remarked.

"Overwhelming, isn't it?"

"I guess."

"But worth the trip. Don't you agree?"

"Oooo-kay!" Emma interjected, and she crossed back to Fee, tugged her by the arm, and nudged her to the door. "See you tomorrow, Fee."

She chuckled as she pulled the door shut behind her. "Later, you two. Happy trails."

Emma leaned against the closed door and looked up at Jackson. She heaved in a deep breath and then used it to puff air up under her bangs to lift them out of her eyes. Then she just waited.

And waited.

Finally, she padded across the living room and eased into the chair. She sat on the edge and crossed her legs, then folded her hands and rested them on her lap.

"You wanted to talk to me?"

Jackson just stood there, staring at her. He looked like he was about to say something, then he sighed and put his hands on his hips. When she was almost certain he'd turned to stone in that position, he dropped his hands and sighed again.

"It was a date," he said, his voice tight against his throat.

"I beg your pardon?"

"The football game," he said as he slowly approached her. Sitting down on the corner of the coffee table, he added, "It was a date."

"Really."

"Really. And if you're actually going to still be around in the future, I'd like to ask you out on another one."

"And it took you all week to sort that out, did it?"

"Well," he began, and then swallowed hard before continuing. "It was really my talk with your father that —"

"My father!"

She stared him down until the heat of it melted him. "He told me about his first wife, and how she died unexpectedly."

Emma's heart beat double-time. "He told you that? Daddy never talks about her."

"I think he thought it might help me. You know. After Desi."

Emma nodded, wondering what her father had in mind with a conversation like that one.

"And did it?"

"What?"

"Help."

"Oh. Yes, actually. It did."

Emma sighed. "I'm glad."

"He doesn't want me to make the same mistakes with you that he made with your mother."

Emma thought that over. "There are too many to choose from. You'll have to be more specific."

"All that really matters, Emma, is that I have very deep feelings for you, and I haven't been able to reconcile them to the residual ones still banging around in here." He tapped his chest several times, and then arched his eyebrow at her. "You know what I mean?"

"I think so."

The rhythm of her pulse started to pick up as Emma speculated about where the conversation might be headed.

"Are you going to leave, Emma? Do you want out of your contract with me?"

She smiled. "No, Jackson. I don't want to go anywhere."

"Are you sure?"

"Well, it was a great offer," she told him, shaking her head. "It's not easy to turn it down."

"But you're going to turn it down," he stated matter-of-factly.

"I already have."

"Can I ask why?" he said softly, and then he reached out and took her hand between both of his. "Why do you want to stay?"

"Why do you *want me to* stay?"

Jackson grinned. "You're not going to make this easy on me, are you?"

"Not at all."

He broke eye contact for a moment, and she got the sense that he was trying to compose himself. She considered putting him out of his misery and just telling him how she felt. Maybe putting it right out there on the table would —

"The thing is," he said, cutting her inner dialogue right in two, "I love you."

Her eyes popped open wide, and her jaw dropped slightly, leaving her mouth open in a tiny round O.

"Huh?"

He smiled. "I love you. And I don't want to make the mistake of not telling you, not showing you, because I think a woman like you needs —"

Emma lifted her free hand and snapped it

to his mouth, holding it there until Jackson fell silent.

"And tomorrow morning when you wake up and remember that you've said this to me," she began, pausing to catch her breath, "are you going to retreat into After Care for two weeks? Start avoiding me? Not call me?"

"After Care?" he repeated through her fingers, and she dropped her hand and groaned.

"It's what men do," she said. "Advance, retreat, advance, retreat. Are you gonna retreat again, Jackson?"

"I am not."

She sighed, and her shoulders dropped considerably. "How do you know? How can you say that now?"

"I just can."

"But later when you think it over —"

"After I think it over, I'll be inclined to freak out a little bit," he acknowledged. "And then I'll remember the glimmer in your eyes and the curve of your smile." He paused to run a finger down the line of her jaw, and he grinned at her. "I'll remember what your hair smells like when I hold you very close, and I'll remind myself how God blessed me one rainy afternoon and gave me the sudden craving for something sweet, and I walked into that little bakery and found you."

She opened her mouth to object, but now it was Jackson's turn to silence Emma, and he placed two fingers over her lips.

"You had flour on your cheek," he recalled. "And then later, when you came to The Tanglewood and tripped over the linens in the lobby, you had icing all over your nose and chin."

She chuckled, and Jackson caressed her cheek before drawing his hand away.

"God blessed my life early on," he told her. "Desiree was the best thing that had ever happened to me. When I lost her, I was quite certain I'd never find that again."

The *rat-a-tat-tat* in her ears turned out to be her own heartbeat, and Emma's eyes misted over with a glaze of unexpected, prickly emotion.

"Why God has chosen to bless me for a second time, only He knows for sure," he went on. "But I'm not going to take it for granted. I'm not going to lose it by tripping over my own two feet. I love you, Emma Rae Travis. And what I need to know is . . . Do you love me too?"

Emma jumped to her feet, propelled by sheer instinct. Her head spun a little as she paced behind the sofa for a lap or two and then made her way to the window and stood in front of it, staring out at the street.

She blinked twice, pushing the tears standing in her eyes to cascading streams down the slope of her face. When she blinked a third time, she was able to bring Fee's car into focus where it was still parked in front of Jackson's. Fee was seated behind the wheel, very still, her head bowed, and Emma realized that her friend was out there . . . *praying.*

A sudden burst of laughter popped out of her, and Emma spun around to find Jackson standing close behind her, his eyes bearing down on her with the embers of a very serious fire burning in them.

"I feel woozy," she told him on a raspy whisper, and Jackson blinked hard.

"Oh. Do you need something to eat? Can I get your monitor for you?"

"No," she replied, and she lifted one shoulder into an awkward shrug.

"What is it then?"

Emma grinned at him timidly as she admitted, "I love you, too, Jackson."

You Are Cordially Invited
To Attend a (Very Secret) Wedding
at
The Tanglewood Inn

The Anonymous Bride & Groom
would appreciate your attendance
in the Desiree Ballroom
at
9:00 p.m.
on
Friday Evening
to witness a private ceremony
in celebration of their
Love, Commitment & Joy

Formal Attire is Requested
and your complete discretion is
required.

(Don't you just love a good surprise?)

27

Emma looked down at the engraved invitation card that she'd found on her desk earlier that same day, and she read it through one more time.

A secret wedding ceremony at The Tanglewood.

She'd been speculating all afternoon, and again now she wondered who it could be. Pearl and Anton tripped across her mind first, but she dismissed the thought with a grin. Anton probably had a few dozen more sessions of After Care in him, after all. No, it wasn't Anton and Pearl.

Several times that day, she'd chuckled at the unlikely idea that she herself was the unsuspecting bride mentioned on the parchment card. She fantasized about how Jackson might have plotted out the event with the help of his sister Madeline; the two of them scheming about how they would get her there without betraying the plan.

And then for the second time since finding the invitation propped up against her telephone, Emma realized there was already a very likely bride and groom on The Tanglewood's radar.

Of course it's Fee and Peter. It can't be anyone else.

She recalled her friend's excitement when she'd shared the news of their engagement. That had to be who it was, and how like Fee to take such a unique and intimate track to the altar.

"Any more thoughts on our bride and groom?"

She spun around to find Jackson standing behind her. This wasn't the first time she'd seen him in a tuxedo, but he certainly took her breath away as if it were.

"I think it's Fee and Peter," she whispered to him.

"I suspect you're right."

"It has to be," she stated with confidence. Then she asked him, "Doesn't it?"

Jackson nodded. "Has to be."

He extended his arm to her, and Emma thought how natural it had become to walk with him that way, arm in arm. In the month or so since he'd declared his love for her, they'd slipped into the effortless groove of a couple. It seemed like such a long time ago when they were foreign to one another, still getting to know each other. She caressed his arm as they reached the foyer.

Jackson tried the door to the smallest of the three ballrooms, but it was locked. With a shrug, he turned back toward Emma.

"You look so beautiful," he told her softly.

Emma glanced down at the beaded top of her scarlet red dress. She ran her hands over the black chiffon skirt and straightened the thick velvet sash that tied at the waist in a soft, smooth bow.

"I bought this dress two weeks ago with no idea where I would wear it," she told him.

"Fashion destiny," he teased.

Emma grinned at him. He was so handsome that it was almost painful. Jackson slipped his arm around her waist and drew her toward him, pecking her lips with a soft kiss.

"I love you," he murmured.

"I love you too."

"Hey!" Fee called out, and Emma watched her cross toward them in a sleek black dress with a full-length red hooded cape tied loosely over it. She released her loose grip on Peter's hand. "So what's going on? Do you guys know what this shindig is all about?"

"Oh, come on," Emma said on a chuckle. "You can come clean. We know it's you two."

Peter glanced at Fee, and the two of them laughed.

"We thought it was you," he said.

Emma angled her head toward Jackson, and he shrugged. "I don't know, then."

"Whoever it is, they have great taste in music," said Pearl as she and Anton rounded the corner. "I just saw Ben Colson down in the lobby."

"Ben Colson," Emma repeated. "Who in the world is getting married here tonight?"

Norma and her husband Louis arrived at just that moment, and Norma rubbed her brother's arm as she stepped up beside him. "I was kind of hoping it was you and Emma."

"Us?" Jackson scoffed. "Not likely."

Emma's heart thumped a couple of fast beats, and she bit her lip. *Do you have to be so quick to balk at us as likely candidates for marriage?*

"I just meant that this wouldn't be our style," he said, instantly aware of her thoughts. His attention was diverted as Madeline and Georgiann rounded the corner, both of them so elegant in their long, beautiful dresses.

"Maddie, did you arrange this event?" Jackson asked her. "Who are we here to see?"

Madeline gave them catlike smile. "You'll see, little *bruthah.* Just five more minutes, and all of your questions will be answered."

Madeline poked a key into the door and turned it. When she pulled it open and exposed the elaborate decorations of flowers and candles on the other side, the whole group of them gasped and sighed in unison.

"How lovely!" Norma exclaimed.

"Go on in and take your seats," Madeline told them. "We'll get started in just a few minutes."

Emma slid her hand into Jackson's and they headed up the small aisle between two short rows of chairs draped in blue chiffon and tied at the back in large bows. Half a dozen candelabras flanked a short platform covered in dark blue velvet, and arrangements of light blue hydrangea and pink sweetheart roses were placed around it.

Just as they settled into their chairs, Miguel entered from the side entrance, leading Emma's aunt Sophie to a seat in the front row.

"Aunt Sophie? What are you —"

Sophie turned and waved at Emma, then wrinkled up her nose with eager excitement.

And as realization pounced upon her, Emma gasped.

"Oh, Jackson! I know who —"

The opportunity was gone in an instant as Emma's parents walked through the side door. Avery wore a full-length champagne dress with fitted top and long sleeves. The skirt was overlaid with light blue chiffon, the same color as the draping on the chairs, adorned with thin vines, hand-sewn with silver beads. The stem of her simple hydrangea bouquet was wrapped with a pale pink silk ribbon.

When Avery's eyes met hers, Emma burst into tears. She rose from her chair and immediately hurried to her mother and threw her arms around her.

"Are you joking?" she sniffed, and then she caught her father's eyes over the slope of her mother's shoulder. "Are you serious?"

"Your father and I want to renew our vows, Emma Rae. We know how late this comes, but we both want to begin again and make it work this time."

"I'll do it right, Princess," her father said in a soft vow. "I won't let either one of you down."

Emma released her mother and moved on to embrace her father. "I love you, Daddy."

"We love you, too, Princess."

She didn't know that Jackson had joined them at the front of the room until he braced her shoulder with a firm grasp. "Let's sit with your aunt," he suggested, and Sophie hugged Emma when she sat down beside her.

"Thank you all for being with us tonight," Miguel said once he completed the picture on the platform at the front. "It's a very special night for two very unique and special people."

Jackson threaded his fingers through Emma's, and she felt the electricity of it all the way up her arm. She reached over with her other hand and took Sophie's. In a flash, she was reminded of the day they'd gone to the movies together, and Sophie had been singing the part of *Henry Higgins* in the guise of Gavin Travis.

How things have changed! she thought, glancing up at Jackson with a quivering smile.

And with all that change rolling down the river of her life, fueled by the current of answered prayer and a new community of family and friends, Emma took a moment to wonder . . . if only just in that one instant . . . whether there might be more of it ahead for her.

I don't always have to be the baker, she

thought hopefully. *Maybe next time, I'll be the bride!*

"By the power vested in me, and with the blessing of God the Father, His son Jesus, and the Holy Spirit, I now pronounce you husband and wife. Still and again."

As her parents affirmed their love and commitment to one another right there at the front of the room, Emma Rae Travis decided that she would do whatever she had to do. She would take whatever medication necessary, prepare in whatever vigorous way might be required with a balance of protein and keeping some insulin handy.

Whatever it took, on her big day, Emma Rae Travis was *going to bake her cake . . . and eat it too!*

DISCUSSION QUESTIONS

1. What do you think of Emma's career choice, considering that she is diabetic?
2. Fee is a very unique individual, and her loyalty to Emma defines their relationship. What specific role does Fee play in Emma Rae's life?
3. What do you think forms the attraction between Jackson and Emma? Which of their characteristics complemented the other person? Which of those characteristics rocked their romantic boat?
4. How did the death of Jackson's wife affect his future relationships?
5. Did you feel that Jackson compromised part of himself by pursuing his deceased wife's dream? Or did you feel that he used her dream as an excuse to do something unexpected and different?
6. How do you feel about the family dynamics in the book? From Jackson's sisters to Emma's parents and aunt, what do the

various roles represent for Emma and Jackson?

7. How did you feel about the relationship between Emma's mother and father?
8. There are so many peripheral characters in the book. Aside from family members, which characters do you think had the most impact on Emma and Jackson?
9. It's often said that food is the foundation for so many things in life, from family events to social networking. How do you see the role of food in the book?
10. Did you enjoy the recipes and wedding tips in the book? What were your favorites?
11. Before their identity was revealed, who did you suspect would be the bride and groom at the surprise wedding at the end of the book?

AN INTERVIEW WITH AUTHOR SANDRA D. BRICKER

Q: What inspired you to create "laugh out loud" inspirational stories for women?

Sandie: I'm a firm believer in the scripture that says a merry heart is like medicine. I mean, I've always been a bit of a class clown. Even in the worst of times, if I can find something to laugh about, things really start to look up. There's hope in laughter, and I suppose I just knew somehow that my sense of humor came from the Lord. It was a natural progression to use that in weaving my stories. In *Steel Magnolias,* Dolly Parton's character said, "Laughter through tears is my favorite emotion." Rock on, Dolly, because I feel that way, too!

Q: What elements of similarity will readers find in *Always the Baker, Never the Bride* and *The Big 5-Oh!*?

Sandie: The basic stories and characterization are vastly different, but I think all of my stories have one foundational thread in common: a sense of destiny that is tied into God's plan for our lives, told through my kind of unique and rather quirky sense of humor.

Q: How do you as the author connect with the characters you write about?

Sandie: Well, maybe I shouldn't admit it . . . but the truth is . . . every one of my characters has a little piece of me in them, especially my heroines. My gigglability, my klutziness, my love of all things bakery! Even the fact that Olivia in *The Big 5-Oh!* is a cancer survivor, and Emma Rae in *Always the Baker* is a diabetic. I sort of live through my characters, except that they're always thinner and cuter than me.

Q: What do you think readers will enjoy most about *Always the Baker, Never the Bride*?

Sandie: In *The Big 5-Oh!,* it was the cast of characters and the freedom to really make fun of Florida that made it such a party. But *Baker* was truly the most fun I've ever had as a writer. Emma's family and friends, and Jackson's family as well, just rocked the whole book for me. I identified with Emma, and I think I fell a little bit in love with Jackson as I wrote the story. I'm pretty sure readers will fall for them as well.

Q: Where did you do most of your research for Emma Rae's award winning baker character?

Sandie: In the acknowledgments at the front of the book, I credited my mom for making me what I am today: a diabetic with a weight problem. In all seriousness, the woman baked like a crazy person. Cakes, pies, muffins, you name it. Every dessert of my childhood and adolescence was nothing short of an extravaganza . . . so most of the recipes in the book came from her card file. In addition to Mom, I'm a little bit addicted to reality shows like *Cake Boss* and *Amazing Wedding Cakes.* I gained almost 20 pounds while researching and writing Baker, and I'd like to tell you it wasn't worth it. I mean, I'd really like to tell you that. But, you know. I'm just sayin'.

The employees of Thorndike Press hope you have enjoyed this Large Print book. All our Thorndike, Wheeler, and Kennebec Large Print titles are designed for easy reading, and all our books are made to last. Other Thorndike Press Large Print books are available at your library, through selected bookstores, or directly from us.

For information about titles, please call:
(800) 223-1244

or visit our Web site at:
http://gale.cengage.com/thorndike

To share your comments, please write:

Publisher
Thorndike Press
10 Water St., Suite 310
Waterville, ME 04901